CONGREGATION

Also by Virginia Owens

At Point Blank
A Multitude of Sins

CONGREGATION

Virginia Owens

A LION BOOK

Copyright © 1992 Virginia Owens

The author asserts the moral right
to be identified as the author of this work

Published by
Lion Publishing plc
Sandy Lane West, Oxford, England
ISBN 0 7459 3011 5
Albatross Books Pty Ltd
PO Box 320, Sutherland, NSW 2232, Australia
ISBN 0 7324 0854 7

First edition 1992
This UK edition 1994

All rights reserved

Acknowledgments
Scripture references are from the King James Version

A catalogue record for this book is available
from the British Library

Printed and bound in Great Britain
by Biddles Ltd, Guildford

Dramatis Personae

Harriet Autry—elderly widow grieving over the sale of the church she's attended for thirty years.

Tony Winston—a converted ballerina with a past.

Denny McCready—the junior warden with a secret passon for the rector's wife.

Mollie McCready—the bright, bold teacher of Somerville High's gifted students and Denny's second wife.

Clyde Mapes—irascible rancher and vestryman at St. Barnabas.

Jack Tatum—bachelor history professor at Somerville State and St. Barnabas's long-suffering pillar.

Leslie Rittenhouse—wealthy lay reader who's been relieved of her duties by the rector.

Wendy Sanderson—at fourteen, a model acolyte and baby-sitter who suddenly turns punk.

Arlen Canby—increasingly alienated from his congregation after three years as rector at St. Barnabas.

Dan Kamowski—sent by the bishop to conduct the final service at St. Barnabas and the only Episcopal priest recruited from prison.

CHAPTER • ONE

JUST AS IT HAD FOR FIFTEEN YEARS, the key to the side door grated in the lock and then balked. Harriet Autrey shifted the church door's considerable weight slightly to the left, using the key as a lever, and silently called on the Almighty to blast the door to kingdom come. As her hands had grown weaker during the past decade, Harriet's anathemas had grown stronger. This morning, however, she couldn't have told whether her indignation was directed at the recalcitrant lock, the swollen and tender joints in her hands, or—well, she wouldn't want to put a name to the other object of her anger.

"The last time," she said in a hoarse whisper, not checking herself as she usually did when she heard her own voice in the silence. She needed to hear a voice this morning, even if it was only her own. It frightened her to think about all that was coming to an end with this final service at St. Barnabas. Including the building itself.

She stepped into the side vestibule and dropped the key into the purse pocket reserved for it, taking special care to register where she had put it. Harriet hated misplacing the key as much as she did using it. She paused in the dark space a moment to catch her breath, not eager to face what was waiting for her inside, what she would have to pass by on her way to the sacristy behind the organ.

It would be an hour before the congregation started arriving, but Harriet had wanted to give herself plenty of time for this last preparation. How fitting, she thought, that the last service should be a funeral. Next week bulldozers would level the building. But its physical destruction was the least of St. Barnabas's problems.

She hadn't seen it that way at first. Rumors about selling the church to a development company wanting to build high-rise apartments on the edge of the university campus had started making the rounds over a year ago. The Daughters of the King meetings had buzzed about the plan in angry undertones, like bees trapped in a bottle. *St. Barnabas—imagine! . . . The only Episcopal church in Somerville.*

The Daughters of the King were mostly older women like herself whose family connections to the church included decades of service on committees and vestry, families for whom the church marked the significant events of their lives with baptisms, weddings, and funerals. If any of them had been asked on a theological exam whether the church was the building, they would have answered of course not—it was the people.

But in their heart of hearts, St. Barnabas was indeed this not very picturesque brown brick building at the corner of M and 20th, on the western edge of the Somerville State University campus, not some ethereal, disembodied notion of spiritual community. It was the concrete steps they had climbed Sunday by Sunday. It was the plain, heavy oak doors with the mildew stains along the bottom edge, and the admittedly ugly parish hall that never looked pretty enough for receptions, no matter what shade they agreed to paint its cinder block walls. It was the stone-floored narthex with the perpetually broken water fountain and the schefflera plant by the front entrance, which only visitors used. Most of all for Harriet, it was opening the door and being momentarily arrested by the thrumming stillness inside, as though she were listening to someone breathe beside her in the night.

How many times had she come in the side door off the street, intent on the details of setting up for the Eucharist, only to be stopped in her tracks as she stepped into the nave, her eyes pulled toward the altar where sunlight, filtered through the pebbly Plexiglas panels, fell across the white altar cloth in red and blue patches? The white lace edging on the cloth was the one frill in their otherwise rather stark church, and it was so old now that the Altar Guild had to keep stitching it back together every time the fair linen was washed. But she loved that strip of lace, especially the way the chipped bachelor-button blue enamel of the altar showed through it.

Every Sunday while she knelt at the altar rail waiting to have the round host pressed into her palm, her eyes wandered to the small hole in the center panel above the altar. Made by a boy's BB gun, she guessed; it had been there at least ten years now. Father Shields had been determined to replace the plastic panels with glass, but they'd never gotten around to it during his tenure. And seen from the back of the nave, you couldn't really tell they were plastic. The light pouring through the colored panels seemed to fill up the sanctuary, to make it swell and float there before the congregation.

Those were the things she regretted losing, the same kinds of little physical details she'd miss if she suddenly lost her home in a tornado or a fire. Those details were still St. Barnabas to Harriet.

Everything else had already been lost, including a good portion of the membership. She would never say this to anyone else, of course—she didn't allow herself to think it often—but at this point setting up for a service was like tending a corpse. *But even corpses,* she muttered to herself now, *have to be tended to.* She took a deep breath and pushed open the vestibule door.

By the time the rumors about selling the church had begun circulating, the congregation had learned not to ask questions outright. If you asked vestry members, they tended to take it as criticism. Feelings got hurt. Accusations were made. It got messy. And the members of St. Barnabas weren't the sort of people who sought out confrontations or enjoyed giving offense. Episcopalians were a minority in the small town of Somerville, but an elite minority. Leave the church splits to the Baptists, they always said. Baptists, being the majority denomination in town, could afford to split.

Nevertheless, the congregation had kept its ears to the ground for rumblings. And, she was ashamed to admit now, it was the rumors about selling the church that had upset the older members most—as if the building's physical existence had been their insurance that everything else would be all right. Eventually. They'd seen priests come and they'd seen them go, and they figured they could wait this one out too.

But that was before St. Barnabas had gone on the auction block.

Even now it seemed impossible. Harriet lingered beside each pew as she made her way up the aisle, letting her long, bent fingers trail along the backs, remembering who sat in each one as a matter of long habit. The Tollivers usually slipped into the back pew on the right. Betty always looked worried and solicitous of Ned, while his face was either frozen in desperation or, on good days, a shining pink mask stretched tight across the bones. They sat in back so that after they'd been down for Communion they could slip out without having to talk to people after the final prayer and benediction.

On the left and a little farther toward the front had been Sandy Stickles's spot. She had worn those big, outrageous hats after her hair fell out from the chemotherapy. She hadn't even been buried from St. Barnabas but from the funeral home. Like a Baptist.

"I'm not going to have that sorry so-and-so hovering over my wife's body like some kind of vulture." That's what her husband had said at the hospital—right in front of Sandy's mother, a lifelong member at the cathedral in Houston.

The McCreadys always sat right in front of Sandy. Mollie McCready and Sandy had been friends ever since they got their divorces from their first husbands about the same time. They both taught at the high school, and if it hadn't been for Mollie, things would have gone a lot worse for Sandy at the end.

The rumor was the McCreadys had almost split up over the troubles at St. Barnabas. Denny had been elected junior warden two years ago. There hadn't been many younger men left in the church by then to take care of the maintenance and the repairs. Everyone thought things might take a turn for the better with him on vestry, but it hadn't worked out that way. His knees had been just as weak as everyone else's.

Harriet shook her head and reached over to straighten the prayer books and hymnals in one of the pew racks. Why had it taken her till her eighty-second year to dis-cover that men had no more courage than women? If Marvin had still been alive, what would he have done? Her husband had been senior warden several times at St. Barnabas back in the sixties and seventies when there were some real troubles to deal with. Marvin Autrey had always handled priests and congregations alike with a firm hand. He'd gone to the bishop himself when Father Zilke started turning up drunk, first at vestry meetings and then at Morning Prayer on Wednesdays.

When St. Barnabas had its first black communicant in the sixties, Marvin had faced down an irate contingent at a vestry meeting and told them they were welcome to go to any of the other churches in town that were still segregated. And some of them did for a while. But the ace in the hole for St. Barnabas was, if you were an Episcopalian, it was the only show in town. The segregationists weren't about to sit through a thirty-minute sermon, and they were suspicious of the celibate priests at the Catholic Church.

Further down the aisle, Harriet stopped and leaned against the row where Jack Tatum sat on alternating sides, whenever he wasn't the lay reader. For a long time everyone had counted on the plump bachelor professor, the holiest person they had at St. Barnabas, to pull them through. Jack supported his widowed mother, hosted foreign students during the holidays, and was the only person Harriet knew who had actually visited someone in prison.

But maybe holy wasn't enough, Harriet thought. Or maybe holy wasn't exactly what they thought it was. At any rate, he hadn't been any more effective than Denny McCready. Jack went about with a perpetual look of anguish on his fleshy face now, sidling into corners when anyone approached him looking either resolute or angry.

Holy was certainly not a word Harriet had ever thought of associating with her husband, Marvin. In fact, just the opposite. Shrewd, stubborn, unemotional. That was Marvin. Perfect senior warden material. Even so, she was glad he had never been tested with this particular kind of trial. He might not have done any better than Daniel Mabry or Ty Singletary. They were both lawyers too and had served consecutive terms as senior wardens. But the troubles at St. Barnabas had only gotten worse under their administrations. Now they had reverted to their old pattern of coming to church only at Christmas, Easter, and the baptisms of their grandchildren. They didn't relish failure either.

Harriet passed by what she knew everyone called "the little old ladies' pew," where she herself sat, then paused at the front pew on the gospel side. The new family that had been coming to St. Barnabas only about three years now sat down there. They were converts. You could always tell the ones who weren't cradle Episcopalians. They crowded right down toward the front as if they wanted to devour everything—the sermon, the music, the priest, everything. They never could seem to take it all in, as though there might not be enough to go around.

Maybe there wasn't. The sanctuary lamp hung, extinguished and empty, behind the altar. It had not been lit for over a year now, since they no longer kept the reserved sacrament in the brass-and-enamel tabernacle on the retable. How often had she come into the church to clear away after Communion and found the lamp burning like a red and ever-wakeful eye? Now it seemed a dead crater, a blind socket. And maybe that was best, considering all that had happened. Maybe they all ought to be hiding from God, relieved to have his gaze turned away from them.

It still seemed impossible. A nightmare. She'd hardly been able to take it in when Mollie McCready called to tell her. But there they stood in plain, undeniable daylight. Two little coffins, one on the gospel side and the other on the epistle side of the chancel, separated, not close to one another as she had hoped. One of the funeral palls hung down too far, almost to the floor. The Altar Guild had had to borrow an extra white one from the Roman church. They couldn't put a black one on a child. Harriet shook her head; she ought to have brought a needle and thread or at least some pins to shorten the borrowed one properly.

The small twin coffins looked so lonely, sitting apart. Side by side would have looked more comforting, she thought. As though the little sister and brother were holding hands. A song from her childhood came back to her faintly.

Two little babes . . .
Stolen away on a bright summer's day,
And lost in the woods,
I've heard people say . . .

How did the rest of it go? Harriet flexed her swollen joints in an effort to remember.

And the robin so red,
As they sang overhead,
Gathered strawberry leaves
And over them spread.
And all the day long,
They sang a sweet song
For the two little babes
Who died all alone.

Something like that. Or maybe it was Hansel and Gretel she was thinking of. She got so confused these days.

Their funeral would be the last service at St. Barnabas. And it would be done by a strange priest, someone the bishop had sent up from Houston, someone who didn't even know them or their difficulties. For the last time Harriet would lay out the corporal, the purificator, and the lavabo for Eucharist. Next week St. Barnabas Episcopal Church would be a parking lot at M and 20th. Would the strange priest even know that? Or care?

Harriet sighed and wished there was a way to make the coffins look more comfortable. Marvin would have thought she was silly. But there had been precious little comfort for any of them for three years now. They had been like the Israelites wandering in the desert. Only without a Moses to lead them. Some had wandered off to other churches in town.

One woman, another widow who'd been a member of St. Barnabas even longer than Harriet, went to First Christian now. At least, she told Harriet, you could get Communion there every week. It made the church sound like a reliable vegetable market. And some people were driving thirty miles to St. Cuthbert's down in Olney where, Harriet heard, they had a wonderful choir and a day school. It was mostly the ones like her, too old to drive far or too set in their ways to give up, who had stuck it out at St. Barnabas.

And now it was all over. Not suddenly, certainly. They had watched its slow death, the way one watches a cancer patient die, piecemeal. But death, even after a long illness, is always a jolt. She closed her eyes and imagined the black expanse of asphalt already under her feet. Worse than a desert.

Harriet had been on the Altar Guild at St. Barnabas for the last fifteen years. It was Father Hummel who had asked her to join, soon after Marvin died. She knew the priest had thought it a sort of consolation prize. But the job had made coming to church easier after she no longer had a husband to sit with. She could get there early, set up for the service, and then be in her pew by the time the rest of the congregation started filtering in.

Fifteen years ago she had been the youngest member of Team III, which did the third Sunday of every month and the noon Eucharist every Wednesday. Irene Spinneyton, imperious and arthritic, had been the head of the guild then. She had taught Harriet how to take the black silver stains out of the purificators with Haggerty's Jewel Cleaner and to remove the wine stains with lemon juice. Irene had always been so particular, insisting on doing all the laundry and repairs herself until she was well into her eighties. She had died—how long ago? It must be four years now, because Irene had still been there when Father Shields had retired. Thank heaven she hadn't lived to see what they had become. Harriet shook her head and murmured aloud, "It would have killed her."

Startled at the sound, she put her hand to her mouth and looked around instinctively. But the church was still empty, just her and the two dead children.

Harriet suddenly felt so weak, she sank into the lay reader's chair by the organ. Touching her face, she was startled to find her cheeks wet. It had been so long since she'd cried that she didn't even recognize the tears at first. They felt as if they came from a long way down, from the bottom of a dry well into which a little water had seeped, a trickle of thin water. Not hot and salty, the way she remembered tears, but just a little leaky dampness. She let them dry on her face without wiping them away. Then she pulled a handkerchief from her sleeve and wiped her nose. Who was she crying for, she wondered. Marvin? The two children? Her own death? Or for them all?

Harriet had never been very good at unraveling emotions. In fact, of late she hadn't even been too good at having them. So she sat there, feeling the dampness on her face evaporate and probing the soreness in her chest. This was sorrow, she told herself, marveling that she could remember it. "Sorrow." She said the word over again, purposely aloud this time. It had an antique ring to it. It wasn't a word people used much in everyday speech anymore. The closest they came was "sorry." But just to say the word "sorrow" was like drawing a bow across cello strings.

Earlier in her life, just a few years ago even, Harriet would have been embarrassed by such thoughts. Before they had gotten lost in this desert. But now—she shook her head and two more drops spilled over the edges of her reddened eyelids. Why had they been so backward, so hesitating? Why had they kept on pretending that it didn't matter, as it died around them, cell by cell?

That's why it had to come to this—two dead children, one on the gospel side and the other on the epistle side. That's what it had taken to open their eyes.

CHAPTER • TWO

TONY WINSTON TURNED OFF the ignition, removed the keys, and dropped them into her pocket. She never carried purses. She considered them encumbrances that made a woman look slightly off balance. And balance was very important to Tony.

A dancer for almost twenty years before she finally quit the ballet company and started teaching, she still held herself upright, as though always on the alert, ready to make an entrance. In fact, the only physical accommodation she had made to her change in professional status was cutting her hair. She had always worn it wound in a copper coil at the nape of her neck, but when she started teaching she'd had it cropped short.

"I don't trust women with short hair," he'd said.

She could still hear his voice, thin and insistent, inside her skull. She shook her head sharply, trying to rid it of the imagined voice. If it *were* only imagined. She crossed herself, not quickly, but making the sign deliberately, from her forehead down to the bottom of her sternum and across to either shoulder.

She sat in the parking lot for another five minutes, staring across the street at the church. She could hardly bring herself to open the car door. Just like the first time she'd come to St. Barnabas. She had driven around the church several times, approaching it from every angle, telling herself this was foolish, that she hadn't darkened the door of a church since junior high school and certainly had no business in one now.

Finally, though, she'd turned into the parking lot, as if giving up an argument reluctantly and unconvinced. All right, she'd told herself, you've gone to all the trouble of getting up on Sunday morning and putting on a suit and heels; you may as well get something for all your trouble. That was how she had talked herself into making that first, fateful entrance.

She got out of the car now and locked the door, eager to get inside the church before other people started arriving. She didn't want to have to make awkward small talk with the other members who'd stuck it out.

What must he be feeling now? There had been a point when she tried to put herself in his place, to figure out why he acted the way he did. But it was like trying to imagine what a rock thought.

It was almost a year now since she'd been inside St. Barnabas. But for the six years before that, she'd been in and out of the building almost daily—collecting trays of newsletters to take to the post office, sacking canned goods for the food pantry, cleaning out cupboards in the Sunday school rooms. Surprising even herself with the sudden domestic urges she'd never felt toward her own home.

If any of her friends in Dallas—if Mance—could see her now, she had often thought, they'd never believe it. The last time she'd seen Mance . . . but Tony never allowed herself to go beyond that point. No going back, she'd said, not even in memory. And for five blissful years she'd felt herself getting stronger and stronger. She never seemed to run out of energy. She went to the nursing home on Thursday afternoons with Denny and Jack, she made needlepoint crèches for the Christmas bazaar, she tutored on Tuesday evenings. Quietly. Anonymously if possible. What had happened to her need to perform, to have people notice, she'd wondered.

"You're doing too much," *he'd* said when he'd been at St. Barnabas three months. "This is unhealthy. Obviously you're using the church as a substitute for—" The unspoken phrase hung in the air like a threat. "—something else," he'd finished innocuously.

Why hadn't she told him? Why hadn't she said it then? *You bet your booty, buster. I have enough passion inside me to scare the pants off of you. And I'm pouring it out just as hard and fast as I can here. All the places I've wanted to put it and couldn't, and even the place I did put it and shouldn't are all rolled up into this place now. It's a pool, a well, an ocean that can take as much as I can pour out. And don't you dare try to pull the plug on it.*

But she hadn't said that. She hadn't managed, in fact, to pull those words to the surface of her own mind until at least a week after he'd called her into his office to tell her he'd removed her from the Stewardship Committee. She had sat there stunned and inarticulate. Only later did she lie awake in the middle of the night, making up speeches to him, to the vestry, to the congregation. Not that speeches would have made any difference.

Tony wasn't sure anything would have made a difference. She was coming to believe he was invincible. He had, she feared, some kind of power on his side that had rolled over them all, even the strongest, leaving them flattened. Limp. Impotent.

A week after removing her from the committee, he'd come to her apartment. That's when he'd made the remark about the short hair. He was angry because she had told one of the members of the vestry about the meeting in his office. He'd accused her of trying to undermine his ministry out of some kind of Freudian jealousy. "You'll never have another job in this church," he'd shouted at her. "Not as long as I'm here!"

It was then she'd started dreaming of Mance again. In the dream they were together, the three of them. She was comparing the priest's sallow, narrow face to Mance's, whose heavy, dark eyebrows lifted in mock surprise, his mouth pulled up on one side in a wry smile. Then Mance turned to the priest, lifted one hand laconically toward her as if resigning his claim, made an ironic little bow, and walked away.

She had run after him in the dream, panting and crying. And when she had almost reached him, he turned around—but it was no longer Mance's flushed, full face. It was her father's, looking the way she had last seen him in the hospital, wasted and drawn by bitterness and pain.

Tony crossed the street and slipped in the side door of the church. Someone had turned the lights on already, illuminating the chancel like a stage awaiting a performance. Even now it made her catch her breath. She bowed precisely to the altar, though she knew no host waited there, and slid into one of the back pews. Lowering the kneeler silently, she settled her skirt across her calves, folded her hands on the back of the pew, and bowed her head. She didn't want to have to talk to anyone.

Twelve years. It still astounded her that she'd been able to do it. Walk away like that after twelve years. Where had she gotten the strength? She had always had great confidence in the power of her own will, but injuries and time had taught her that there were some things even willpower wasn't equal to. What she and Mance had wasn't marriage, she'd often reminded herself. But it was twelve years. Even being the other woman became a settled habit after that long.

Not that Mance hadn't been willing to leave his wife. For the first five years he had pleaded with Tony to marry him.

"Are you crazy?" she'd told him. "You have three children. You have a responsibility as a father. And besides, what would I do with three kids anyway? I'm no good with children."

"Their mother would get them," he'd answered, adding quickly, "I mean, she'd fight for them, and no judge would give them to me." Tony had been disturbed, rather than flattered, that he would give them up so easily for her.

So she'd brought up money. A divorce would be expensive, she said. His wife's family owned a ranch, which they'd be willing to mortgage to prosecute him.

She had never actually met his wife, but in the early days of the liaison Tony had gone to places where she could observe the woman unobtrusively. Shopping at the same supermarket, lingering near her booth at a crafts fair, eating at the McDonald's where she took the children after their swimming lessons in the summer.

Tony's spying was from curiosity rather than guilt, and after she discovered Mance's wife to be an ordinary type—neither much different nor worse than most married women she knew—she'd lost interest. In those days, Tony still had a theory that there were a not-very-large number of types in the world, most of them immediately identifiable by certain physical characteristics. Buck teeth, angular gestures, eyes that drooped at the corners, slumping posture—each physical trait indicated a personality category. Only rarely did she come across anyone who did not fit a type.

Mance himself had been a type. She'd first met him when he showed up at her dressing room door with his little daughter after a Christmas performance of *The Nutcracker* one year. He'd promised Jessica he'd take her to meet one of the dancers after the show, but it was obvious that Mance, not his daughter, was the starry-eyed one, taken in by the tinsel and magic of the production.

Jessica was tired and cross and wanted to go to the bathroom. Exasperated with the child, Mance had finally sent her down the hall to find one while he stayed and talked to this being who was like a creature from another world to him.

And the West Texas cowboy made good in oil tools had never gotten over that initial dazzlement. He'd loved taking the pins out of her hair and watching it uncoil into burnished waves that he'd crush wonderingly in his big hands. His appetites were demanding, but if she didn't feel like seeing him, all she had to do was say she had a rehearsal, a master class, whatever, and Mance was immediately subdued. Sometimes she thought her career as a dancer meant more to him than it did to her. The worst fight they'd ever had was over her quitting the company and cutting her hair. Even her moving a hundred and fifty miles away to open a studio in Somerville hadn't hurt him as much.

She would never have married him. She knew that. Not even if he'd been unattached. His wife was actually a great convenience for Tony, who came to see over the years that Mance never felt safe unless he owned whatever he desired. Perhaps that's why they'd made it for twelve years; she hadn't belonged to him. She could love him—and she did—without the muddle of marriage. And never being able to lay claim to her publicly kept her ever-alluring to him.

That's what she had confessed to Father Shields before her first Communion. To her, the adultery seemed almost inconsequential beside the fact that she'd chosen to stick with Mance as a convenience.

"He was there when I wanted him, but I could always send him back to his wife when he was in the way."

The old priest had rubbed his large nose thoughtfully. "Maybe she felt the same way about you."

"She never knew. She wouldn't have stood for it."

"Twelve years? That's highly unlikely I'd say." He'd leaned back in his chair and stared out the high window of his office at two squirrels chasing one another up a pecan tree. "Maybe she was just as relieved to have you there to take him off her hands from time to time. Maybe there was a subtle complicity going on."

The idea had shocked Tony. "That sounds," she drew up her shoulders and shivered, "I don't know . . . incestuous."

He'd turned suddenly and smiled at her with his watery eyes. "Yes. Doesn't it?"

And that, she'd suddenly seen, had been the point of the confession. She had come in with the intention of doing God a favor. To own up, bravely, to this rather outrageous sin she'd lived in for the twelve preceding years. Being skilled in stoicism and willpower, Tony had seen that as her duty. She had already decided that if she went through with this project, joining a church, being baptized—giving herself to this Other Man who was even more demanding than Mance—she intended to do it right. No holding back. All or nothing.

Even after Father Shields had told her gently that confession wasn't required in the Episcopal Church, she had insisted, showing up at his office on the Saturday evening before the bishop's Sunday visitation, when she was to be baptized and confirmed.

She had expected to feel good about it. Confession would be therapeutic; she would get it off her chest and start with a clean slate. She had expected to feel relieved, clean, even vindicated. As though the virtue of confessing canceled out the vice she was renouncing.

She had certainly never expected to feel diminished, smaller, humbled. She wasn't sure she had ever experienced that feeling before. *Used,* she'd said to herself, *for twelve years*. The idea was galling. It wasn't being used by Mance that bothered her; after all she'd consented to that. But being used by someone she hadn't chosen to submit to. It made her feel dirty. A convenience for his wife. And then she felt angry.

"Now we're getting somewhere," Father Shields had

said. "Now you're feeling what you may have caused someone else to feel. A good sign." And he'd smiled happily, as though she were a child making headway with the multiplication tables. "That's the nature of sin, isn't it? Not a simple straight line between cause and effect. But reverberations. A web entangling everyone involved. And everyone gets caught and degraded in the deception. Yet all the while we're telling ourselves we're the one in control, that we're the spider, not the fly."

She had gone home and shivered all through the night like a frightened child. And had come the next morning to her baptism still frightened—frightened enough to go through with it. A child needing protection, after all those years of never asking anyone for anything. Not even Mance. Least of all Mance. Afraid that his protection would also mean ownership. Yet realizing now that ownership was absolutely the case here.

"Tony, will you help me?"

She jerked her head up from where it had rested on her clenched fists. Harriet Autrey, her glasses hanging on the end of her nose and her hair in wispy disorder, touched her shoulder tentatively. Tony was startled at the woman's appearance. The last time Tony had seen her, a year ago, Harriet had looked old. Now she looked undone.

Harriet drew her hand back. "I shouldn't have disturbed you. I'm sorry. I just—"

"No, no." Tony got to her feet quickly and lifted the kneeler back in place. "What do you need?"

"The cork," the older woman said, lacing her long fingers together and then pulling them apart again. "I've broken it off. I can't seem to get everything organized. I'm so afraid . . . people will be coming—"

Tony put an arm around Harriet's shoulder and aimed her up the aisle again. "Don't worry," she said. "We'll take care of it. You just tell me what to do."

The sacristy, around behind the organ, was a small

room, not much larger than a pantry, lined with shallow shelves. Along one wall was a narrow counter with a formica top and a number of long drawers for altar linens and vestments. It looked like a wet bar to Tony, with its small sink for washing the chalice and paten.

Father Shields had laughed when she had first made the comparison. "That's exactly what it is," he'd said, starting to wheeze. "A wet bar. A holy wet bar. But don't let the Altar Guild hear you call it that. To them it's a piscina. See this pipe here?" He bent over and pointed to a drain angling over to the wall. "It goes to the outside. Runs right out on the ground behind that oleander on the west side of the church. Can't have anything consecrated running into a common sewer." He straightened up and tugged his coattails down in back. "As though we weren't all sewers."

Tony had never served on the Altar Guild herself, nor had any inclination to. But the priest had insisted on showing her all the "trappings" of the church, as he called them, before her baptism.

She hadn't been sure she wanted to see behind the scenes. What looked grand and courtly from out front looked self-conscious and fussy from the sacristy. Little diagrams were pasted to the wall, showing how to lay out the credence table beside the altar and how to fold the linens, each piece having a different, antique name. Lists of special days and their colors, rules about floral arrangements, addresses of wine merchants and convents that sold Communion wafers were taped inside the cabinet doors.

"I feel like Dorothy discovering the wizard's machinery in Oz," she told him.

"Of course," he said. "That's why I wanted you to see it. I don't want you floating around in some romantic haze about all this ceremonial stuff. You've been a performer. You know all the fabrication that goes on backstage to bring it off for the audience. Don't look so shocked. Why should it be any different here? Do you think we've got some kind of magic up our sleeve?"

But she was shocked. "A performance?" she echoed his term. "You mean this is all just—" She waved her arms, gesturing futility.

"Yes," he said happily, "just a play. That's what the Eucharist is. A play we put on. We're like children, you see, putting on a play for our Father. He's the audience, not us. And like most parents watching their children perform, he's delighted with our efforts. The ladies in the Altar Guild," he gestured widely now, "they're children here too. Very intent, like children making mud pies. You mustn't look down on them for that. Most children get absorbed in their play and take it seriously. That's all right. If their Father doesn't mind, why should you be offended?"

Ever after she'd noticed how his eyes lit up when he lifted his arms for the opening acclamation every Sunday. She'd recognized the gleam of the performer there. And the child.

But when *he* had come—Tony had a superstitious fear of saying his name, even silently in her head—that had all ended. A barrier, almost palpable, like a gray transparent membrane, seemed to encase the chancel. The new priest read through the eucharistic prayer at a fast clip in a dull monotone. There was no hint of delight or anticipation in his voice. In fact, the whole event appeared painful to him. Not just a duty, but a punishment. Once, at the point where the priest holds out his arms in a gesture of symmetry and openness, he had swung his right arm in from the elbow and looked at his watch. It was like catching Baryshnikov checking on the time in the middle of a *pas de deux*.

There'd be yet another priest today. Someone the bishop kept in perpetual exile in various mission churches, Mollie McCready, who knew all the diocesan gossip, had told her.

"See?" Harriet said now, holding the bottle of wine out to her. "I don't know if the cork was dry or old or what. But it broke off before I could even start pulling on it."

"Have you got a pocket knife in here? Or an ice pick? We'll probably have to push it on through."

Harriet opened a drawer and rummaged through it fretfully. "I think there used to be an old pipe tool in here that Irene kept for that very purpose. It's just that this has never happened before. I've never had to use it. What does a pipe tool look like anyway?"

Tony reached over and picked out a hinged, stainless steel instrument from the clutter in the drawer. Mance had smoked a pipe. What if *he* had found out about Mance? What would he have threatened her with then? She pulled out the leg with a flattened end and inserted it into the neck of the bottle.

"Don't break it now," Harriet fretted. "Maybe we should just get another bottle."

"If this doesn't work, we will," Tony said patiently, and hit the tool sharply with the heel of her palm.

"After all, we won't be needing them anymore, will we?" the older woman said.

Tony looked up. Harriet's eyes were red and she was pulling a handkerchief from her wristband. "You know what I'm going to do after this is over?" she said fiercely. "I'm going to come back in here and pour out every last bottle of wine. Right down the drain."

Tony gave one last push to the cork. It went through, crumbling into several pieces. "We'll need to strain this."

"I don't care what anybody says," Harriet went on. "I don't think the wine should leave here, do you? It's almost as if everything here is contaminated. This ought to be the end of it. Of everything."

Tony dropped the pipe tool back in the drawer. "I'll help you," she said.

CHAPTER THREE

DENNY MCCREADY GAVE THE furnace housing one last swipe and dropped the rag into a box with the empty light bulb cartons, plastic detergent bottles, dirty sponges, and the rest of the household detritus a building collects. He wanted to take the box out to the garbage bin before the service began. Having seen both Harriet and Tony arrive, he planned to go out through the back hall past the Sunday school rooms so that he wouldn't run into them. Or anyone else.

Why was he bothering to take out the garbage? he asked himself. What was the point now? There wasn't any reason to keep things picked up and tidy anymore. His responsibility as junior warden was over. Or would be as soon as this service was done and he'd turned off the thermostat and locked up for the last time. This was it.

But he couldn't bring himself to pick up the box and leave the furnace room yet. He had always liked it in here where it was close and dark and he could hear the domestic noises of the church coming to him muffled and distant. He felt safe then.

Also he was in no hurry to face the funeral for the

priest's children. Cassie's children, he made himself add. They were Cassie's children too. No one at St. Barnabas suspected how he felt about Cassie; saying her name was a self-imposed penance he performed now whenever he thought of her. It jolted him like a painful electrical charge.

How did it happen, he asked himself for the hundredth time, that two people as obviously suited to each other as he and Cassie should have been brought together too late, after they'd already married someone else? It didn't seem fair.

Actually it was not himself he put the question to; it was God he wanted an answer from. *And why, if you couldn't have let us find one another in time,* he whispered into the warm darkness of the furnace room, *why did you have to bring us together at all?*

And as with all those hundred times before, the warm darkness was silent.

Everything about Cassie was soft. Her pink skin was soft—she never laid out in the broiling Texas sun turning her hide to tanned leather the way Mollie did. Nor did she diet constantly like Mollie so that you could see her bones sticking through like a bicycle frame. Cassie looked mellow and buoyant. How many times had he imagined himself sinking into that soft, slightly moist flesh?

She had a habit when she was nervous of rubbing her palms up and down her thighs. Or she'd hug her round upper arms and rock herself slightly back and forth. Habits left over from childhood probably, but gestures of such urgency and vulnerability that it would almost make him cry to watch her. He'd never see her do that again.

Denny ran his hands through his thick, grey curls. If once, just once, it could have been Cassie's fingers in his hair, how he would have been comforted. He could almost feel them now, cool and consoling, stroking his temples that ached from clenching his teeth in his sleep. His tight, constricted heart would have melted with relief. Even the cholesterol plaque Mollie was always harping at him about would simply melt away, leaving his arteries slick as a whistle. His love for Cassie was that strong. She was enfolding comfort, warmth, security. She would love him like he was; she wouldn't always be poking at him to be different.

He could see her eyes shining up at him in amazement and admiration now. How long had it been since anyone had looked at him like that? Not since the kids were little, he was sure. He couldn't remember Mollie ever looking at him that way. What he needed was someone to believe in him—in him, not in some imaginary picture he could never live up to.

Denny pulled himself up short. He'd put all that behind him, even before this terrible thing had happened. He remembered the exact day. It had been on the final day of reserve training maneuvers last fall when they'd been caught in a blue norther out in the field in Oklahoma. He'd shivered all night inside his sleeping bag, checking the green glow of his watch every thirty minutes to see how close it was to sunup. It was at such times that visions of Cassie came to him most vividly. He imagined how her skin would smell—like fresh cut grass in summer.

Denny was in the habit of praying for things he wanted badly. He'd prayed to get his present job at Southwest Savings and Loan. Then he'd prayed later that the company wouldn't go under. In both cases it had worked. On the other hand, when he prayed that Mollie would take a more lenient attitude toward his two children on the weekends they spent with him, it hadn't worked so well. The older his kids got, the less they liked coming to Somerville from Houston. And Mollie's brusque ways didn't help matters any. Of course, if the kids had had their way, they would have spent most of the weekend sleeping and the rest of the time playing video games. Both he and Mollie had tried to get them interested in sports—baseball, tennis, hiking. Anything. But the more Mollie prodded, the more they resisted. Now they only came on holidays and one week in the summer. He had given up pleading with Mollie to humor them a little.

"I'm only going to all this trouble for you," she'd said, obviously hurt. "But if it doesn't matter to you that your children grow up to be couch potatoes, it sure doesn't matter to me."

That's when he started pleading with God instead. But even God had turned a deaf ear to this particular supplication. When the kids were there, it was like an armed camp at home. After his success with the job and the financial stability of Southwest Savings, it took him aback that his prayers for domestic harmony had so little effect. What was he doing wrong? There must be something he was missing here, he thought, something he didn't understand.

If Father Shields had still been there, he would have talked to him about it. But by then they were between priests at St. Barnabas, and the shifting lineup of fill-ins didn't allow for comfortable conversations. It would have taken a while to explain the situation all over again to each new priest, and you never knew how he might feel about divorce and remarriage. Denny certainly didn't want any lectures. All he wanted was to figure out how he was praying wrong about Mollie and the children getting along. It was obvious to him that Jesus would want them to. So what was the holdup anyway?

No answer had come, but a new priest had. A permanent one. And with him had come Cassie and their two children, the youngest one still a baby then. That had been in the spring, and by the next fall Denny had been lying on the hard, cold Oklahoma clay, fantasizing about Cassie's genial, consoling flesh in order to keep from freezing to death. He imagined her snuggled in the sleeping bag with him, their legs twined together.

And suddenly he'd found himself praying. *Please, God, please.* He didn't dare formulate a request any more specific than that. What could he say anyway, how could he have put it? *Please give me Cassie and take away Mollie?* You couldn't say that sort of thing to God. But his yearning was so strong that he knew if he denied it he might die right then and there in his sleeping bag. So he rolled all his longing, all his desire for tenderness given and received into those long-voweled syllables, like a child imploring a parent.

And, like a stone dropping into the depths of a still pond, he had gotten an answer. Not in words, of course. But suddenly, before he had time to notice it happening, his mind had been relieved, lightened. He felt reassured, even peaceful. Somehow or another it would all be taken care of. He was certain of that. He didn't have to think up the plan. Someone else would take care of that. His peace, in fact, was so great that he vowed to suppress all his lustful imaginings about Cassie as a sort of thank-you note to God.

For he'd been certain that night in Oklahoma, and he'd been even more certain the next Sunday when he saw Cassie in church, herding Russell and Heather into a pew toward the front. The church was having financial problems and couldn't afford to pay someone to keep the nursery. Besides, Russell and Heather were the only small children left. And they were a handful, swarming all over Cassie during the prayers, crawling under the pews, banging on the kneelers with their shoes. It was distracting, and several people made stiff comments about it to him as junior warden. He, however, didn't mind at all. The ruckus the kids caused gave him an excuse for staring at Cassie.

As the year wore on, though, his certainty about that message in Oklahoma wore off. Thanksgiving came and went, and then Christmas. Nothing changed. Mollie was heavily involved with the Gifted and Talented Program at her school. She didn't have much time or energy for him. He was always a little awed by Mollie. She was much more absorbed by her work than he had ever been, and he felt uneasy about that, as though it were unnatural somehow.

He began spending more time down at the church, changing light bulbs and furnace filters, repairing wobbly kneelers, even stripping the wax from the kitchen floor and putting down a new coat. Not because there was much hope of seeing Cassie there—she rarely came except for services—but just because he liked being in the only place he ever saw her.

He tried to get Mollie to invite the Canbys over for dinner. "You know what trouble they're having with the congregation. Don't you think it would make them feel a little better if someone took a friendly interest in them?" he'd asked her.

"Friendly interest? Are you kidding me? You might as well try to be friends with a fish! Heaven knows I feel sorry for that wife of his—he certainly has the wool pulled over her eyes. Sometimes I think she must be simpleminded. Maybe I'll just call her up and invite her to lunch. But I'm not having that man in my house, Denny. You can just forget it. Did you hear what he did when the Breits had them over?"

Of course he'd heard, but Mollie recounted it again anyway. "First he calls Marie up and announces that dinner can't be at six after all, but at seven. Doesn't ask—just announces. Then they bring those two little hellions, who proceed to tear up the living room while both parents just sit there and watch. Then as soon as dinner is over, he lays down his napkin, jumps up, and says he has an appointment somewhere and rushes off, leaving his wife and kids there for the Breits to take home. The man is a Neanderthal, Denny. He's socially retarded. No, it'll be much better if I just invite Cassie to lunch. Buy her a Happy Meal with a toy or something."

He was stung by her sarcasm but didn't dare show it. Mollie thought he only felt sorry for Cassie. Most of the members at St. Barnabas pitied the priest's wife. They reminded one another of that fact constantly, although they usually tacked some mention of her naiveté onto the end of their remarks.

Their attitude toward the priest, however, was another matter, although for the first few months everyone had bent over backward to reserve judgment. After all, Father Shields and the diocesan Committee on Ministry had drilled into their heads the difficulty of switching priests and the inevitability of change. And by and large, people had been sincere in their efforts to welcome the new rector.

The comments about how he stumbled through the service were at first good-natured. The congregation even went along meekly with the changes he made in the service—cutting out the doxology and one of the hymns so it would be shorter, using a different tune for the Benedictus, going entirely to Rite II.

All right, they figured, it was his show. Let him do it the way he wanted. If he wanted to stand down between the two front pews to preach, they could handle that. His sermons were certainly more intellectual than Father Shields's had been. Maybe that would bring in more young people.

They felt a little uneasy, though, when he refused to read aloud the names of the sick in the parish during the Prayers of the People. He told them it was because they should respect people's privacy. Maybe sick people didn't want everyone knowing they were sick. It might even lead to a lawsuit, he said.

The vestry members had looked around at one another, bewildered. What was this man talking about? Lawsuits? For prayer? As though sensing the first stirring of misgivings among them, he had quickly adjourned the meeting.

Not long after that the priest had called each vestry member into his office for a private consultation. None of them were ever sure what he'd said to the others because he had first made them promise they'd keep the details of the meeting secret.

Of course, he hadn't used the word "secret." He'd said "confidential," which sounded, at the time, not sinister but responsible. Even virtuous. He'd talked about how bad it was for rumors to be floating around a church, how innocent people could get hurt and misunderstandings arise. All of that seemed to make sense then. But afterward, they'd all felt a little off-balance, unsure of what it was right to talk about with whom. People began to get edgy with one another. Denny suspected there'd even been trouble between some couples when vestry members refused to tell their spouses what had happened in the meetings.

Meanwhile, Denny found himself spending more and more time down at the church. The building hadn't been in such good shape in years. Maybe he was trying to compensate for the growing ill will in the congregation; he had a way of feeling vaguely guilty when things went bad.

But he knew also he spent a lot of time at the church simply because it was the place he was most likely to see Cassie. And when they chatted around the coffee urn on Sunday mornings, he could bring up little domestic details like the dripping faucet in the women's rest room or whether to buy sugar-free Kool-Aid for the children in the nursery. Matters that Mollie couldn't have cared less about, Cassie took seriously, frowning in concentration while he explained how he'd installed the new dripless faucet.

He'd been afraid for a while that her husband would notice the way he always sought her out, or how he couldn't take his eyes off her during the service. Mollie, he knew, figured he was just trying to be extra nice to this woman caught in the middle of an unfortunate situation. But the priest seemed completely oblivious to Denny's attentions to his wife, which were, on the surface anyway, innocent enough.

Denny could at least console himself with the knowledge that he had never spoken a word to Cassie that could have been considered out of line. But somehow that didn't make him feel any better. He had never told her how much he'd loved her. And now it was too late.

The closest he'd ever come was after the last parish meeting. There had been a particularly ugly scene over the memorial fund accounts. People were on the verge of making accusations. They'd certainly implied that the meager information on the yearly budget report wasn't their idea of financial disclosure—and that some of the numbers didn't add up. But Denny hadn't paid much attention to it. After all, Ty Singletary was the treasurer, and as a lawyer in a small town like Somerville, he couldn't afford any funny business with the books or he'd be finished. Denny had slipped out the back and gone to check on the ham keeping warm for the church dinner they always had after the annual meeting. He didn't want it to get dried out.

The meeting had grown so rancorous though that a lot of people hadn't stayed for the dinner, including a number of the women who always cleaned up afterward. Cassie had put on an apron and started scrubbing pans in the sink, a way of keeping her back to everyone else in the kitchen, he suspected. When he picked up a cup towel and started drying the pans stacked in the drainer, he could see she was blinking back tears.

He couldn't help himself. He reached over into the soapy water where her hands were submerged and gripped one of them. "Cassie," he said, "sweetheart. Please don't cry." He called her that—sweetheart—the comforting way you might talk to a child who'd been injured.

She hadn't been offended. She looked up, her eyes still swimming and her lower lip gripped between her teeth.

"I just wish there were some way I could protect you from all this," he went on.

She dropped her head for a moment, closed her eyes, and—he could have sworn—squeezed his hand under the dishwater, then rushed from the kitchen. Harriet Autrey had looked at him strangely as she dumped the paper plates and Styrofoam cups in the garbage can beside the sink.

Cassie must have gathered up the kids and taken them home, because he didn't see her again that day. And he hadn't seen her the next Sunday either; the children had supposedly come down with the flu. But he ran into her at the grocery store the following Saturday.

When she caught sight of him, she stopped and put her hand to her mouth in a charming, involuntary gesture. It was impossible for her not to speak to him, of course. His own heart was pounding, and he stumbled over his words awkwardly. She kept her eyes on the contents of her grocery cart, which included Russell who was tearing open a box of Captain Crunch. They didn't talk long; both of them were flustered. But when she allowed herself one glance up at him, her face had been suddenly suffused with pink. He had to put out a hand and steady himself against a shelf of bottled spaghetti sauce.

Denny was no fool. He'd been involved with women before. In fact, that's how he'd lost his first wife and ended up married to Mollie. Although, in all fairness, he had to admit Mollie had pretty much taken the initiative there, just as she did in most things. He knew he had no right to lead Cassie on, to take advantage of her unhappy situation. He'd read in *Psychology Today* about hostages becoming emotionally involved with their captors out of sheer gratitude when they were treated well. He knew Cassie must feel trapped at St. Barnabas, held hostage by her husband's growing alienation from the people. Denny was one of the few members of the congregation making an overt effort to be nice to her, and he was certain she felt grateful, as simply and naturally as a child.

He would not lead her on, he promised himself repeatedly. He absolutely would not do that. He would not take advantage of the situation. Nevertheless, after their meeting in the supermarket, he believed again and wholeheartedly that his Oklahoma prayer had been heard and that this encounter had been a reminder, an assurance of that.

Denny wouldn't have said that to another living soul, of course. Not even to Jack Tatum, who was his prayer partner. He wondered if Jack had ever loved a woman in his life—as a woman, that is. Jack, of course, loved everyone, but not the way Denny knew he loved Cassie. So he'd kept his secret from everyone except God, and even with him he didn't harp on the subject.

Maybe he should confess though. The priest coming to do the funeral today, he'd probably never have to see him again. Maybe he should confess all this to him. What if somehow his confessing would help Cassie recover?

Denny stood up suddenly and picked up the box of trash. It was all too much for him, trying to figure out what worked with God—if he'd be willing to make that kind of a trade-off or not. Denny felt angry and defeated at the same time. The two little coffins waiting in there in the church were bad enough. Terrible. But not so bad, not so terrible to him as the limp, grey body of Cassie Canby, violated by a tangle of plastic tubing, lying up on the sixth floor of the Watson County Hospital, a body they'd told him might never come to consciousness again.

And he couldn't even wish for her to wake up. For how could she live with the knowledge of what she'd done? Even this visiting priest probably couldn't answer that.

CHAPTER • FOUR

CLYDE MAPES TURNED OFF THE ignition of his pickup and started to open the door. Then he stopped with his hand still on the handle and scanned the parking lot. Tony Winston's blue Mustang was parked across the street. Harriet Autrey's ten-year-old grey Oldsmobile was edged up to the back door of the church. McCready's Suburban was over by the trash bins. Other than the hearse, drawn up by the side door, waiting, that was all. Where was everybody anyway? Singletary and Mabry ought to be here by now. And Tatum. Where was Tatum?

He leaned back and sighed. No way was he getting out and going in that church until someone else got there. He hated standing around making small talk with women, and McCready would be busy. He was always bustling around the church these days, though what he found to fix when the whole thing was coming down next week anyway, Clyde couldn't imagine.

He didn't mind old lady Autrey so much. She'd been friends with his mother for years. He'd say something about the weather and she'd ask how his mother was. Neither of them would mention the funeral. But he sure didn't want to run into that Winston woman. A dancer.

What was a dancer doing in church anyway? And what was she doing here today? She hadn't shown her face in months. So why was she here now? Had she come just to gloat? He'd always thought there was something funny about her, right from the start. He should have known she'd be one of the troublemakers. None of that bunch had ever fit in at St. Barnabas. They'd all come from someplace else, every one of them. It was always your outsiders who liked to stir up trouble.

Clyde had lived in Somerville all his life. Not in town, of course. The ranch was actually closer to Niobe than Somerville, but Niobe wasn't anything but a post office and a filling station. He'd gone to school here in Somerville, all twelve grades. His father's funeral had been right in this very building. But his mother's wouldn't be. That was the one thing that had disturbed Clyde about selling the church. Where would they have Mama's funeral?

The rancher shifted uneasily against the vinyl truck seat. Maybe he should have talked it over with Mama first. But the preacher had told them to keep it confidential. The vestry members were the responsible parties, he'd said. The congregation had elected them to make these kinds of hard decisions. They wouldn't be living up to their responsibility if all they did was throw it back in the people's laps. It was a hard decision to make, all right. But somebody had to do it. No use getting people stirred up, the priest had said. Keep your own counsel about this. Or words to that effect.

And Clyde had certainly agreed with him on that. Lord knows, he didn't want to have to start explaining all the ins and outs of the situation to every Tom, Dick, and Harry. Or worse, to all the little old ladies. Including Mama.

Clyde was grateful to his mother for the way she'd stood by him during all the troubles at St. Barnabas. He'd figured that Daughters of the King bunch would

start worrying her, trying to get some information out of
her since he was on vestry. But she'd set her jaw and
never divulged a word. Not that she knew anything, of
course. But when the Daughters started gossiping about
how poorly things were going at the church, Mama
stopped going to the meetings out of loyalty to him. He
figured that had cost her something. She'd known most
of those women all her life. They were her closest
friends—and every year she had fewer and fewer friends
left. They were dropping like flies these days.

Poor Mama! He'd have to talk to her now that it was
all over. Ask her where she wanted to be buried from.
Maybe she'd just say the funeral home. That would sure
be the easiest. Let the professionals do it.

Where were the others anyway? He slammed his
palm against the steering wheel. Tatum ought to be here
already. Surely he'd be the lay reader today. Who else
was there anymore? When the bishop had called the day
before, he'd said that all the vestry members were to
show up for the funeral. He'd made that very clear. He
was sending some strange priest up to do the funeral and
they needed to support him. It was the first time Clyde
had ever actually talked to a bishop, except for nodding
at one in the reception line after confirmations. He
hadn't expected him to sound so gruff. Clyde hadn't
been talked to in that tone of voice in a long time.

Great, he'd thought, another outsider priest. But he
told the bishop that he'd intended all along to go—
though actually, at that point, he hadn't quite made up
his mind. Mama was having another spell with her heart,
and she didn't need to be exposed to that kind of a situation. Louise said she had to take the kids to their swimming lessons, but he suspected that was just an excuse.
Louise had been Church of Christ before they married
and never had felt comfortable about the Episcopal way
of doing things. And after Clyde, Jr. got in trouble with
the law that time and had his name in the *Somerville*

Courier, she didn't much like going to St. Barnabas anymore. Clyde made a mental note to talk to that Cartwright girl who came to St. Barnabas, or used to. What was her name? Beth Marie? Anyway, she worked at the paper. She ought to be able to keep that from happening again.

Clyde might have eased out of the church along with Louise if it hadn't been for Mama. He figured that as long as she was still alive he'd have to go. And too, after he got elected to the vestry, he didn't have much choice. Wouldn't you know all hell would break loose once he was on the vestry?

Clyde, like his father before him, generally felt all this church business was a big waste of time. When people started talking about God and their spiritual life—whatever that was—he could feel his heart begin to speed up and he had to clear his throat a lot. He'd edge away, go outside, and smoke a cigarette, inhaling deeply. Feeling something real like cigarette smoke rolling around inside him was reassuring. He had tried probing around inside for his soul—other people mentioned theirs so casually—but he never was sure he'd actually located it and was haunted by the fear that he might not have what everyone else seemed to be born with.

Clyde had hoped that if he stuck with the church, his kids would stay out of trouble and behave themselves. He'd been disappointed in that. The oldest, Clyde, Jr., was failing half his subjects at school. Then one night last fall they'd got a call from the sheriff to come down and get the boy at the county jail. He'd been picked up when the deputies broke up a drug deal in a convenience store parking lot. Clyde had managed to get him off with a suspended sentence and within a month had gotten him confirmed at St. Barnabas. But he couldn't help feeling like the boy was still edging toward disaster. He smiled too much for one thing. And he got phone calls late at night after the rest of the family had gone to

bed. The next morning he'd always be particularly eager
to please. Too eager.

Casting about in his mind for something to do, some
measure to take, Clyde remembered what his own father
had told him when he'd taken off for the Army right out
of high school. "If you ever get in trouble," Ron Mapes
had said, "you look up the preacher and go talk to him.
He'll help you out." So Clyde had asked his son if he
wanted to go in and talk to the preacher. But Clyde, Jr.
hadn't wanted to go. And Clyde couldn't say as he
blamed him.

As a vestry member, Clyde had considered it his duty
to stand behind the new priest, to close ranks. But personally he didn't have much use for the man. Preachers
had changed since he was a boy going off to the service.
He hadn't seen anything strange in his father's advice at
the time, and in fact, if he had gotten in any serious
trouble, he would very likely have followed it. Most
preachers had seemed trustworthy enough, reliable. And
they usually had the kinds of connections that could do
you some good. But nowadays—well, they talked a whole
other kind of language, one he didn't understand at all. In
a way, it was even worse than talking about souls.

When this new one had started talking about "Christ
events," for instance, Clyde wasn't sure just exactly what
he meant. Clyde knew all the Bible stories about Jesus,
of course. Mama had seen to that. Whether he believed
them was another question, and one he wouldn't have
felt comfortable answering straight out. That's why he
hadn't been sorry to see Father Shields go. Clyde had
always felt panicky around the old priest, as if he might
ask something like that at any minute. But somehow
Clyde felt sure this new man would never ask that kind
of question. And he never talked about anybody's soul, a
real relief as far as Clyde was concerned.

On the other hand, Clyde was never sure just what
the new priest was talking about. He used words like

"proactive" and "cognitive dissonance," words that the rancher had never even heard before. Once he'd preached a sermon about "your shadow self." That struck Clyde as even creepier than "soul." You could feel around inside for your soul, but a "shadow self" sounded like something that might sneak up on you from behind. At first he'd thought maybe the preacher was talking about the feeling you get when you've done something wrong—your conscience, more or less. At least a conscience was something you could feel, almost as strong as smoke in your lungs. Sometimes worse.

Then just when he'd figured out that this "shadow self" was a preacher-word for the bad part of you that did those things your conscience said you ought not to do, the priest started saying how you ought to "embrace" this shadow self and not reject it or try to pretend it didn't exist. It was just about then that Clyde figured out what the man really meant.

He might have known. It didn't seem like you could get away from it these days. They even wanted to teach it in the schools. It was all over the TV. You picked up a magazine while you were waiting to get the inspection sticker on your vehicle, and there it was staring you in the face. Sex.

Clyde squirmed uncomfortably in the truck seat. That "shadow self" talk might have been a tip-off right there that the preacher and his wife were having trouble. But whatever had been going on, Clyde figured it wasn't his fault and he didn't intend to take any of the blame for it. It wasn't the vestry's place to pry into the private life of their priest.

Where was Tatum and all the rest of them? The bishop must have called them too. Maybe they hadn't caved in as easy as he had. Maybe they had told him to blow it out his barracks bag. No. Tatum, at least, would never do that. In fact, he'd probably want to be here. But Mabry and Singletary? Both of them were lawyers, after all. Slippery. He wouldn't trust either one any farther than he could throw them. Not those two. He wondered how they felt about this whole shooting match now.

All the vestry members had pretty well stuck together after questions about the budget started coming up. Their own reputations were on the line. Clyde admitted he wasn't good at numbers. He might as well try to read Greek as a financial report. At home Louise balanced their checkbook and Mama always kept the ranch accounts. In fact, he tended to nod off whenever the treasurer gave his report at the vestry meetings. St. Barnabas had known good times and bad times, but they'd always gotten by one way or another. It wasn't something he worried much about except when some woman got on the vestry and wanted to start supporting all the drunks and deadbeats in town.

And he still wasn't convinced they'd done anything wrong. After all, they were the vestry, and if they wanted to make a short-term loan to the preacher out of the memorial fund to make a down payment on a house, Clyde didn't see why they shouldn't. He figured the preacher might as well have it as those bums down at the rescue mission. At least there'd be something tangible to show for it.

Besides, it was nobody else's business, not even the bishop's. It was Somerville money after all. They didn't need some guy in a little pointy hat down in Houston telling them how to run their own affairs. And the preacher had paid it back within the year, just like he said he would. So Clyde didn't see what the big fuss was about.

When he remembered that particular vestry meeting, the one where that doctor, who wasn't even a baptized member, came and shot off his mouth about "financial disclosure," Clyde winced. A lot of people had said things they shouldn't that night. Thank goodness he wasn't one of them. And if the others had just sat there stony-faced the way he had and kept their mouths shut, St. Barnabas would be in a whole lot better shape today.

He'd been so confused by the reams of computer paper they were handed that he hadn't known what to say anyway. But Singletary had to start arguing with the guy. And pretty soon people were shouting at one another. They ended up having to pay for another audit of the books to put all the rumors to rest. Luckily they were able to get David Whitehead, Singletary's cousin, at a bargain price.

Clyde hoped they were all happy now. At least they could see that money wasn't the real problem—it was all that "shadow self" business. He just hoped this out-of-town priest wouldn't try to make them feel guilty today. Nobody could have predicted what had happened.

He leaned his forehead on the steering wheel and closed his eyes. *Oh God, I can't stand any more. How am I ever going to look at those two little coffins in there? I hate this place. I'll be glad when the bulldozers come next week. I don't want to have to think about this any more. It's eating me up. What happened? What went wrong? Please, God, please. I didn't want this to happen. I'm not to blame. Please, God.*

A picture of the children's faces as they'd appeared in the newspaper flashed into his mind. *Lord, have mercy. Don't hold this against me, Lord. Make Mama understand. Nobody meant for this to happen. Why do you let people do things like that anyway?*

Clyde's hands gripped the steering wheel and his clenched jaw made his lower lip protrude. He was on the point of putting the key back in the ignition, starting up the truck, and easing out of the parking lot, when he saw Jack Tatum's pale blue Ford coming slowly up the hill toward the church.

"Thank God," he breathed.

CHAPTER • FIVE

FATHER DAN KAMOWSKI SHUT the office door behind him softly. He wasn't a man who did things softly as a rule, but he didn't want anyone to know he was there. Not until the last minute. He had parked in the lot across the street and entered the church by the front door, which he knew, at least in this part of the country, parishioners rarely used. Dan wanted to avoid the members of St. Barnabas as much as possible. He recognized a no-win situation when he saw one. They would come flocking around him from all sides, wanting his opinion, wanting reassurance, wanting him to say what could have been done to keep it from happening.

He'd been in this convocation for fifteen years now, moving from one mission parish to another, sometimes to specially created assignments, all because he couldn't keep his mouth shut. He figured it was time he learned how to do that. He and Dell weren't getting any younger. It wouldn't be many more years till he could retire. And he'd just as soon it be at River Point, where they'd finally got enough money together to put down on a house of their own.

"No more rectories," Dell had shouted from the front porch after they'd signed the papers. And he'd swept her up and carried her across the threshold. He might be in his sixties, but he could still do that.

No one looking at Dan Kamowski would have questioned his physical strength. He was six feet six, weighed two hundred and fifty pounds, and, though a lot of it sagged around his middle now, he looked as if he might have played tackle for Notre Dame at one time.

Actually, his alma mater was the Texas State Prison System. He was the only priest in the diocese, or the whole nation as far as he knew, with a prison record. Five years in the Ferguson Unit for car theft and two counts of fraud. The only reason he hadn't done twenty was the intervention of the prison chaplain at Ferguson, a Dominican priest who had floundered into the Episcopal church during the sixties. Father Berkowitz, who had married a nun who later left him to go live on an ashram in the seventies, had been serving his own kind of sentence, listening to confessions that, as he put it, would scare anybody celibate.

Dan had started going to Mass in prison simply to get a few minutes of peace and quiet. The chapel was never crowded, and you could usually find a place to sit where you could relax and feel relatively safe for at least half an hour. But once he'd heard Father Berkowitz's accent, he was hooked. He'd listened to the drawl and twang of Texas voices for so long that he sometimes felt he was being slowly smothered in white gravy. Hearing the nasal New Jersey tones of the priest was more comforting than he had expected. And at that point, Dan had thought he was beyond comfort.

He had grown up in the Bronx, among what might as well have been a family of bears. The women were as religious as they were allowed to be, as much out of nostalgia for the old country as religious conviction. And probably, he later realized, out of that same desire for peace and quiet that brought him to the chapel. The men in the family scarcely spoke to the women except to complain, to order, or to rage. And with their children they spoke only to order and rage. As a boy, he was expected to learn how to fight—and to win. When he was drafted at the end of World War II, he had to learn to curtail the fighting. They only wanted you killing Japs, not your platoon leader.

He'd been sent to Texas, of all places, for training. To his family, Texas might as well have been the moon. But in San Antonio he'd met Dell, a redheaded clerk at the post exchange. She was tall, and a wonderful dancer. That was enough for him. He lied to her about being shipped out to the South Pacific in order to get her to marry him. The day after the wedding, he told her his orders had been changed. And as a matter of fact, the war came to an unexpected end a few weeks later with Hiroshima. Even with all he confessed to Dell later, he never had told her the truth about that. He sometimes wondered if she'd ever figured it out.

They moved on from Texas to St. Louis, where his Uncle Tadeusz was running an operation of ambiguous character. His uncle had taken one look at Dell and offered him five thousand dollars to leave her. "I can fix it," he told Dan. "An annulment. It'll cost me another couple of thousand, but I can handle it. This woman," he shook his head, "she don't understand our ways. She'll ruin you. And you're a good boy. You got a head on your shoulders. We can use you."

Dan had walked out of the sooty red brick building and never gone back. They had to leave St. Louis. His uncle saw to it that he couldn't work there. Back in Texas he wound up selling dubious burial insurance to people—black and white—living in shanties along the river and in lumber camps. It made him uneasy. Not because it was a scam, but because his buddies back in the Bronx would have considered it a job for a broken-down bum, not a man in his prime.

When the insurance office folded overnight and Dan

found himself served with a warrant, he was genuinely surprised at having been set up by his employers to take the fall. Somehow he had been lulled into thinking these red-faced, sweaty Texans with their earnest way of leaning toward you and talking right into your face were the gullible ones. He'd been regularly pocketing some of the premiums he collected, and they had never seemed to notice. Then one day they just weren't there anymore. But the sheriff was—warrant in hand.

Out on bail the next day, he'd found a Chevy with the keys still in it and taken off for the Louisiana border. A couple of Texas Rangers were waiting for him just this side of the Sabine River. Though Dell had wired Uncle Tadeusz in St. Louis and his family in the Bronx, he'd never heard anything from them.

After Dan started going to Mass regularly in prison, Father Berkowitz would stare at him stonily when he slipped the host into his mouth. "The body of our Lord Jesus Christ, broken for you," the priest would say, and come down hard on that last word.

Hey, what is this? Dan had wondered. What's going on here? This guy's trying to get next to me. I ain't done nothing.

He'd skipped Mass the next time. The day after, one of the screws showed up at his cell, rattling his keys. "I got a order you got to go see the chaplain," the guard said, eyeing him suspiciously.

Father Berkowitz barely looked up when Dan opened the door to his office. "You been baptized?" he asked curtly.

Dan shrugged. "I guess so."

"Okay," the priest said, turning his back and opening a file cabinet. "You gonna be my acolyte from now on, you hear?" He swiveled his chair back around and handed him a sheet with purple ink on it. "Here. This tells you how to do it. You can read, can't you?" The guard took Dan back to his cell.

After that, he served at every service. Eventually the routine and ritual began to wear a groove in his weeks, like a pleasant habit. It didn't take him long to memorize the entire service, and he found himself whispering snatches of it at odd times during the day.

Not long afterward the warden called him in to tell him he looked like a good candidate for the college program they were starting. He told Dan he wanted him to sign up for a couple of courses. Dan had barely scraped through high school, but the books and assignments offered such a welcome relief from the boredom of prison that he actually studied and did reasonably well. Not until he'd completed fifteen hours did he discover that it was Berkowitz who'd suggested him to the warden.

That made him uneasy. What did this guy want from him anyway? Few words, other than what was necessary for running the chapel service, had passed between them up to that point. He felt like he was getting in over his head, into something he didn't understand.

"What's going on?" he asked the priest bluntly one day. He was folding the vestments and putting them away after a service.

The priest hadn't pretended not to know what he was talking about. Nevertheless, the answer took Dan off guard.

"Time," Berkowitz said. "Time is what's going on. Got that? Your life. Down the drain. You gotta wife out there. You think she's gonna wait for you twenty years? She don't even have a baby to take up her time. You ain't got a son, Kamowski. What's with you anyway? You're already dead. Wake up!"

It hadn't been what he expected to hear from a priest. In prison you trained yourself not to think about things. You kept your eyes on whoever was around you, waiting for trouble, but you didn't think. Thinking could drive you crazy.

He hardly allowed himself to think, even about Dell. She came every visiting day, but as soon as she was gone, he tried not to remember her, not to anticipate the next visit. She might not come the next time if he did. It hurt too much to expect things. It hurt too much to hope. Berkowitz is right, he said to himself. I am dead. All I'm doing is waiting to stop breathing.

He began to have terrifying dreams, so that he was afraid of going to sleep at night. At odd moments during the day his heart would start racing and he'd break out in a sweat. He suffered from headaches and stomach cramps. Finally he confronted the priest.

"You gotta stop it," Dan told him.

"Stop what?"

"This hex, this curse—whatever it is you done to me."

"Ha!" the priest barked in his face. "It's a curse, all right, but I ain't the one put it on you, Kamowski. And the only way it's going to stop is when they carry you out of here feet first."

The answer stunned him. Dan went back to his cell and sat there in shock. What was he going to do? He hated the priest! He'd been holding it all together before Berkowitz came along. Now look at him. He felt like he was dissolving, coming apart at the seams.

Dan barely made it through that night. The next morning he told the boss on his ramp he needed to see the chaplain. Dan's size alone had kept the other prisoners from making too much of his chapel assignment, but they had nicknamed him Choir Boy. Now the guard looked at him and leered, but took him to the chaplain's office.

"You gotta help me," Dan told the priest as soon as he was through the door. He clamped his teeth together to keep his jaw steady.

Berkowitz looked up wearily. "I can't help you," he said, and went back to filling out a form.

"What you mean you can't help me? Ain't that your job? Ain't that what you supposed to do? You got some kinda special cross or something, don't you? Ain't there something in that book that can undo this hex or evil-eye or whatever it is?" Dan pointed to the priest's prayer book.

The priest looked up again, irritated. "Get this straight, Kamowski. I don't play around with that kind of garbage. You want that, you go to the Mexicans or maybe one of them root doctors we got in here from Haiti."

"You can't do nothing about it? You telling me God can't do nothing about voodoo?"

The priest shrugged. "God can do whatever he wants to."

"Then get him to make this stop. I'm going crazy, you hear me?" His voice sounded like glass cracking.

"Why should he, huh? Why should he?" Berkowitz laid down his pen finally and looked at Dan. "Why should he waste his time on some bum like you? Your life's down the toilet anyway." He picked up the pen and tapped it on the desk, staring at it. Then he looked up at Dan again. "You didn't get into this world on your own steam, you know. Your parents probably didn't give it much thought either. It was him gave you this life, and you've thrown it away. It ain't worth a plug nickel now, thanks to you."

"But I thought—"

"You thought what?" the priest said.

"You said . . . you always say . . . every time, you know, about 'given for you.'" Dan stumbled over the words, could hardly bring them out.

Berkowitz sat back in his chair. "You got that wrong. I didn't say that. That's what he said. I'm just quoting him, that's all. I gotta admit it don't make a lot of sense to me."

"What do you mean it don't make sense? You're a priest, ain't you?"

"That don't mean it's gotta make sense. For one thing, you ain't worth it, Kamowski."

Dan stood there frozen. The priest's pen began scratching across the form in front of him. Berkowitz, it suddenly occurred to him, was right. And it was that knowledge that lay at the bottom of all his terror. *He wasn't worth it.*

Berkowitz signed his name at the bottom of the form with a flourish and laid the pen down. "Nobody's worth it. But that's not why he did it."

Dan found he couldn't speak at all now. He was suddenly so tired he couldn't bring out a sound. He lowered himself to a chair in silence.

"Who knows why he did it? Maybe he's crazy. You read this book here," the priest laid his hand on a Bible among the litter on his desk, "it'll tell you it's because he loves us. What does that mean? All you and me know of love, Kamowski, is desire. Lust. You want something—" he leaned toward him, snatched a piece of paper from the desktop, and crumpled it abruptly in his fist "—you take it. Is that what he means by love? Grabbing you and making you a prisoner? No. I've seen too many fall through his fingers. Ones like you, Kamowski. Squirming loose."

He dropped the wad of paper into the basket beside his chair. "You want loose, he lets you go." He sat back again. "Go on. Get out of here. Nobody's forcing you."

"No!" It was the first word Dan had been able to speak. The sound of his own voice startled him, and he lapsed into an embarrassed silence.

The priest rubbed his forehead wearily. "Get out of here, Kamowski. You're wasting my time."

Dan felt panicky; something was slipping away. He could almost touch it. "But how do I know—" he started.

"You don't," the priest broke in. "You don't know nothing. I don't know nothing either. I don't have a single shred of evidence to show you—not a splinter from the one true cross, not a scrap from baby Jesus' diaper. All we got is what somebody said they saw thousands of years ago, Kamowski. The way I see it, you either want it to be true or you don't. If you want it to be true, that's hope. You start with that. And maybe someplace down the road you cross over the line between hope and faith. Hope's all you got now, and I'd advise you to go with that. It's like parole—not as good as a full pardon, but better than staying inside this tomb."

Looking back, Dan had often wondered just when he'd crossed that line. He had expected it to be straight—a single, horizontal mark, like the finish line of a race. Instead, it was like a meandering river that the highway you were on kept crossing. Sometimes you were on one side of the river and sometimes the other. And you weren't always sure just which side it was. But one thing he knew. He never had felt dead again—not like he had in prison when he'd trained himself not to think, not to wait for Dell to come.

He looped the cincture around his stole on either side now and cinched it up. And what about the priest who usually vested in this room, he wondered? What side of the river was he on now, after such a disaster? He'd seen Arlen Canby at diocesan council a few times and at a convocation meeting. Thin and angular, the man moved among his fellow clergy like a jerky chicken, obviously ill at ease.

Dan could see Canby wasn't the type who would fit into Somerville easily. He looked more like a prep-school adolescent than a priest. And Episcopalians, especially in small towns, liked their priests either old or affable. This guy should have been in the city, say at All Saints in Houston. A staff priest. A junior executive. The question was, why had he agreed to come to a place like Somerville in the first place?

Dan picked up the clergy directory on Canby's desk and thumbed through it. The bio entry for the Somerville priest showed that he had previously been on the staff of a large church in New Orleans. During that time he'd also gotten a graduate degree in sociology. Dan snorted softly and closed the book. Maybe he'd come to Somerville to study small town society. Maybe the New Orleans church had gotten a new rector who wanted to pick his own staff. Or maybe Canby's wife had wanted to get the kids out of the city. But to Dan's way of thinking, the bishop had made a mistake in letting Canby come to St. Barnabas. The guy didn't fit in here.

Dan figured he knew something about being a misfit in the Episcopal church. But as Berkowitz had pointed out, for him it was either crime or the church. Those were the only two systems he knew how to operate in. After Dan's parole, Berkowitz had put him in touch with a parish priest who hustled scholarships, seminaries, and the bishop to get him ordained. Dan had sometimes felt—and often looked—like a dancing bear, displayed to confound the critics who accused the church of being elitist.

Arlen Canby, however, should have been the fair-haired boy of the diocese. From the rest of the description in the directory, he looked to be a prime candidate for bishop himself one day. His father was a doctor. He'd gone to private schools, universities, and the most prestigious seminary in the country. He'd married at the appropriate time, after he'd finished seminary. Had two children, a girl and a boy. So why had the bishop stuck him off in a small church like St. Barnabas that only lately had struggled out of its mission status and was now on the brink of dropping into that ecclesiastical abyss again? Why had Canby accepted the position? St. Barnabas had to be a disappointment to such an up-and-coming priest.

Dan glanced through the mail that had piled up on the rector's desk during the last week. Among the church equipment catalogues and newsletters from other parishes in the diocese were a program of upcoming events from the Jungian Society, an AIDS newsletter, and a fund-raising appeal from the Houston PBS station. It wasn't the sort of mail Dan got himself, but he knew that half the clergy in the diocese were probably on the same mailing lists. There was also, he saw, a renewal notice for a publication called *Yellow Silk*, whatever that was. And, of all things, a gun catalog. The rector of St. Barnabas certainly hadn't struck Dan as a gun kind of guy.

He shuffled the catalog back to the bottom of the pile. What another priest got in the mail wasn't any of his business. His business, as the bishop had made clear, was to come in, get the funeral over with, and get out again as quickly as possible. Reassure the congregation as well as he could, but answer questions cautiously. Don't talk to reporters at all, especially about the children. If the press wanted any information about the church's stand on suicide, Dan was to refer them to the bishop; that was his job.

It had not escaped Dan's attention that when any problem in the diocese came up that was even remotely connected with crime, the bishop handed it over to him. Other priests might have reputations for fund-raising or mediating church disputes or running retreats. Father Hoepker down at St. Bede's was even their token charismatic. But Dan, supposedly, had been given the gift of understanding the criminal mind.

The problem was that Dan usually didn't find much difference between the criminal mind and anyone else's mind. If there was a difference, it was mostly a matter of degree. Certain levels of dishonesty and violence were tolerated by the general population. But the thought processes a clerk went through when taking home a pen from the office were not really any different than the twists a car thief's mind took. The same person who kicked his dog on a bad day could, conceivably, shoot somebody tailgating him on the freeway. Those were quantitative, not qualitative, differences.

Nevertheless, Dan also knew that once in a while— and not always in prisons—he came across people who were a mystery to him. He couldn't imagine doing the things they did. Crimes of greed, lust, passion, anger— all those were more or less natural, he could see. You figured to get something out of holding up a convenience store. You at least expected to feel better after you'd bashed somebody's head.

But killing yourself and taking your kids along with you—that didn't make any sense to him. It was like something from one of those Greek plays where characters married their mother or ate their children. It was unnatural. And, he had to admit, it rattled him. He wondered what the police had felt when they discovered the priest's wife slumped over the steering wheel of the car and the children already dead in the back seat.

Why had she done it? Somebody young like that, with her whole life before her? What had made her that desperate, that unhappy?

And where was Canby? Dan had tried to reach him by phone, but only had gotten a recorded voice saying he was not available.

Well, Dan couldn't blame him. He wouldn't have wanted to talk to anyone either. Especially a stranger.

He wiped his large, sweating palms on the skirts of his alb, crossed himself, and opened the door. However much he dreaded facing the congregation and their questions, he didn't want to stay in this man's office alone any longer.

CHAPTER • SIX

JACK TATUM WOULD NEVER HAVE
thought of getting a baby-sitter for the nursery
if Mollie McCready hadn't called him about it.
"You never can tell how many people might
show up," she said. "Even if they haven't been
there in a long time. And mothers are certainly
not going to want to take their children in where they'll
see the coffins. I just think it would be a good idea, Jack."

So Jack had called the Sanderson's granddaugher and
asked if she'd keep the nursery during the funeral. The
girl hesitated so long before answering that he started to
apologize.

"But of course, you might want to be at the service
yourself," he said. "I should have thought of that. Maybe
you're supposed to be the acolyte."

"No," she said. "I haven't done that for a long time.
You haven't noticed?" She sighed audibly into the
phone.

Jack began to stammer out a vague apology, but she
broke in abruptly. "Okay," she said. "All right. I'll do it."

The Sandersons' granddaughter. That's what Wendy
had always been known as at St. Barnabas. No one ever

said she was Jeanette Sanderson's daughter. Jeanette had taken off two days after Wendy was born and had never shown herself in Somerville again, leaving her parents, Bert and Ilamae, to care for the child. Who the father was they never knew; some thought Jeanette probably didn't know herself.

The Sandersons had Wendy baptized when she was eighteen months old. By then it was clear that Jeanette wasn't coming back to claim her. "You can do a lot better job of raising her than I can," she'd written to her parents from California. Which, considering how Jeanette had turned out, the Daughters of the King found a questionable assumption.

Nevertheless, the Sandersons, in their mid-fifties then, had taken on the task without a word of complaint. They hadn't even discussed it. There it was, laid in their laps, quite literally; the idea that they had any choice in the matter or that, given one, they would choose otherwise, never occurred to them.

Bert and Ilamae were in their late sixties now, and Wendy had never given them cause to regret their course of action. Growing up in the tranquil environment of a middle-aged household had made her a mild, measured creature. She performed well at school, and to reward her, they had bought her a computer. She spent several hours every evening in its green glow. Ilamae worried about her eyes.

The older ladies at St. Barnabas fussed over Wendy; the younger mothers tried to coax her into the kind of youthful, exuberant behavior they suffered from their own children. But though she came to the Youth Council outings and seemed, in her own quiet way, to enjoy them as much as anyone, Wendy proved to be implacably placid.

Unlike the other youngsters, she always genuflected before entering her pew, then pulled the kneeler down, slid onto it, and prayed for about thirty seconds—which was considered an appropriate length at St. Barnabas.

Anything more would have been "showy." During the summer she came with her grandmother to the morning meetings of the Martha Circle and helped work on the needlepoint ornaments for the annual Christmas bazaar. If Ilamae and Bert had failed with her mother, it was generally conceded that they had redeemed themselves with Wendy.

She had, of course, been an acolyte, one of the more dependable and even attractive ones, her long blond hair tied back in a blue ribbon and her lips pursed in reverent concentration as she lit the altar candles. She had even accepted the new priest's liturgical changes without comment. The other acolytes, who thought memorizing their first set of stage directions an act of heroic proportions, chafed under the demands of Father Canby. They stumbled and fumbled through the services, looking sullen and rebellious. They wore their dirtiest Reeboks, once they knew it irritated him, and hitched up their robes so that their shoes and jeans showed at the bottom. Wendy alone performed flawlessly and without complaint. And when the other youngsters began to drop away from their duties, she remained steadfast.

Little was ever said in the Sanderson household about Wendy's absent mother. On the child's birthday every year a card would arrive signed only "Jeanette." Inside would be a check for twenty dollars. When Wendy was old enough to wonder who this mysterious person was, Ilamae and Bert had told her about her mother. They told the story with as little embellishment as possible, not only because they didn't want to turn the child against her mother but also because they simply didn't know much more to tell. Wendy continued to call Ilamae "Mom."

The Sandersons were uncomplicated people who, having grown up in hard times, approached difficult tasks by doing what had to be done and hoping for the best. The best in this case meant Jeanette not reappear-

ing to disrupt their lives, and Wendy herself not "brood-
ing," as Ilamae put it, over the parents she had never
known. The Sandersons figured there was a good deal
they didn't understand about life themselves—including
their own daughter—but they accepted these murky
areas as inevitable. You did what you could and went on
with your life.

Wendy, it seemed, was following in their footsteps, a
fact for which they both gave fervent thanks every day.
Then, "something happened"—a phrase that was used a
good deal as time went on under the new priest's regime.

Wendy's calm, reliable demeanor made her a favorite
baby-sitter among the young mothers at St. Barnabas,
and the children found her agreeable if not exciting. It
was not surprising, then, that Cassie Canby began asking
her to baby-sit regularly.

Wendy was a little shocked the first time she sat with
the priest's children. Having seen the interiors of many
homes by now, she knew they were not all as tidy as her
grandmother's, but never before had she seen the kind
of disorder she found at the Canbys. She stumbled over
jogging shoes and children's sneakers as she came in the
door. Piles of clothes straight from the dryer were
dumped on the living room sofa. Newspapers and junk
mail littered the dining room table. Dishes, dirty for
more than a day, covered the counters in the kitchen.

Mrs. Canby waved her arms at all this and laughed a
little desperately. "Excuse the mess, Wendy. We have a
hard time getting organized." The two children, Russell
and Heather, had pulled themselves up onto the back of
the sofa and were turning somersaults into the pile of
laundry.

Her husband—it was hard for Wendy to think of him
as the priest without his suit and clerical collar—came
down the hall, his hair still wet from the shower, dressed
in jeans and a cowboy shirt. He nodded at her but did
not speak.

"We're going to a country western dance at the fair-grounds with the Mabrys," Mrs. Canby said. "I guess the number's in the book if you need to reach us there. But I think everything'll be all right. If the children get hungry, you can fix them a peanut butter and jelly sandwich. Or cereal. They like the colored kind."

"When do they go to bed?" Wendy asked.

"Oh." Mrs. Canby paused to study the question as though it were one that had never occurred to her before. "Sometime around nine, I suppose. If they're tired by then."

"Do they get baths first?"

"If you'd like that." Mrs. Canby's face brightened. "I'm sure they would."

Her husband opened the coat closet by the front door. "Let's get going," he said.

Both the children threw their arms around their mother's legs and clung like leeches. "We want to go too," the little girl howled.

"Turn Mommy loose, sweetheart," Mrs. Canby said. "Next time. You can go next time. We'll bring you something, all right? A surprise."

The promises failed to stop the howling, but her husband was holding the front door open impatiently. Wendy helped her detach the children's sticky fingers from her skirt.

"Bye-bye, sweeties, see you later." And Mrs. Canby slipped out the front door and closed it behind her.

Both children made a lunge for the door, but Wendy managed to capture them and settle them on either side of her on the sofa. She had just pulled a storybook from under one of the cushions and was trying to interest them in it when the front door suddenly opened again.

"I forgot to mention," the priest said, "we always keep our bedroom door closed. The children are not to go in there. Not under any circumstances. Nor you either, of course."

Wendy looked at him blankly.

"You do agree to that condition, don't you?" He looked very serious.

Her eyes widened. "Sure," she said.

He nodded brusquely. "Good," he said and closed the door.

Wendy had never seen hard-core pornography before. Of course she'd seen copies of *Playboy* at school, but nothing like what she found in the Canbys' bedroom. Not the first time she baby-sat; it must have been the third or fourth time.

Each time she stayed with the Canby children, she was given the same warning about not going into their parents' bedroom—and always by the priest. Despite her placid nature, Wendy's curiosity was eventually piqued.

She found herself trying to invent reasons why she might need to go into the bedroom, but nothing had sounded very plausible until the night Russell started running a fever while the Canbys were guests at a Rotary Club dinner. As the couple were leaving, Mrs. Canby mentioned that the little boy had "the sniffles." And later, after eating a bowl of canned spaghetti, he had thrown up all over the kitchen floor. When Wendy wiped his face, she found he was burning with fever. While she was tucking him into bed—after putting sheets on it—it occurred to her that she ought to check his temperature.

She sat on the side of his bed a moment, considering. Surely, she said to herself, they wouldn't keep a thermometer in the hall bathroom the children used. That would be too dangerous. It would only make sense that the thermometer would be kept in the medicine cabinet in the bathroom connected to the Canbys' bedroom. And she really needed to check Russell's temperature.

Heather was watching TV in the living room. Wendy opened the door to the master bedroom quietly. The bed was unmade and clothes were lying on the floor. Beer and Pepsi cans littered the nightstands and dresser. The clutter didn't surprise her. Nevertheless, she felt a vague disappointment. She'd been expecting—what?

In the bathroom she checked the medicine cabinet for a thermometer. Lots of pill bottles with medication she couldn't pronounce, but no thermometer. The drawers in the vanity yielded nothing except makeup, soap, and hairbrushes. Maybe they did keep the thermometer in the children's bathroom.

As she was leaving the bedroom, however, the notion struck her that it might be in one of the nightstands. She pulled open the drawer of the one nearest her and froze. A gun, small and stubby, lay on top of several magazines. Are these people crazy? That was her first reaction. Who would keep a gun like that with small children around? No wonder he was always talking about staying out of the bedroom and keeping the door closed.

Then she noticed the cover of the magazine under the gun. She frowned, not quite able to figure it out. What was the woman in the picture doing anyway? She moved the gun carefully aside with one finger and slid the magazine from under it, turning the pages back over the edge of the drawer.

Once, when she was six or seven, Wendy had been given an Advent calendar with little windows that folded back to reveal various figures—angels and shepherds and kings. It was the same year that her grandparents had first told her about her mother, and somehow, with each little cardboard shutter she opened, Wendy kept expecting to see her mother's face looking out at her. She knew she would recognize her mother when she saw her and that she would be smiling a special smile just for her.

Wendy had the same feeling now as she turned the pages of the magazine. She had figured out the circumstances of her birth years ago. She no longer expected to find her mother in an Advent calendar. Jeanette was one of these women. Wendy was certain of it. She searched their faces—sullen, pleading, fierce, contemptuous—waiting for the shock of recognition. She turned each page with dread, rather than the hope that had flickered each time she had opened a new little window of the calendar. She wanted to stop, to shut the magazine and close the drawer, but the dread was mingled with a fascination that glued her to the pictures. Only when she looked up to see Heather standing at the bedroom door did she close the magazine.

The little girl was staring at her wordlessly.

"I was looking for the thermometer, Heather," Wendy said, her voice made uneven by the lie. "Do you know where it is?"

The little girl shook her head and stuck her thumb in her mouth. Trying to shield it from Heather's view, Wendy slid the gun back over the magazine and shut the drawer. "Let's look in your bathroom," she said.

She herded Heather ahead of her into the other bathroom and rummaged through the cabinets and drawers. Her hands were shaking and she could feel panic swelling in her chest. What had she done? What if Russell got worse? Had Heather seen the gun? Would the Canbys be able to tell she had been in their bedroom?

There was no thermometer to be found in the children's bathroom either. Giving up the search, she sponged Russell off with cold water and sat beside him, holding Heather in her lap.

"I couldn't find a thermometer," she told Mrs. Canby when they got home.

"Oh, heavens! I keep it in the kitchen, up with the aspirin, in the cabinet over the sink," she said. "I didn't think. I should have told you."

The priest drove her home. He usually didn't talk much except to ask her stiff questions about what classes she was taking in school or how her grandparents were.

Tonight he was even more silent than usual. She looked at him out of the corner of her eye once and saw his jaw clenching and unclenching. When they were about halfway home, he finally broke the silence.

"You couldn't find the thermometer?" he asked.

Wendy felt her stomach lurch. "No."

"Where did you look?"

"Oh. In the medicine cabinet." Her voice sounded weak even to her. She kept her eyes straight ahead and felt, rather than saw, him turn and look at her closely as he pulled up to a stop sign.

"Did you look in our bathroom?"

"No," she said quickly. "No, I didn't."

Slowly a kind of smile spread across his face. The car didn't move. "It's all right, Wendy. You can tell me the truth. You can trust me with your secrets."

She frowned and clenched her fists in her lap. "That is the truth," she said stubbornly.

"It's all right, Wendy," he went on as though she hadn't spoken. "It's natural for a young person to be curious. I just don't want you getting the wrong idea. Maybe if we talked about it."

She didn't say anything. She could feel him staring at her.

"You can talk to me, you know. That's what priests are for. Sometimes things, new things, can be pretty confusing. You're at a point in your life where you're changing. Even your body's changing. You may look in the mirror at yourself—your body—and feel like you don't recognize who you are anymore. I understand you don't have a mother to talk to. And your grandmother, well, maybe you're afraid she won't understand. But you can talk to me. Ask me anything you want. Anything at all."

He lifted one hand from the steering wheel to gesture, spreading his fingers upward. She was suddenly afraid he was going to reach over and touch her, pat her knee or her shoulder. She edged closer to the door.

"I want to go home now," she said.

He frowned and nodded, then eased the car across the intersection. "Of course," he said stiffly. Wendy wasn't sure if she had hurt his feelings or made him angry.

He was right, she thought. She was confused. There were lots of things she wanted to know about. But she couldn't even put them into words right now. And she didn't like him talking about her looking at her body in the mirror. How did he know anyway? She suddenly felt as if she wouldn't be able to breathe again until she got out of the car.

He cleared his throat. "I just want you to know I'm available," he went on in the same soft tone. "Sometimes when you're young, discovering new things about the world, about your own feelings, an older person can help. Can make you see it's okay. If you're confused, they can explain things to you. Someone with more experience can make the new feelings seem—natural, not so frightening. You can learn how to enjoy them."

They turned the corner onto her street. Wendy stared straight ahead and said nothing.

"You've got to have somebody to talk to, Wendy. Remember, I'm there for you. Anytime. Just call. You can trust me with your secrets."

The car slid along the curb smoothly and silently. He turned out the headlights. "You will remember, won't you?"

Wendy mumbled "yes" and jerked the car door open.

"Wendy—" he called after her. But she pretended she didn't hear him.

The porch light was on and she already had her key out, but her hand was shaking so badly that she was still fumbling with the lock when she heard his step behind her.

"Here, Wendy. Give it to me. I'll do it for you."

She looked up at him there under the porch light. He

was smiling down at her, gently, one side of his mouth pulled up higher than the other.

"It's the least I can do for you, isn't it? I'm a priest, remember? I like doing things for people. I'd like doing things for you." He held out his hand. "Let me do it for you, Wendy."

Mutely, she handed him the key.

Wendy didn't baby-sit again after that night. Not for the Canbys or anyone else. Her regular customers were distressed, but she wouldn't relent, and eventually they gave up asking her.

"It happens to them all sooner or later," Mollie McCready said. "Baby-sitting's not glamorous enough anymore. They want to work at Pizza Hut or something."

The next Sunday Wendy told Ilamae she had an upset stomach and couldn't go to church. Later she told her grandmother she wanted her name taken off the list of acolytes.

"But they need you, sweetheart. There's hardly anyone left to do it, you know," her grandmother said.

"I don't care," Wendy said flatly. "I'm not going to do it anymore."

Her grandmother looked up from the pie crust she was trimming. "What's wrong, Wendy? Is something wrong?"

Wendy sighed heavily, shook her head, and disappeared into her bedroom. She dropped her books on the floor and fell across the bed. How could she tell her grandmother what was wrong when all she felt was this vague but constant uneasiness? Is this what had happened to her mother too? Was she like her mother—this mysterious woman she only knew by the one word "Jeanette"? Had her mother had these same uneasy feelings—things Wendy didn't even have names for? Had she suspected things about herself—and had to leave home, leave her, because of them?

She flopped over onto her back and ran her hands over her ribs and down her sides. Kids at school joked about this kind of thing all the time. Sometimes they bragged about the weekends when their folks were away.

But all that was like . . . like little toy boats or twigs bobbing on the surface where life was sunny and ordinary. This was different. This was like the ocean itself, like sinking down beneath the surface, where the light was murky and everything indistinct, in slow motion. She didn't know how to describe it. But the other kids wouldn't know what she was talking about.

There were only two people in the world she knew for certain would understand what she wanted to know. One was her mother. The other . . . the very thought made her flinch. Somehow he knew—knew everything. Knew she'd opened the drawer, moved aside the gun, turned the pages of the magazine. It was like he could see into her mind, like they had this secret together.

She thrust her fingers into her hair and pulled it as hard as she could. Pain was the only thing that could arrest her attention, that could stop her mind from running away. Pain somehow made her rush back inside herself, like sucking a genie back into a bottle.

She got up and went to her dresser and rummaged through a little straw basket of odds and ends, pulling out a pair of tweezers. Then, leaning close to the mirror, she began methodically pulling out her eyebrows, hair by hair.

It took almost an hour and hurt a lot. Sometimes little drops of blood oozed out of the tiny holes where the hairs had grown. She would lick her finger and wipe the blood away. When she was finished, she stood back and stared at her face. It looked bald, skinned, blank. She hardly recognized herself. She looked like a different person.

Maybe she was. The other Wendy, the one who had lived in her grandparents' quiet house for fourteen years, was gone, lost. And she didn't know who this person in the mirror was. A stranger. Someone who frightened her. What might she do next?

He knew though. He had read her mind that night. He knew about this person in the mirror. He could tell her.

Dropping the tweezers back in the little basket, she picked up the phone from the nightstand and pulled it into the middle of the bed with her. It was almost five o'clock and he might have left the office already, but it was worth a try.

Wendy hadn't slept all night. In fact, she'd had hardly any sleep since her grandmother told her the terrible news. She still felt as if the top of her head were coming off, and she seemed to observe herself from outside her own body, as if she were watching a movie. No one else appeared to notice anything strange about her though. Or else they had gotten used to the abrupt changes that swept over her lately.

Her grandmother had been pleased when Jack Tatum called and Wendy agreed to keep the nursery. Her grandfather's doctor had scheduled some kind of test for him in a Houston hospital, and they wouldn't be able to attend the funeral themselves.

It would be the first time Wendy had been to St. Barnabas for a service since April when she last baby-sat for the Canbys. She doubted there would be any children to take care of. And if some did show up, they wouldn't recognize her now. Not only was her face bald, but she had shaved one side of her head.

She put on the softest dress she had, a pink one her

grandmother had made her the summer before. It was a little tight across the chest now and the waist was too high, but it lessened the effect of her bald face. She brushed her hair to the side to cover the shaved half of her head. She had never intended to frighten any children.

CHAPTER • SEVEN

H E COULDN'T PUT IT OFF ANY
longer. He'd gone back in the house
before he even started the car—first
for his keys and then for his prayer
book—postponing the inevitable
moment when he'd have to pull into the parking lot
behind St. Barnabas, get out of the car, and open the
back door to the parish hall.

Jack Tatum drove at a snail's pace through the streets
of Somerville, wondering if Mabry and Singletary would
be there. They hadn't called to say they wouldn't come
to this final, terrible service; nevertheless, he had a sinking feeling Mabry's Lincoln and Singletary's Chrysler
wouldn't be in the parking lot when he pulled in.

Jack drove an eight-year-old Ford himself. Lanelle
Chambers, from the education department, had insisted
on going with him when he bought the car from Poor
Henry's Motors, the local Ford dealer.

"I can't believe you're not going to Houston to buy a
car," Lanelle had fussed. "You can get a much better
deal there. They give bigger discounts because of the
volume."

Jack, however, was willing to pay the difference in
order to avoid the high-pressure Houston salesmen.

They knew him at Poor Henry's. He'd been buying cars from them for twenty years, ever since he came to Somerville State right out of graduate school and started teaching history. He'd never sought a position at any other college and he'd never bought a car from any other dealer.

Lanelle Chambers figured if she could ever get him to the altar, he would prove as faithful to her as he was to his employer and automobile dealer. But if Jack Tatum had a more deeply embedded character trait than perseverance, it was stubbornness. Lanelle sometimes pointed out to him that these were just different names for the same thing.

Her infrequent shopping outings with him were motivated as much by revenge as romance. She knew it embarrassed him when she hooted at a salesman's first offer, one Jack would have accepted if he'd been alone. But if he was determined to be a bachelor the rest of his life and to deprive himself of the comforts of her considerable flesh and succulent cooking, then he deserved to be made periodically uncomfortable.

His mildness only served to make her more abrasive. She knew he would never refuse to let her go along, would not even lie to avoid her company. His church friends could call that pious if they wanted to, but Lanelle knew it was nothing more that pure-D cussedness. Jack was as obstinate as a balky mule. Not only would he never propose marriage, he wouldn't even admit, by trying to avoid her, that the danger existed.

Jack, in truth only vaguely aware of Lanelle's feelings, was, however, painfully conscious of the upheavals at St. Barnabas. He had often felt during the past year that though he had successfully avoided the quagmire of marriage, he was nevertheless having to suffer through a divorce. He'd felt the separation from former members of the congregation that keenly. And those friends could understand his sticking with the

church no more than Lanelle could understand his
patronizing Poor Henry's.

His perseverance—or stubbornness—made for some
strained situations at times. He'd continued to see the
former members, though he knew Arlen Canby didn't
like it. At the same time, however, the priest put him on
just about every committee he formed. But, then, there
weren't many people under sixty left at St. Barnabas.
Denny McCready was still junior warden, but Singletary
and Mabry had faded into the woodwork. And Clyde
Mapes was only waiting till his term on the vestry was
over. Then he'd disappear too.

What did all that matter now though? He shouldn't
even be thinking about the problems at St. Barnabas at a
time like this, Jack told himself. He should be thinking
about—praying for—Cassie Canby and the children.

Poor Cassie, sweet Cassie. How could she ever have
brought herself to do such a thing? Jack had no idea what
it was to be a parent, but he figured a mother would have
to be desperate beyond all imagining to try to kill her
children along with herself. And Arlen? What would this
do to him?

The priest was a troubled man, certainly. And not a
popular one. He had shown Jack, in confidence, an
anonymous letter he believed had come from a hostile
parishioner. A terrible, virulent letter. *Scum*, it said.
Filth. We know why you want women priests in the church.
Temple harlots! It had gone on to predict certain out-
landish acts being performed in the sacristy. Jack had
been profoundly shocked. He found it impossible to
believe that the letter had come from anyone in the congregation.

Arlen Canby had pointed out the Somerville cancel-
lation on the envelope. "Don't we have someone in the
congregation who works for the newspaper? That young
woman who lives out at Point Blank. What's her name?"

"Beth Marie Cartwright? Surely you don't think—"

"No. Of course not. I meant maybe we should turn this story over to her. Maybe a little publicity would flush out whoever's responsible."

Jack inhaled slowly, then blew the breath out in an even slower sigh, trying to convey pensiveness rather than the dismay he felt. "There are some religious cranks in Somerville, no doubt about it," he said. "But publicity about this might do more to damage St. Barnabas than help it, don't you think?"

The priest raised an eyebrow and dropped the letter back into a file folder. "I guess you're right. I should put the welfare of the whole church ahead of my own problems. Well. We'll just keep it to ourselves then, Jack. I haven't shared this with anyone else. I do wish I knew who hated me so much though."

Jack couldn't imagine anyone at St. Barnabas writing such a letter. He could understand why people didn't find Arlen Canby a good priest. He certainly was short on pastoral manner. But Jack could also see, in a way others either couldn't or wouldn't, that the man suffered from terrible fears and hungers. The hunger drove him on and the fear held him back. But toward what was he driven? And what fear stopped him? There were times when the priest would pause in the middle of a sermon, his face drawn, almost contorted, and, having lost his train of thought, would look suddenly terrified, as though he couldn't possibly go on.

After seeing the anonymous letter, Jack had tried to draw the rector out in a gentle way, but he always became brusque and businesslike. It was obvious that it would take more than gentleness to soften his defenses. And now this. He couldn't picture the man, already on the edge, surviving this tragedy.

Jack winced as he pulled into the back parking lot and saw Clyde Mapes sitting in his pickup, waiting. The rancher got out slowly as Jack opened his own car door. Clyde's face was flushed—not a good sign—and Jack felt his own smile slipping. He knew he was no good at dealing with Clyde's volatile temper.

"You lay reading?" the rancher asked as he ambled up, twisting his neck from side to side inside his collar to indicate his discomfort with a tie.

"I believe I am," Jack said. Long ago he had developed the strategy of couching statements in the most tentative way possible. He had avoided many confrontations that way; the provisional seemed to pacify people. The habit had served him so well that he wasn't even conscious of it anymore.

"I gotta say this is the goshawfullest mess I've ever been involved in," Clyde declared, folding his arms across his chest and rocking back on his boot heels. He stared belligerently at Jack.

No, you don't *gotta* say it, Jack thought to himself. Aloud he murmured, "Terrible, terrible," and shook his head, looking down. Then, after an appropriate pause, he added, "Is Father Kamowski here yet?"

Clyde shrugged, as though to let Jack know he did not intend to be put off by an irrelevant question. "That his name? You think the bishop is trying to tell us something, Doc, sending some mission priest up here to do the funeral?"

"Tell us something?" Jack repeated. He was active enough in diocese affairs to know that Father Kamowski had a prison record. Obviously Clyde wasn't aware of that or he'd be even more offended.

"You know. Like this is some kind of statement. The bishop saying he doesn't think much of St. Barnabas."

"Oh. I don't think that's the case, Clyde. Father Kamowski is well-respected in the diocese."

Clyde laughed shortly. "Sure." He looked up, squinting into the glare of the sun. "When's those bulldozers supposed to be here?" he asked. "I want to bring the kids by to see. Figured they'd get a kick out of that."

Jack's chin dropped and his mouth made a little o.

Then he shook his head. "I'm not sure, Clyde. You might check with Denny about that." He opened the door to the parish hall quickly before the rancher could ask him any more questions.

It was dark and stuffy inside the big, windowless hall. The commercial-grade carpet was a practical dirt-color. At one time the cinder-block walls had been covered with enormous banners made by the children in Vacation Bible School. The banners had come down soon after Arlen Canby arrived. Jack supposed someone on the Memorials Committee knew where they were now. Maybe Mollie McCready. He'd like to know. He'd even like to have one.

He had never asked though. It might have caused a problem. The priest might have thought—well, who knows what he might have thought? Anyway, Jack didn't want to risk causing more trouble, and he had sensed fairly early on that the best way to keep the peace was to keep quiet. Jack was good at sensing potential trouble.

But not good enough, he reproached himself now. He hadn't anticipated this final tragedy. Cassie Canby had never said a word to him about being unhappy. In fact, he had noticed a new exuberance in her lately; she had even started holding up her hands during the Gloria, swaying slightly back and forth. It wasn't the kind of thing he would do himself, but Cassie looked as absorbed and beautiful as a child while she sang. He didn't pretend to know much about women, but she had actually seemed happier lately. So how could he have known?

No one had. None of them could have predicted the two little coffins in the chancel. Or the hospital bed where plastic tubes were feeding narrow tributaries of colorless fluids into Cassie's passive and inert body. None of them.

He knew what the others would say. Or at least what they'd think. That somehow this was her husband's fault. He was overbearing and manipulative—especially toward women, they'd say. And they'd be thinking that this never would have happened if Jack had stood up to the priest.

"You're just being used, Jack," Leslie Rittenhouse had told him months ago. "Can't you see that? You have more credibility with this congregation than anyone. You've been here twenty years. The old people trust you. If you stay, they figure they should too."

"But I *should* stay," he'd retorted. "It's my church. And theirs too."

Leslie had laughed the same way Clyde Mapes had out in the parking lot just now. Short and bitter. "Really?" she said. "Other than paying the bills, just what part do the people play, Jack? Is that why he revoked my lay reader's license? He polled the membership and discovered they were dissatisfied with my performance?"

"I can understand you being unhappy about that—"

"Unhappy!" she'd exploded. "I'm not unhappy, Jack, I'm hopping mad. Angry. I could spit nails. Look at me!" She grabbed his arm. "This is anger, Jack, not unhappiness."

He could see that. Streaks of red had crept up Leslie's neck, and her eyes were bright with tears. The sight terrified him. He had to admit he could stand the priest's cold disapproval better than Leslie's frontal assault.

It wasn't that he didn't understand why people had been upset. Especially after the disastrous vestry meeting the previous spring when Linda Hooper had been attacked—there was no other word to describe it. He would admit that. She'd left the meeting in tears, and afterward the rest of the vestry had dispersed without much comment, ashamed of having allowed it to happen. Jack had been the only one who even tried to intervene on her behalf.

Linda was forty and often made edgy jokes about still being single after six years of widowhood. Jack was vaguely aware that she wore bright, vivid colors and had heard her described by younger men as "hot to trot." It wasn't a phrase Jack would have ever used himself, but even he had sensed Linda's frustrations.

For the last couple of years she had put a good deal of that pent-up energy into sponsoring the church's youth group. And certainly it had been more active under her leadership than at any time since Jack had been a member at St. Barnabas. She put together trips to the beach, spaghetti dinners to raise money for camp, and even got the teenagers interested in Bible study. Maybe she worked so hard at it in part because she was trying to raise her own two teenagers alone.

Linda was also active on the Altar Guild, a job she'd taken on originally to please her husband, a man Jack remembered as pompous and overbearing. After he had died suddenly from a heart attack, Linda had confided in Jack about her struggle with family finances; she had never paid a single bill before. Nevertheless, she'd been elected to the vestry during Father Shields's last year there and had made an excellent clerk, taking far better minutes than Orville Kelly, who'd tried to get by with dictating them over the phone to the church secretary.

After the new priest arrived, Linda had, if anything, worked even harder at St. Barnabas than before. She refused to listen to any rumors about the rector and nipped any complaints she heard in the bud. "A real team player," Ty Singletary, the senior warden then, had called her. Until the fateful vestry meeting.

Jack still squirmed when he thought about it. The vestry had always met in the parish hall, sitting around one of the big folding tables they used for potluck dinners. There was plenty of room that way, and the coffee urn was handy. Father Canby, however, had moved them into his office. It was a bit of a squeeze getting ten adults in the small room, but he said it provided greater privacy and confidentiality.

That was where they'd been when it happened, sitting knee to knee, with no place to put coffee cups or papers. Canby had passed out printed agendas, one of his innovations meant to correct what he called their "loose leadership style." They'd discovered, however, that the main point of the agenda was not what was on it but what wasn't. They were not, the priest made clear, to discuss items not printed on the agenda. And if they had any matter they wanted included, it was necessary to call his office a minimum of three days before the meeting. Such an "instrument"—as he called it—contributed to the orderly dispatch of business.

Most of the vestry members did well not to forget the meeting itself, let alone think far enough ahead to call in an agenda item three days in advance. Except for Linda. Near the end of that night's list was an item called "youth program proposal." Jack had assumed that was her contribution.

From the first, he could hear the tension in Linda's voice when she read the previous month's minutes, and he sensed there was going to be trouble. Ty Singletary kept shifting in his folding chair and moving his shoulders up and down inside his suitcoat.

The first item concerned the Memorials Committee. "Under our new bylaws," the rector explained, "this committee is actually responsible for more than just spending the money donated to that fund. I'd like them to be in charge of everything we might think of as the decor of the church. I don't think we're doing ourselves any favors by allowing our sentiment to overcome our good taste. For example, new people who come to St. Barnabas don't know our children. Certainly they don't have the same attachment to their handiwork that we might. You see what I mean? At home we might stick our children's crayon drawings on the fridge, for instance, but we wouldn't hang them on our living room walls. I think the Memorials Committee would be an appropriate venue for making these difficult decisions."

No one said anything. Jack scanned all the faces. Denny McCready was rubbing his palms up and down his thighs. Clyde Mapes frowned as if trying to understand just what the priest was talking about. Across from Jack, the other woman on the vestry shook her head slightly, as though she did understand. She said nothing, however. The rest looked blank.

Linda cleared her throat and leaned forward slightly in her chair. "Have you spoken with the Sunday school teachers about this?" she asked.

"Oh, no. That would be the place of the Memorials Committee itself. I don't want this to be my decision. That's not the point." Jack noticed that the pitch of the priest's voice had risen slightly.

"Who's on the Memorials Committee?" the other woman asked.

Father Canby consulted a sheet of paper, as though to refresh his memory on the subject. He read out three names, two women and a man. "I've also asked Ty here to be on the committee. Of course, as senior warden he's automatically an ad hoc member of all our committees. But I want him to take a leadership role here. The reason being that, as I say, we want to be proud of our church when visitors come, just as we'd want to be proud of our homes. I wouldn't want us to be embarrassed by— you know—tacky stuff. I'd like to think that we'd have nothing in our church that the Singletarys, for example, wouldn't have in their own tasteful home."

Ty swallowed hard and rubbed his hands together. Denny glanced over at Jack, who instantly looked away. He knew if Denny caught his eye, they'd both laugh out loud. Ty Singletary as an arbiter of taste and culture? The man had money, yes, but so far as Jack knew, his taste ran to knotty pine and Jack Daniels.

Linda broke the uneasy silence. "Gee, Ty, I never thought of you as an interior decorator before." Singletary grinned sheepishly, but Linda's voice was edged with irony. Jack saw Father Canby look pointedly at her. He was not smiling.

By the time they had moved down the list to "youth program proposal," everyone was tired of the metal folding chairs and the cramped quarters. They were startled to attention, though, when the priest moved to "go into executive session."

"What does that mean?" Clyde asked.

"Only that we'll be discussing some sensitive matters that we need to keep confidential, both for our own protection and that of others," Canby said, not looking at Clyde but down at his notes.

Clyde shrugged. No one else said anything. Linda sat up a little straighter. Jack noticed she'd begun to flex one foot up and down.

"If there's no objection then, we'll proceed. With the understanding, of course, that whatever is said now is not to leave this room or even be discussed among yourselves later."

Several people frowned, but no one said anything.

The priest looked up from his notes. "I'm afraid this is going to be rather painful, but it's come to my attention that certain of our parents aren't completely satisfied with the way the youth program is being carried on in the church. They have a particular complaint about activities not being properly supervised. That kind of thing."

Linda pressed her lips together and started tapping her pencil on her notepad. It was obvious to Jack that she had known somehow that this was coming.

"I would like to suggest that it's time we started thinking about revamping our youth program altogether," the priest said. "This seems to be the moment."

"Just a minute," Linda broke in. "If there's been

complaints, as sponsor of the youth group I want to know what they are and who they come from."

The priest looked down at his notes and gave the merest sigh. "I'm sorry, Linda, but I can't divulge any names. If you think about it, I'm sure you can understand why."

"No. I have thought about it, and I can't think of why. Why don't you enlighten me." Her tone was getting sharper.

Jack cleared his throat. Everyone else was silent.

The priest sighed again, more audibly this time, and glanced briefly at the ceiling. "I had hoped it wouldn't come to this. I certainly don't want our discussion to become acrimonious. And there's no one blaming you in particular. I want you to understand that, Linda. We all appreciate what you've been able to accomplish. But that—what do you call it?—lock-in you had last month. Well. Some of the parents weren't entirely satisfied that the chaperons were as . . . responsible as they could wish."

"Which chaperons?" Linda demanded.

"It certainly wasn't you, Linda. Be assured of that."

"There was only myself, Maryellen, Leffler, and my friend Josh Frederick. Did they object because I've been dating Josh? Maryellen and Leffler—they're college students—almost kids themselves."

"Exactly."

"What do you mean 'exactly'?"

"Well, if they're kids themselves, they can hardly be suitable chaperons, can they?" He paused and looked around at the group. "But it's not my intention to get into personalities here—"

Linda broke in again. "Is it because I was there with Josh? Was that it?"

"Please, Linda. That's in the past. Let's put that behind us now, shall we?"

For a moment it looked as though she were about to

retort, but then she blinked rapidly and stared down at her agenda.

"At any rate," the priest went on rapidly, "I have here a proposal for a program I've designed for this coming year—" He paused and reached over to hand a sheaf of copies to Ty Singletary to pass around.

"Just a minute," Linda said. She was swinging her leg again. "What about the program we currently have? What's wrong with it? We have more kids coming than we've ever had."

The priest gripped the sides of his clipboard. Jack could see his jaw working. "Maybe so," he said. "But those same kids aren't coming to church, are they?"

"That's hardly the fault of the youth program, I'd say," Linda shot back. "If they're not coming to church, I think I'd look elsewhere for an explanation."

By now the other vestry members were shooting alarmed glances at one another. Jack's mouth had come open, and he was making little murmuring noises in his throat. He saw the priest's eyes narrow and his jaw tighten again.

"I'm sorry, Linda, but we've got to move on. I've tried to be kind. But if you insist on disrupting the meeting—"

"Disrupting!" The word exploded from her.

"Umm," Jack said and held up a hand.

"I am responsible for the conduct of this church," Canby said, his voice rising. "I cannot allow this kind of thing to go on. I'm afraid I'm going to have to ask for your resignation as sponsor of the youth group, Linda. You're obviously too emotional at this point in your life to be able to handle it."

"What! What the devil are you talking about?"

He sighed heavily and looked around at the others again, as though appealing for their understanding. "It's evident you are in no condition to be handling youngsters who are themselves at a difficult time in their lives regarding their own sexuality."

Linda sat back, stunned.

"You've forced me to go much further with this than I ever intended. But if you insist on having everything out in the open like this, I must tell you that I believe you are doing entirely too much at St. Barnabas. You need—for your own good—to be relieved of some of your duties here. It's obvious to me—and I believe I have some expertise in these matters—that you've never really gotten over your husband's death, Linda, and that you're trying to compensate somehow for his loss by, well, what you probably perceive as service, but which to an objective observer looks perilously like compulsive, even neurotic behavior."

"I, uh, I'm not sure this is the place for saying these kind of things," Jack finally put in. His own voice was shaking, and he could feel little rivulets of cold sweat making their way down his sides. He heard a murmur of assent around him from the others. "We might be saying things here we would regret later."

Canby turned toward him instantly. "Exactly," he said. "I couldn't agree more. Let's do move on."

"Move on?" Linda said. She was blinking back tears. "You say those kinds of things about me, make all kinds of innuendos, and then you say we should move on?"

"I'm not impugning your character here. Please understand that. I'm only saying that people sometimes make God a psychological substitute for whatever is missing in their lives. As your pastor, I believe it's best that you take things a little easier for a while. Turn over some of your responsibilities to others. Your work as clerk of vestry has been very valuable to us all." He scanned the members' faces as though soliciting their support. "Now we really do need to move on."

Linda stood up, her agenda and notepad falling to the floor. She started toward the door, then turned back to pick up her purse from where she'd left it beside her chair. Everyone watched silently. Jack put out a hand toward her, but she ignored him and turned toward the door, visibly fighting back tears. He got up and followed her out of the office.

Out in the darkened parish hall he called to her to wait.

"Not now, Jack. Please."

"Are you all right? Would you like me to drive you home?"

She was fumbling for her keys. "What? And contaminate yourself by associating with some sex-starved slut?"

"Please, Linda. I don't think he meant it that way. Let me talk to him. Maybe I can help."

She turned and looked at him as she opened the back door. She was silhouetted by the light from the parking lot, and he couldn't see her face. "You waited a little too long for that, didn't you, Jack. I'm afraid you missed your chance."

After the door closed behind her, he had stood there in the dark, waiting for the meeting to break up. He hadn't known what else to do.

Jack opened the door to the closet where the lay readers' robes hung. They never had considered the new proposal for the youth group. And it was a moot point now. There was no youth group—in fact, no teenagers— left at St. Barnabas. He tried to remember the last news he'd heard about Linda. She had kept in touch with Mollie McCready for a while. Somewhere he'd heard that the children were living with their grandparents in Houston now. He wasn't sure where Linda was.

CHAPTER EIGHT

A rape," Leslie Rittenhouse had said to Jack Tatum when she heard about the vestry meeting. Not from him, of course. He hadn't said a word about the fiasco to anyone. She'd learned about it from Mollie McCready, who had known the instant she saw Denny's face that night that something terrible had happened. And when Denny held back, invoking Canby's request for confidentiality, Mollie's response had been both withering and profane. Finally he'd spilled it all.

Leslie barely knew Linda Hooper; the two women certainly weren't close. Linda was entirely too impulsive for Leslie, who prided herself on her ability to analyze problems and address them logically. Nevertheless, having been a divorcée herself, Leslie could sympathize with the widow's struggle to raise two children alone, not to mention the exhaustion from playing social games meant for younger women.

"What you witnessed was a rape," she'd told Jack.

"Rape," Jack had repeated, startled, echoing her word rather than questioning it.

"What else would you call it?" she demanded. "Spiritually violated? Is that any better?" And before he could answer, she added, "You can call it what you want,

Jack, but that's what it amounts to. I mean, he publicly humiliated the woman, stripped her bare right there before the entire vestry."

She didn't add her implicit indictment against the rest of the members—that they had all sat there and allowed it to happen. "Without a word of protest," as she explicitly put it to Tony Winston later. With Jack, however, she merely allowed the reproach to hang in the air, unspoken but nonetheless palpable.

Jack's mouth drew up into a small, round pucker. They were sitting, as they did every Wednesday morning at 7:30, in a booth at McDonald's where they "reunioned," a term used in a diocesan program for encouraging lay spirituality. They were supposed to pray—which they did—and discuss whatever spiritual projects they had going in their lives. Originally the group had included two other people. But after the troubles at St. Barnabas began, the other two had dropped away. Now it was only Leslie and Jack.

In the past they had both looked forward to their Wednesday mornings as a delectable little nugget in the middle of the week when they could savor the other's instant understanding, an experience that Jack, at his age, had almost despaired of finding with a woman. As for Leslie, her second husband, Felix, was a doctor firmly entrenched in atheism.

"If there is a God," he had told her before they were married, "I don't see how it concerns us in the slightest. It's simply not part of our species' scope. Do bacteria wonder if there are people? It's a waste of time." Not that Felix did not contribute generously to St. Barnabas. He'd even gone to church with Leslie up until the time the new priest had revoked her lay reader's license. He liked to sing, he said.

The Rittenhouses had agreed not to argue about religion after they were married. They were both reasonable people, and responsible for their own souls. Still, Leslie hadn't realized how big a hole not being able to talk about God would leave in her marriage. That's why she went to her Wednesday McDonald's breakfasts with the baggy bachelor, feeling the kind of anticipation she might have felt for an illicit assignation.

There was even something comfortably domestic about the arrangement now. Over the past few years she and Jack had watched the decor at McDonald's change from a yellow-and-orange antique automobile motif to a mauve-and-aqua undersea theme. She had tried to analyze what kind of marketing research brought about such changes in the Somerville McDonald's. "We're over a hundred miles from the coast, for heaven's sake. Why all these fishes and seaweed in Somerville? It doesn't make sense."

Leslie's analytical bent irritated her friends only slightly less than the way she seized on occasions to be instructive.

"Who cares?" Tony said when Leslie began analyzing the announcement of "An American Folk Mass" in the *St. Barnabas Banner,* the church's weekly newsletter. "'Bring a covered dish and the words to your favorite hymn,'" Leslie read aloud. She always read the newsletter aloud to Tony, who threw hers away unopened. "What's this supposed to be anyway? A sing-along? A hootenanny? They're having it at the Watsons. Of course. Marge Watson couldn't turn down Jack the Ripper if he showed up on her doorstep and invited himself in. Listen to this. 'A time for sharing will follow the simple eucharistic meal.' Sharing. Do you think they'll share what went on at the vestry meeting?"

"Why do you read that stuff if it upsets you so much?" Tony said.

It was a question Leslie often asked herself. She'd already transferred her membership to St. Cuthbert's in Olney, even though she had to drive an extra half hour to get there. It was a wonderful church—with three choirs, a food pantry, and a middle-aged, literate priest with respectable proportions of both angst and faith. If his Eucharists were not dramatic, they were at least sincere.

It had been Arlen Canby's bumbling, unfocused celebration of the Eucharist that first put Leslie off. He cut out every optional prayer, discouraged the old ladies from genuflecting, and instructed the ushers to keep people moving at the altar rail so that Communion wouldn't take so long.

"Thin, psychological, and unbelieving," was how she had described the new priest when he first came to Somerville. "You know the type," she told a friend in Houston. "He pictures himself in a cassock, swishing around the church, guardian of the great secret that there is no secret. Trying to keep it from the little old ladies so they won't despair. Trying to break it to the rest of us gently."

"Come on, Les, give him a chance," her friend had said. "You're always so critical. You take all this too seriously."

"I agree with the first part. I am critical, although I don't necessarily see that as a flaw. I mean, is being gullible preferable? But the second part I absolutely deny. There's no such thing as taking this too seriously." She said this with a composure she found admirable.

"You sound like a fanatic," her friend said flatly. "You give me a headache. It's a wonder you have any friends at all. Why don't you and Felix come to dinner Friday evening? But don't talk about that priest of yours, at least not unless he does something really amusing like running off with the organist."

To Leslie's mind there was nothing even remotely amusing about Arlen Canby. She had tried to see him as some kind of comic figure for a while, Ichabod Crane in a cassock. It didn't work. He wasn't funny.

Still, she had hung on at St. Barnabas, raising an occasional eyebrow, complaining privately to Felix and Jack.

And, at first, the priest had openly courted Leslie's approval. He'd even asked her to go to Dallas with Jack to attend a conference on a new program for theological lay education. The week after the conference, he called and asked her to come by his office.

"A debriefing," she said to Felix, who only smiled blandly. She got her notes together and went.

She hadn't liked it when the priest got up, walked around behind the chair she'd taken across from his desk, and shut the door to the office. She suddenly felt nervous, closed in. Nevertheless, she took out her notebook and with deliberate calm put on her reading glasses, preparing to give him a brief summary of the conference. She noticed that his attention seemed to wander as she talked about the program and the procedure for setting it up.

Finally he broke in. "Of course, you realize that I'd have to approve the materials you would be using beforehand."

She hadn't expected that. "But the bishop's already approved them. I don't think there's any problem. I mean nationally—"

"Still, I need to know what's going on, especially what's being taught in my own church."

"Of course," she said with cool courtesy. "I have the books. I can bring them by for you to look at."

"And then there's the structure. I think we'd need to lay down some guidelines for the group right from the start."

"That's spelled out in the material too. No group over twelve. One leader in each group. Everyone who signs up makes a two-year commitment."

"I'm aware of all the basic stuff," he said stiffly. "I'm talking about certain ground rules."

"Ground rules?" she echoed.

"Yes. You see we have to consider group dynamics here. If a small group of people makes a commitment to one another such as this, well, it has the potential of becoming quite intimate. Especially over such an extended period of time. All kinds of relationships can spring up unexpectedly. If you see what I mean." He was twirling a pencil between his fingers and looking down at the blotter on his desk.

"I'm afraid I don't," she said cautiously.

He sighed heavily, as though restraining exasperation. "I don't think I need to spell it out for you. Men and women in the same group. They meet once every week for two years. In the evening. They talk about very intimate, personal matters, things perhaps they have not revealed even to their own spouses. In such an atmosphere people can form deep attachments, develop very close bonds." He paused and looked up at her pointedly.

She waited, uncertain of just what he was getting at.

He let the pencil fall from his fingers and leaned toward her over the desk. "I think we would need to require everyone entering such a group to sign a statement to the effect that they won't have sex with any other member of the group. For those two years."

She sat there a moment, not sure she'd heard him right. Then it was too late to laugh. It was obvious he was quite serious. She swallowed and took a deep breath before she spoke. "Well, I certainly haven't considered that possibility. I suppose when you're dealing with human beings, anything can happen. But I don't see that signing a statement would keep anyone from—doing that. I mean, if you were going to commit adultery, you surely wouldn't balk at breaking a much lesser promise, would you?"

He leaned back in his chair. "I'm afraid this is not negotiable," he said in a tight voice.

She looked around the office, puzzled as to how to reply. "Well. I personally wouldn't sign such a statement. Nor do I think any responsible adult in their right mind would."

"Then," he said, the tension suddenly going out of his voice, "you won't be leading the group at this church."

And that was that. She was too stunned to even think to ask whether he had made the same stipulation to Jack. She never asked Jack, and he had never volunteered any information about his own interview with the rector. All she knew was that Jack had been chosen to lead the lay education group at St. Barnabas and that she had been dropped from the project.

All right, she'd thought at the time. I can live with that. I don't like it, but I can live with it. Inevitably, however, it had caused something of a rift between her and Jack. She found herself being more reticent at their Wednesday morning meetings. As for him, she sensed a new uneasiness on his part to discuss anything connected with the rector of St. Barnabas. And when the program went under during the winter after some of the members dropped out, Leslie had felt a certain sting of satisfaction. She was pretty sure the group had never been asked to sign a statement that they wouldn't sleep with one another.

"It's your hair," Tony told her.

"What's wrong with my hair?"

"It's short. He told me he doesn't trust women with short hair."

"Why ever not?"

"He suspects they're lesbians, I imagine," Tony said flatly.

"But most women my age have short hair."

"Would you stop trying to be logical about this?" Tony said again.

Felix, who had always been genial enough about her religious dedication, frowned at this latest episode with the new rector. Ever since Father Shields had retired, Felix had gotten a little lax about going to church with her. Now, however, he never missed a

Sunday. Does he think I need protection from this jerk, Leslie wondered.

Nevertheless, if Felix's father hadn't died the next fall, and if Felix hadn't decided to make a rather generous contribution to the memorial fund in his memory, things might have rocked on a while longer without any further incident between her and the rector. She never asked Felix why he would want to make a contribution to the church on behalf of his father, who had not only lived out in California, but had originally inoculated him against faith. It was one of those questions it was pointless to ask her husband. A shrug would be his only reply.

However, when the financial statement was handed out at the annual parish meeting in January, the memorial fund balance was considerably below the Rittenhouse contribution alone. It was an awkward matter for Leslie. Felix wasn't at the meeting or he might have questioned the figures then and there, although not being officially a member of the congregation, he might not have been allowed to speak. And Leslie's growing reticence kept her from speaking up. Already, she knew, people were aware of her dissatisfaction with the rector. If she questioned the accuracy of the figures in the general parish meeting, she was certain the priest would add that to his list of grievances against her.

When she showed the financial statement to Felix that evening, however, he scowled. "When is the next vestry meeting?" he asked. It was two weeks away. In the meantime, he had Leslie round up the annual statements for the past few years from any member who still had copies so that he could compare them. Then he went alone to the vestry meeting. "You'll only antagonize them," he told her. "Asking people about money always makes them defensive."

"I can't believe those people," he said when he came home. He loosened his tie and cranked the recliner back while she fixed him a drink. "I wouldn't have been allowed to speak at all if Jack Tatum hadn't finally pointed out that state disclosure laws endorsed such enquiries."

"So what did they say?"

"That they've just elected a new treasurer. That they're in the middle of auditing the books. That they're sure it's only an accounting error. That they'll let me know as soon as they get it figured out."

The next morning the phone rang around nine. It was the secretary at St. Barnabas. She said Father Canby wanted to know if Leslie could meet with him at the church at two that afternoon.

She paused before answering. "Tell him I'll be happy to meet him at the church. But not in his office." She didn't intend to get cornered there again. "Tell him I'll be at the altar rail praying at one. I'll meet him there at two."

Why had she said that, she wondered as she drove into town. She hadn't thought it through at the time; the notion had simply leaped to her mind and onto her tongue. She didn't like outrunning her rationality that way. And he would certainly interpret it as some kind of pious nonsense. Nevertheless, she had to admit she liked the idea now that she had time to think about it. It might be a little melodramatic, but perhaps the altar would sober them both. She assumed he was angry about Felix's appearance at the vestry meeting. She hoped to reassure him that he was not being personally accused of any misconduct, but that her husband just wanted to know where his money had gone.

Nevertheless, her hands were cold as she folded them on the altar rail. She read several of the prayers out of the Book of Common Prayer to calm herself—"For the Unity of the Church," "For the Parish," "For Clergy and People," even "For Our Enemies."

She knew her knees wouldn't take a whole hour of kneeling, and after about fifteen minutes she retreated to the front pew where she sat looking up at the hole in the red panel of Plexiglas. Maybe the memorial for Felix's father could do something about those terrible plastic windows.

A minute later she was startled to hear a step behind her. "I take it you've finished your orisons," the priest said. "I'd just as soon get on with this if we could."

Leslie looked up, stung by his tone. "Not really," she said. "I was trying to listen for the Lord's voice in all this. But now that you're here . . ." She stood up and joined him in the aisle. He needn't think he could intimidate her by standing over her like that.

"I'll get right to the point," he said. "Because of your quite evident hostility toward me and my ministry, I've decided to revoke your lay reader's license."

She reached behind her for the pew back. "You what?"

He repeated what he'd said, his voice more strained the second time.

Leslie turned away and took a step toward the altar. Still not saying anything, she ran her finger slowly along the edge of her prayer book, trying to sort out her options as quickly as she could. He had, she supposed, the right to take such action under canon law. He would have made sure of that before announcing his decision. But would she have any right of appeal to the bishop?

He suddenly broke the silence. "As your pastor, Leslie, I have to tell you that it's plain to me why you're acting in this vindictive way."

She turned to stare at him. He went on quickly before she could speak. "And I want you to understand I have a good deal of sympathy with your plight. It hasn't been very many years since the Episcopal church started ordaining women to the priesthood. No doubt if ordination had been an option for you when you were a younger woman, you would have taken it. Your devotion to the church is obvious. Perhaps you've felt you have a vocation, but that you've been thwarted in that. Now you're married, comfortably well-off. It's too late for you to start now. Please believe that I do indeed sympathize with what must be an extremely frustrating situation."

"I don't think you should say any more," Leslie said.

"I'm afraid I must. I know this is painful for you. But I have a duty to the members of this congregation. I cannot allow your own frustrated ambitions to tear St. Barnabas apart. It's not my fault you weren't born a man. Or weren't born later so that you could be a priest. But I will not allow you to take out your frustrations either on me or this church."

Leslie stood there, speechless for once. He stared back at her, his hand twitching slightly by his side and his head canted back on his long, thin neck.

"You're lucky I'm not a man," she finally said. "If I were, I'd knock you down, right here in front of the altar."

For the first time, a smile stole onto his face. The left side of his mouth raised slightly. "So much for spirituality," he said. He glanced pointedly at his watch. "I'll be returning your license to the bishop this week. I'll see that the secretary sends you a copy of the cover letter."

"Fine," she said. "I'll be writing to the bishop myself."

He shrugged again. "I have another appointment now. I'll leave you to your prayers." He turned and started back down the aisle. When he got to the door, he paused before pushing it open. "If you get any messages from Jesus there, be sure to let me know."

She went home and immediately wrote to the bishop, detailing the state of affairs between herself and the priest. She tried to sound as objective and analytical about the situation as she could. She never got an answer. That same weekend a priest in one of the suburban churches in the diocese committed suicide. It was the third one in five years.

"That settles it," Tony told her. "You can forget the bishop riding to your rescue. He's going to be walking on eggs with the clergy. He can't risk another priest flipping out like that."

Mollie agreed. "The bishop's into damage control right now. Canby's obviously a weird duck. Everyone knows that. One parishioner more or less isn't going to make much difference. But the bishop sure can't afford to have another priest go off the deep end."

And now, parking her Mercedes in her old spot at St. Barnabas, Leslie couldn't deny a fleeting thrill of vindication. Maybe the suicide of a clergy wife didn't weigh as heavy as a priest's, but how did the bishop calculate the death of the children? And maybe if he had listened to her, had paid attention to the letters from this backwater little parish, two children might be alive today and their mother whole and well.

Felix had told her there was no hope for Cassie the night they brought her into the hospital. "A quick death would have been more merciful," he'd said. "She'll be a vegetable. She could live for five, maybe ten years like that."

If Felix had had any faith, even in embryo, that was dead now too. Instead of his mild bemusement at his wife's religious fervor, he had become bitter over the past few days. He had refused to come to the funeral. "Ghoulish," he'd said. "Vultures." She hadn't tried to argue with him.

There was even some sense in which Leslie felt responsible herself. She had, after all, loaned to Cassie Canby, in a fit of magnanimity before her final showdown with the priest, a book by Ursula Donleavy, a popular speaker at women's retreats. It was both mildly feminist and mildly charismatic, and, though Leslie wasn't particularly interested in the charismatic part herself, she had hoped the book would put some starch in Cassie.

Later, after Leslie had transferred to St. Cuthbert's, she had come across a brochure advertising a Donleavy retreat at St. Winifred's Cenacle House in Houston. She'd sent it to Cassie along with a friendly note. It was no more than a gesture, a way of letting the poor girl know Leslie didn't blame her for her husband's behavior. She hadn't really expected Cassie to go.

But she had. And, from all reports, had come back a changed woman. Not only was she observed to be generally less apprehensive around her husband, but she began holding up her hands during the doxology and swaying from side to side.

"You should see!" Mollie McCready told Leslie when she ran into her in the grocery store. "It's wonderful. Arlen nearly wets his pants every time. It's worth sitting through those ghastly sermons that nobody understands just to see the look on his face when Cassie gets the spirit. Poor girl. It's probably all she's gotten for a long time." Leslie was glad now she'd resisted the urge to claim credit for Cassie's transformation.

She waited in the car, watching the people, mostly the older members of the congregation, trickle in for the funeral. They kept their heads down, avoiding the van with the logo of a Houston TV station parked across the street. She consciously resisted the urge to feel sorry for them. Everyone left at St. Barnabas must be terribly upset by this. But they had all buckled under, wouldn't stand up to the sorry so-and-so. And now, somehow, she was sure, this was the result. She only felt sorry for whatever poor priest had been sent by the bishop to do the service.

The hearse was drawn up along the side door of the church in the shade of a tree. Even Cassie's parents would be inside the church by now.

Leslie looked at her watch. There was no way to put it off any longer. She picked up her prayer book and handbag from the seat beside her, got out, and locked the car door.

CHAPTER NINE

DAN KAMOWSKI WASN'T SURPRISED at how few people turned up for the funeral service, considering the circumstances. Churches were usually full when old or important people died. When children died, congregations turned out to support the parents. But in this case, the parents themselves weren't present. A few local clergy were there as a courtesy, and three of the grandparents sat in the front pew reserved for family members. The little-old-lady pew was full, but the rest of the nave was thinly sprinkled with obviously uncomfortable parishioners.

The responses from the congregation were dogged rather than hearty. *Holy God, holy and mighty, holy and merciful Savior, deliver us not into the bitterness of eternal death.* Kamowski was grateful for even a small attendance. He hated listening to his own voice reverberating off the back wall of an empty nave.

He read the service at a deliberate pace. *Deal graciously with your people in their grief. Surround them with your love, that they may not be overwhelmed by their loss, but have confidence in your goodness and strength to meet the days to come.*

He was especially concerned about the grandparents'

strength. Their names, along with the parents', would ordinarily have been inserted in the place of the generic pronouns of the prayer. But Dan hadn't been able to decide whether to include the mother's name too. It was a delicate point.

He had spoken to her parents briefly in the foyer before the service. All he had discovered was their name—Armstrong—and where they were from—Wisconsin. Dazed from two sleepless nights at the hospital, the couple leaned together on the front pew, sitting during the entire service, except when they came forward to receive Communion. Kamowski suspected they weren't Episcopalians. Maybe Lutheran.

Rupert Canby, the other grandparent, sat apart at the far end of the pew. He had already been in the chapel praying when Kamowski finished vesting. Was it to avoid talking to the priest? As soon as the service began, the man stood and visibly squared his shoulders. Where was his wife? Was he divorced? Widowed? If there was another grandmother, surely she would have come. Or would she? Maybe she wasn't the kind of woman who could face the two little coffins. Maybe she was with her son.

While the Old Testament lesson was being read, Kamowski let his eyes, hooded by their heavy lids, rove over the congregation. They all looked as if they were being slowly roasted alive. *It is good that a man should both hope and quietly wait for the salvation of the Lord.* Dan wondered if anyone in the congregation knew how that passage began. He had memorized it in prison: *He hath filled me with bitterness, he hath made me drunken with wormwood. He hath also broken my teeth with gravel stones, he hath covered me with ashes.*

Could these people, sitting there staring at the twin coffins, possibly believe the final verse? *For he doth not afflict willingly, nor grieve the children of men.* None of them looked convinced, even though Jack Tatum, the lay reader, a big man he'd met before on some diocesan committee, delivered the line with considerable fervor.

Psalm 23 they read in unison, stumbling through the familiar phrases together. Then Tatum started in on the epistle. His voice sounded almost pleading. *Behold, what manner of love the Father hath bestowed on us, that we should be called the children of God.*

Over the years Kamowski had grown used to the wild mood swings of the lectionary readings, but he could still remember how they used to explode in his head, contradictions coming together like a pair of volatile chemicals. What kind of father makes his children drink wormwood and breaks their teeth with gravel? *We shall be like him,* Tatum continued, *for we shall see him as he is.* Like him? A brutal father? One that tortures and afflicts his children? How could the congregation sit there so meekly and give no sign of shock at these contrarieties? How could the lay reader bring himself to mouth such words? *We shall see him as he is.* And what would that be, finally? The best thing Kamowski knew about the human race was its ability to cling to the hope that this potentate of the universe, this cosmic bully, was not as he sometimes appeared to be.

It was his turn. Kamowski rose slowly and made his way deliberately to the center of the chancel to read the gospel appointed for the burial of a child. All the gospel readings for funerals were from the gospel of John, and Dan had always been wary of John. He much preferred Mark—straightforward, no nonsense, a stubborn caution underlying its declarations. In contrast, the strange, chantlike repetitions in John made him uneasy. *Mine own will . . . the will of him that sent me . . . the Father's will.* All the boundaries, the clear definitions seemed to dissolve in John. Whose will was it anyway? Whose will that these children were dead?

"I will raise him up at the last day." Dan punched the line hard. He figured the three figures in the front pew needed whatever hope he could supply this morning. Though where did anyone get the courage for a second life? Wasn't once enough?

Nevertheless, by the time they got to the antiphonal prayer before Communion, the congregational responses had picked up. *Comfort us in our sorrows at the death of these children; let our faith be our consolation, and eternal life our hope.* Kamowski said the words with a kind of weary conviction. And the response, stronger than before, traveled toward him across the chancel, lifting him like a gradual tide: "Hear us, Lord."

Before the service, Kamowski had had a word with the mortician about the Houston television van parked on the side street. After the service, when they came down the church steps with the coffins, he was relieved to see that a patrol car had pulled across the intersection, effectively blocking the van. A motorcycle cop stood in front of the hearse, his arms folded across his chest, staring stonily in the van's direction.

The crew had come spilling from the vehicle as soon as the church doors opened, but they stayed on the other side of the street. The mortician, who'd been mopping his face and neck with an oversized handkerchief in the near-noon sun, signaled to his driver, who bundled the grandparents into the long, gunmetal-blue limo drawn up behind the hearse. Kamowski had never seen a funeral procession get under way so quickly.

Only a few people made the short trip to the cemetery a couple of miles outside Somerville. The three grandparents, Tatum, the junior warden and his wife, and a couple of women from the congregation. Pinewood Cemetery, north of town, was the only place newcomers to Somerville could be buried, the mortician had explained. What plots were left in the old town cemetery had long ago been bought up by natives who wanted to be buried with their ancestors.

The county had gone for a month without rain, and

crickets were coming out of the dry cracks in the ground. They clung to the skirt of Kamowski's alb as he made his way to the canopy set up over the grave site. When he shook them off, they left behind brittle bits of leg that had caught in the fabric. Dell wouldn't like that, he thought.

The committal service in the Book of Common Prayer was mercifully brief. "Rest eternal grant to them, O Lord," he said.

And those who'd come from the congregation knew the response by heart. "Let light perpetual shine upon them."

When he gave the dismissal, he was glad to find that their voices—probably because they were all under the canopy—did not sound thin and diluted as they usually did in the open air: "The Lord is risen indeed. Alleluia." He was grateful. It was over.

But not quite over, of course. A pair of workers, discreetly sitting in the shade just out of view, would come as soon as the hearse and limo had left and lower the two small caskets into the clay hole. Kamowski would have to say a few words of condolence to the grandparents. That would be sticky. No one had said anything about lunch for the mourners, the usual custom in this part of the country. Maybe he would escape that.

But what about Arlen Canby? And his wife in the hospital? What should he do about them? He ought to look in on his fellow priest, say something—what, he couldn't imagine at this point. And he should go by the hospital, even though the woman wouldn't be aware of his presence.

Kamowski closed his prayer book, stuck it under his arm, and made his way to the other side of the grave where the maternal grandmother, Mrs. Armstrong, was sunk in a metal folding chair. The priest could see the mortician moving toward her too; the man would be gently but insistently helping her up and guiding her by a firm elbow grip away from the grave as quickly as possible. Kamowski caught his eye and, raising a thick finger, gestured for him to wait.

Mrs. Armstrong was a small woman, probably no more than sixty, although she looked older. Her recent ordeal had taken an obvious toll. Kamowski was surprised when, extending his own large palm to her, he found it gripped with more strength than he had expected from a woman her size. Tightening her grasp, she pulled herself up from the chair, lost her balance slightly, took a half step forward to steady herself, and clutched the priest's other arm for support. Then she stared up at him—she came only to the midpoint of his chest—and said in a high wavering voice, "I have something to say to everyone."

Her husband, himself a small man, put a hand on her arm. "Janie," he said.

"Let me be," she said, keeping her eyes on Kamowski. Then she repeated, this time not just to the priest but to all those gathered around the grave, "I have something to say."

Everyone froze, as though caught in a camera frame. As though they'd been waiting for this moment. Rupert Canby, who'd been standing at the foot of the caskets, did no more than shift his eyes toward the woman. His head didn't even turn, and he kept his hands clasped in front of him. The junior warden's wife touched her husband's arm; he looked at her, frowning slightly. Jack Tatum's mouth collapsed into a small o in the middle of his face. The two other women exchanged quick glances.

Still steadying herself on Kamowski's arm, Mrs. Armstrong turned to look at them all, her eyes coming to rest on the coffins. When she spoke, it appeared that she was speaking to the dead children.

"My daughter," she began, her voice already breaking, "did not kill these children." She took a deep, quavering breath. "Cassie absolutely could not have done that. She was a good mother. If you know her at all, you know that."

She lifted her eyes now from the coffins and her head tilted upward slightly. "And she did not try to kill herself either. I want you to know that. Cassie did not try to kill herself. She did not. I know this. She did not." On the second repetition, her voice broke completely.

Her husband stepped over the dry clods of red clay to his wife and put his arm around her. She loosened her grip on Kamowski's arm, but looked up into his face. "Believe me," she said more quietly. "This is important."

"Come on, honey," her husband said. "Let's go get in the car. There's not any more we can do here. Let's get back to Cassie."

"Will you be at the hospital?" Kamowski said. "I'm coming by there. We'll talk then."

Mr. Armstrong nodded, turning his wife toward the waiting limo. But under his breath he said, so only the priest could hear him, "She's right. My wife's right."

Then the mortician moved in behind the departing couple as though to shield them from the others, signaling to the driver to open the limo door. None of the group around the grave moved until the door had closed on the Armstrongs. Then, collectively, they breathed again. Tatum's mouth closed, and he looked steadfastly at the ground. The two women stared at him just as steadily, as though determined to catch his eye. Rupert Canby turned grimly from the grave and started toward the line of cars without a word.

As soon as he was out of earshot, the junior warden spoke up. "She's right," he said, looking around at the rest. "Her mother's right. Cassie couldn't do that. Not to herself. And certainly not to her children." His wife laid a hand on his shoulder.

The man turned to Kamowski as though he were the arbiter, a judge he was appealing to. "She didn't do it," he repeated.

Kamowski nodded in a noncommittal way that could be taken as either agreement or dismissal. "We should go now," he said.

Everyone turned quickly away, looking relieved—except, Kamowski noticed, the junior warden's wife, who stood beside the grave a moment longer. She even reached out and touched the metal of one of the caskets. Her face was rigid with pain, and then something else. She looked suddenly very angry.

CHAPTER • TEN

THAT'S IT," HARRIET SAID BREATH-lessly. "That's all."

There had been only three bottles of Communion wine left in the sacristy after the funeral, but opening them and pouring their contents down the drain of the piscina had taken an amazing amount of her energy. Maybe it hadn't been a good idea after all. Her hands were shaking. She wished she was home already with her feet up.

"What about the wafers?" Tony asked, mopping off the counter with a paper towel.

"What?"

"The wafers. The Communion wafers. Shouldn't we dispose of them too?" Tony pointed to the cellophane packages in the cabinet above the counter.

Harriet waved a hand indifferently and tried to keep the impatience out of her voice. "I suppose." Why didn't these younger women take any initiative? Couldn't Tony see how tired she was?

Without a word Tony swept the remaining packets into a paper sack and rolled down the top. Then she got a box and started packing away the chalice and other service pieces for storage. It took no more than thirty minutes for them to pack up what was left in the chancel and sacristy and carry it out to Harriet's car.

"I can take all this home with me if you'd like," the younger woman offered before closing the trunk on Harriet's car.

"No. Thanks, Tony. Everything else is stored at my house already. It's probably best to keep everything in one place."

"You sure you don't want me to drive you home and help unload all this?"

"No, no. I'll do fine." She looked at Tony and hesitated for a moment. Then she said, "Actually, I just need to be alone for a while. You understand. I need to collect myself. I feel like—I don't know—I need to gather my thoughts, if you know what I mean."

"Certainly." Tony could almost hear Harriet's interior mechanisms grinding away, trying to process the events of the day. She was worried about leaving her alone, but on the other hand, she understood how Harriet needed solitude now.

"I tell you what," Tony said. "When you get home, don't bother carrying all this in. I'm going to run by the hospital and see if there's anything I can do for the Armstrongs. Then I'll come back by your place and help put all this away. How's that?"

"Fine," Harriet said, regretting her interior complaints.

"I'll be off then," Tony said, pulling her car keys out of her pocket. "I may be a while. I'll stay at the hospital till the Armstrongs get back from the cemetery."

"Fine," Harriet repeated. "You go on. I'll get my purse and lock up."

As she went back into the church, however, she wished Tony had waited. She didn't like being in the empty building alone. When she came that morning, she had only felt sad. Now she was vaguely uneasy. Her footsteps echoed as she crossed the stretch of stone floor between the parish hall and the sanctuary. She retrieved her purse from the sacristy and, from long habit, locked the door to the little room. Then she retraced her steps down the aisle. She had just left the nave and started across the stone floor again when she thought she heard a noise coming from the hallway leading to the Sunday school rooms. She stopped, thinking perhaps it was only the echo of her footsteps. But as she stood there immobile, she heard it again, a muffled sound from down the hallway.

Surely no one was still here from the funeral. The service had been over for at least an hour. She was halfway down the hall before it occurred to her that it might be vandals.

The noise seemed to be coming from the last room on the left, the nursery. No. It sounded more like a child playing. Frowning, Harriet pushed open the door.

The girl sitting in the middle of the floor lifted her bald, swollen face.

"Wendy?" What in the world had the child done to herself?

She was surrounded by a circle of stuffed animals, blocks, and dolls, and she had been crying. The girl rubbed her nose on the sleeve of her pink dress and stared up at Harriet. "I saw them," she said.

"Saw who?" Harriet asked, her mind still on vandals.

"The children. In their coffins."

"You were here? You've been here the whole time? Whatever for?"

"The children," Wendy repeated.

Harriet took a step toward her.

Wendy held up a hand, palm outward. "Don't!"

Harriet stopped. "What's the matter, honey?"

"Don't break the circle," the girl said. "Don't step over the line."

"All right. But can you tell me what this is all about?" Harriet felt an unaccustomed surge of adrenalin in her veins. What was the matter here? What should she do?

"It's to keep me in," Wendy said. "I have to stay in the circle."

"But why, dear?"

"To keep from hurting anyone. To keep anyone else from being hurt."

Harriet lowered herself slowly into a rocker beside the nursery crib. "But you're not going to hurt anyone, Wendy. You're such a nice girl. Why, I've known you since—"

"No!" The shout echoed up and down the hallway. "You don't know me. I'm not a nice girl. That's why I look like this, so people will know." And she made a face by opening her mouth as wide as it would go and bugging out her eyes.

Harriet cleared her throat carefully. "What do you mean, dear?"

Wendy hid her face in her hands and sighed. "He told me he wanted to help me," she mumbled. "He said he could keep me from being like my mother and having to go away." There was a pause. "But afterwards he said I was horrible, dirty. And now this is all my fault. All mine."

The girl had started to cry again. Harriet sat there silently for a while. She needed to collect herself. Maybe she wasn't understanding Wendy clearly. But she knew something was very wrong here, something that made a buzzing start in her own head. She waited until Wendy raised her face from her hands. Then very quietly and evenly Harriet said, "Tell me what you think I can understand, dear. Tell me all you can."

"The children," Wendy said in a flat voice. "The children are dead."

"Yes. They are. It's very sad. But they're with Jesus now."

Wendy looked up again. "Do you think so? Are they safe?"

"Completely."

A weary smile spread across the girl's face as she slowly stroked a stuffed elephant. "I'm glad they're safe. I wish I was safe. I wish I hadn't helped him. He said I had to—because he had helped me. But all he did was make me bad. Now the children are dead and I wish I were too. I'm nothing but trash!"

Harriet considered reaching out and taking the girl's hand. Maybe she could get her into the car and take her home to her grandmother. "You're not trash, dear. You're feeling confused. We all are. Why don't you let me take you home now. You'll feel better—"

"No! I can't leave. I've got to stay. When the bulldozers come, I'm going to be smashed up with all the trash. They'll take me out to the dump on a truck with all the broken windows and boards and bury me."

Harriet frowned. She felt the ground she had gained with the girl slipping away from her. "Now really, Wendy. You've got to stop this foolishness. What in the world are you talking about anyway?"

The girl drew her hand back from the elephant and pulled her knees up to her chin. "I can't tell you," she said. "I promised."

"What do you mean? Promised who?"

"Him. And Mrs. McCready. My teacher."

Dan Kamowski watched as the limo carrying the Armstrongs pulled away through the wrought iron archway at the entrance of Pinewood Cemetery. He had come with the Armstrongs in that automobile.

The mortician came hurrying up to him now, dabbing at his face with the white handkerchief folded like a bandage. "I'll get you another car, sir," he explained quickly. "I just thought it best to move those folks on out of here. Considering, you know. The lady was awful upset."

Dan nodded. He wanted out of his vestments as

quick as possible. Sweat was trickling down his sides, and the crickets were whirring around his feet again.

Jack Tatum laid a hand on his arm. "I'll be glad to take you back," he said. "I have my car right over here." He pointed to a pale blue Ford sitting in the meager shade of a pin oak.

"Fine," Kamowski said.

"Are you sure?" the mortician asked, stuffing his handkerchief back in his hip pocket.

Without answering, Dan started toward the blue Ford, unbuttoning his alb as he went. He was suddenly angry. At the mortician, at the hysterical woman at the grave, at the bishop, at the stupid crickets. He heard a seam rip as he jerked the robe off. He shook it savagely to get rid of the clinging insects. Dell should have come. She ought to have known he would need her.

Tatum held the door open for him, and Dan slung the robe into the back seat. It would have to be cleaned now anyway. Jack climbed in—they were both big men—and the car sank on its springs. The last straw would be to get stuck out here in the cemetery, Dan thought. He'd seen it happen more than once at funerals when the weather was wet. Thank God for the drought.

He could tell the other man was searching for something to say, but refused to give him any help. After all, he was the outsider here, the Lone Ranger–priest. He'd done what he'd been sent here to do. He wasn't going to work at coming up with conversation starters for these people too.

"We're very grateful to you," Jack finally said. "The congregation."

Kamowski sighed. He hated it when people told him they were grateful. It created the worst kind of obligation. "Just doing my job," he said bleakly.

There was a pause while the car bumped up onto the pavement at the highway. Then Jack said carefully, "I guess it's a pretty hard job, too. Especially today."

"Oh, I don't know," Kamowski said. The fact that Tatum hadn't been offended by his remark had raised him a notch in the priest's estimation. He didn't like thin-skinned people. "I've buried victims before. And I've buried criminals. Hard to say which is worse."

"I guess so," the other man said meekly.

They stopped at a light on the outskirts of Somerville. Dan could almost hear the gears turning in Tatum's mind. He was probably wondering if the treasurer had arranged for a check, and if he should invite the priest to lunch.

Dan remembered his promise to talk to the Armstrongs and his resolve to call on Arlen Canby. He was about to ask Tatum where the Canbys lived when the other man spoke first.

"Cassie's mother—Mrs. Armstrong—she's awfully broken up about all this. I guess that was just a natural reaction she had at the cemetery."

There it was again. The expectation that he understood everybody's motivation when deaths were crimes. "The kids are dead," Kamowski answered sourly. "That's all I know. Just like everybody else. I don't have any special insight. This isn't even my parish. You people ought to know the situation better than I do."

The man driving nodded his head sadly. "You're absolutely right." Then he shook his head. "We've failed. I can't deny it. The congregation has failed the Canbys. I never knew it would have this kind of consequence."

Dan frowned. He hadn't expected abject agreement.

Jack lifted one hand from the steering wheel, then let it drop again heavily. "They were new. They needed—" he gestured again, "something. Something we weren't giving them."

Dan kept his eyes straight ahead. Like most clergy, he liked it when laypeople felt sorry for priests. But he was suddenly afraid that the man might actually start crying.

"You ever been married, Tatum?" he finally asked.

"No. Never have." The unexpected question seemed to steady him.

"Married people have problems all the time. How long have they been here anyway?"

"Three years this fall."

"And you call that new? Looks to me like things ought to have settled out by now. I've never been in any parish that long myself."

Jack glanced over at him, then turned his eyes away quickly. Kamowski caught it though—the look that said, sure, but then you're a special case, aren't you?

As though to make up for the look, Tatum said, "You're probably right. But then that makes it worse, doesn't it? That they've been here for almost three years and yet none of us had any idea that things were so bad. Between them, I mean."

"What about with the congregation? How does this Canby guy get along with the congregation?"

Jack pursed his lips and seemed to be struggling to formulate an answer. "I guess he sort of got off on the wrong foot. With some people."

"Some people? What people? Who?"

Jack opened his mouth and then closed it. Finally he said, "Several, I guess. A lot of them women. But not all."

"Oh, well. Women," the priest said, shrugging.

"But not all of them."

"Sure. If a woman is dissatisfied, her husband's going to be only too willing to use that as an excuse."

"I'm not sure . . ."

"I'm just surprised he hadn't taken care of the situation by now. Three years. Surely in that time—"

Jack moved uneasily behind the wheel. "I think maybe it's more complicated than that."

"The guy's young. And he's following an older priest. Didn't Shields retire right before Canby came?"

"Yes."

"And I guess he was the beloved old priest."

"With a lot of people, yes. Others . . ." Jack shrugged.

"Anyway," Kamowski went on, "it's not unusual for a congregation to have a hard time adjusting to a new priest. Still," he added thoughtfully. "Three years. And St. Barnabas is moving? He must be doing something right if he can afford to build a new church."

Tatum shook his head. "That's not exactly the way it is. I guess the vestry sort of jumped the gun. Sold the building before we really had another place to go to. And our building fund drive hasn't been too successful."

"The bishop let you do this?"

"I guess it was put to him that the college's master plan called for expansion in St. Barnabas's direction. We'd have to move eventually anyway."

"But the college wouldn't insist on eminent domain. I mean the state would never condemn a church. Not in this part of the country, would they?"

"I'd be surprised," Jack said.

"But you got a good deal, didn't you? The money from the sale ought to go a long way toward a new building."

Jack shook his head. "Land prices aren't what they once were, you know. Ten years ago it was a seller's market. We could have gotten maybe twice as much. And now, well, we're going to have to sort of live off the interest for a while. Our operating fund is way down."

"So what are you going to do? I understand the building's being bulldozed next week."

"We're trying to make arrangements to meet in the chapel at the hospital till things get better."

Kamowski sat back and considered the passing view of the town's main drag. It was lined with the same fast-food franchises you'd find in any town. Then they turned at the courthouse square and started up the hill, where a mixture of imitation Georgian classroom buildings and rectilinear dorms rose among carefully tended elm trees.

This is not my territory, Dan told himself again. He could operate all right in a city like Houston, a city eager to please, constantly adapting to whatever economic boom or bust appeared in its headlines. But in a town like Somerville, aloof from outside concerns, moving only skeptically toward a future it hardly believed in, much less approved of, Dan felt out of place. What the people of Somerville knew—the tacit agreements its citizenry made in order to function here—he would never understand.

He imagined it had been that way for Canby too, and he suddenly felt sorry for the guy. But irritated as well. Why hadn't he sized up the situation and just given up? First he alienates the women—something a priest can never afford to do—then he sells the church building before he has another place to go. This guy was a disaster, all right. The bishop should have pulled him long ago. But then, as he knew from past experience, the bishop didn't always operate according to Dan's calculations.

All right, he decided as they pulled into the church parking lot, he'd go by the hospital, see the comatose woman, say a few words to her parents, drop by the Canby home and say a few more words to the husband and grandfather—though heaven only knew what those words would be—and be on the freeway home before the rush-hour traffic started. He wanted to get home to Dell as soon as possible.

"What about lunch?" Tatum asked as he turned off the engine. "We usually have something at the church after funerals, but under the circumstances—" He shrugged apologetically. "We could go somewhere though. I'd like to take you to lunch."

The sincerity in the man's voice surprised Kamowski. He was suddenly on his guard. He opened the door before answering. "If you'll go with me to the hospital afterward," he finally said. Tatum, he was certain, would come up with another appointment he had to attend to after lunch.

"Sure," Jack said. "I can do that."

"And maybe you could take me out to Canby's house after that." The final test.

"Yes," Jack said, although more slowly. "Yes. I could do that."

There wasn't any way out now. "All right," Dan said. "Let's just stay in your car though. You know your way around here. I don't."

"If we're going to the hospital, how about just getting something at the cafeteria there?"

If Tatum hadn't seemed genuinely pleased that he had accepted the offer, Dan would have suspected the suggestion.

"Like I said," he answered with a shrug, "you know this place. You decide."

CHAPTER ELEVEN

THE INTERVIEW WITH THE ARM-
strongs had not gone well. Consequently,
Dan was in a savage mood as he and Jack
Tatum drove out to the Canby home.
After an indifferent lunch in the hospital
cafeteria, he had left Tatum waiting downstairs while he
went up to the Intermediate Care Unit alone. Maybe
that had been a mistake. Tatum had offered to go up
with him, but Kamowski figured the call would be hard
enough without spectators.

He had decided to do the unction service from the
prayer book for Cassie in order to let the Armstrongs
know he took their daughter's plight seriously. After all,
the woman could die at any time.

The actual anointing had gone all right. In his priestly
office Dan considered himself a mere functionary; he had
no control over the ritual's efficacy. He liked that. It made
him feel free of responsibility or blame. He had squeezed
a drop of cinnamon oil onto his thumb from the small
plastic bottle in his hospital kit and rubbed the sign of
the cross into Cassandra Canby's forehead, while her
mind, spirit, soul, or whatever this woman was in the
sight of God, either slept or sat by, invisible and mute.

There was, of course, no question of her taking one

of the papery wafers or even a drop of the Communion wine from the second bottle. Nor had her parents insisted on his touching the miniature chalice to her lips, as family members sometimes wanted him to do with their comatose loved ones. But, as he had suspected, they were Lutherans.

Looking wary and guarded, the Armstrongs had stood on the far side of the bed, not knowing the responses, though they had mumbled a faint "Amen" to some of the prayers. It hadn't occurred to Kamowski until later to wonder if there might be another reason for their passivity. Maybe they weren't really sure they wanted their daughter to recover. If she regained consciousness, she'd have to face the death of her two children. Maybe the only mercy they could imagine now was her death.

Afterward, Jane Armstrong had insisted they leave the room. She didn't want to talk about Cassie in her presence, she said. "I'm sorry if I upset your service at the cemetery, pastor," she began as soon as she pulled the door to behind her. She was obviously avoiding calling him "father." "But I had to say what I did while people were there to hear it. I wanted them to know. This was not our daughter's doing." Her eyes were locked on his face.

Dan had shifted his gaze to her husband, who looked down, then at his wife, then back at Dan. "She's right," the man said in a low tone. "Not Cassie. Cassie wouldn't do that."

"I understand." That was one of the counseling phrases Kamowski had learned in seminary. It neither implied agreement nor specified just what it was he understood. Most of the time it worked. It hadn't worked with Jane Armstrong.

"No. You don't understand," she said flatly. "We're just the parents, so whatever we say no one is going to take seriously. You're just humoring us. But I'm telling you, it is impossible that Cassie did this."

"Mrs. Armstrong," Dan began, then stopped and shook his head. "Maybe it was an accident. Have you thought about that?"

She blinked. "Of course I've thought about that. Don't you think I want to believe something—anything—that would be better than this?" And she gestured behind her toward her daughter's room. "But have you ever heard of anyone accidentally gassing themselves like that?"

"It happens," he said, caught off balance. "It happens in bad weather sometimes. Blizzards."

She looked at him scornfully.

"Maybe something occurred we don't know about," Dan said. "Some freak thing that we'll never know. Maybe she left the motor running—everyone does that here—for the air-conditioning. It would be hot in the garage. The kids were waiting in the car. Maybe she had to go back inside for something she'd forgot. And when she got back, the door locked behind her and she panicked. Carbon monoxide works real quick. Quicker than most people would believe." That really was the best he could do. And he found it almost believable himself.

Mr. Armstrong ventured to look up at Kamowski encouragingly from beneath his thatchy eyebrows.

"This isn't a game," the woman said. "Not to us."

Kamowski was used to making hospital calls. Ordinarily it was a very ritualized procedure. If someone wanted unction, he gave it to them. He read the prayers out of the prayer book. He made the comforting noises the family members seemed to want. True, sometimes they were angry. But then he would sit and listen patiently while they railed at God or a drunk driver or the doctor, and in the end they were grateful to him for serving as the repository of their emotion. But this woman was not recognizing his role. Or hers. It was as though she saw his black clerical clothes as no more than an actor's costume, and she was addressing the person playing the part, not the character he was representing.

He looked down at the rounded toes of his black shoes, taking a moment to make certain internal adjustments. Then he said, looking at her evenly, "So what are you saying? What are the other possibilities?"

Her gaze faltered, and Kamowski felt a small thrill of mastery.

"I'm not—" She stopped and started over again. "All I'm saying is that there's more to this. Everyone is assuming—" She broke off again and shook her head.

Her husband stiffened and frowned at him. "It looks like to us everyone's already made up their minds. No one's even trying to find out if something else might have happened." All he had done was expand his wife's remarks, but it had given her time to pull herself together again.

Making a deliberate effort to lower and soften her tone, Jane Armstrong said, "Do you know Arlen?"

Kamowski shook his head. "I was planning to go by there on my way out of town."

A nurse's aide was wheeling a cart down the hall toward them.

"That's good," she said. "You ought to do that. As much as I'd like to think it was an accident, pastor, I can't believe that either."

The aide stopped at the door of Cassie Canby's room and looked questioningly at Mrs. Armstrong.

"I have to go now," she said. "I always help." She followed the cart in through the wide doorway before he could ask her what she had meant.

In Jack Tatum's car now, already impatient with the professor's driving, Kamowski found himself angry with this woman who had forced him out of his official character. Her face came to him more clearly in recollection after this second encounter. Before, even after the scene at the cemetery, he had thought of the Armstrongs as a conglomerate, not even physically separate beings. But now he recalled her distinctly as small, muscular in a way he took to be necessary to farm wives, with the kind of icy blue eyes and wind-reddened cheeks that he associated with movies about immigrants. Her fingers, he had noted, were rough and the fingertips squared off—a startling contrast to the delicate features of her face.

It angered him that she had managed to complicate matters for him. He had wanted to do nothing more than act as the conduit for the standard comforts of the church. These people's pain was more than he could fathom. Nor did he want to try. A functionary. That's all he aspired to be.

But now Jane Armstrong had laid on him the burden of doubt. Not so much about what had happened in the garage. He still felt the Armstrongs were in the classic stage of denial about that. But why had she mentioned her son-in-law in that way? What was she implying?

After leaving the Armstrongs, he had found Tatum in the foyer, talking with one of the women who had been at the funeral. She sat sideways on a sofa in the waiting area, her long legs precisely placed at a diagonal and one arm stretched along the sofa's back.

The woman rose as soon as she noticed him coming toward them. No one, certainly no woman, was ever as tall as him, but the priest was surprised at just how much taller than most women she was. About as tall as Dell, he estimated. She extended her hand to him immediately. Unlike Jane Armstrong's, it was narrow and smooth, though just as muscular.

"I'm Tony Winston," she said. "Thanks."

"For what?"

She made a small shrug. "For stepping in, taking on this task. It can't be pleasant."

"It's my job." He knew it sounded callous, unspiritual. But that was how he felt at the moment. And these weren't his parishioners. They weren't his responsibility.

The woman had looked at him with an almost mocking smile. "But it's all right if someone's grateful, isn't it?"

It was his turn to shrug then.

"We're on our way out to see the Canbys," Jack said. "To see Arlen," he added quickly.

The smile had disappeared from the woman's face. "Oh." She hadn't made any further comment, but the memory of that single sound, escaping from her spontaneously, made Dan increasingly nervous the closer they got to the rector's house. Tatum was right, it appeared. Arlen Canby was not universally loved.

Tatum slowed down and turned into the entrance to Thornwood Estates, marked by a glassed-in guardhouse with brick pillars on either side. The little shelter was deserted, however. Perhaps a sign the suburb couldn't afford its pretensions. In any case, Dan didn't like guardhouses.

They wound through several looping streets that followed the borders of a golf course. How could the rector of a church in a town like Somerville afford to live here, he wondered. Tatum pulled up in front of a long, low ranch-style on a corner lot. The double garage, Dan noticed, opened onto the side street.

"You want me to go in with you?" the professor asked.

Kamowski hesitated. It would certainly be easier if he had someone with him who knew this guy. On the other hand, if Canby hadn't even been able to face the funeral, he might not be ready for visitors yet. Especially his own parishioners. "Why don't you wait here," he said, "or drive around for about ten or fifteen minutes. Let me see how it's going first."

Tatum looked relieved.

Dan started up the sidewalk to the front door at a steady pace, aware that the two men inside could be watching and wanting to give them time. Arlen Canby could retreat to the bedroom if he chose, leaving his father to deal with the visitor. Nevertheless, Dan had to ring the bell twice before the door opened.

"Yes?" Canby's father had obviously lost the cool demeanor he had exhibited at the funeral that morning. In fact, he looked almost as wild now as Mrs. Armstrong had when she delivered her graveside speech. His silver hair, combed back in perfect waves earlier, was standing up on one side where he'd run his hand through it repeatedly. His pale eyes swam in a net of red veins.

"I thought I'd stop by and see your son before I left town," Kamowski said.

"Oh. I see." The man glanced over his shoulder into the room behind him, obviously trying to decide whether to invite him in.

Dan stood his ground silently. It would be all right with him if he were turned away, but he wasn't going to make it easy.

"Come in," the man finally said. As Dan stepped into the entry hall, Canby's father stuck out his hand. It looked more like a gesture of defeat than a greeting. "I'm sorry. I haven't properly introduced myself. I'm Rupert Canby."

"Dan Kamowski."

"Have a seat." The senior Canby gestured to the sofa in the living room and took a chair across a littered coffee table from him.

"I just stopped by to see you and your son," Dan repeated. "This has been a terrible blow for you."

"Yes. Yes, it has." Canby's eyes continued to search somewhere behind the priest's broad back. He seemed distracted.

Dan sat there another moment in silence. The other man took a deep breath and let it out slowly. His eyes finally came to rest on his own knees.

"I know you'd like to see Arlen," he said. "But he's not here. Just now."

Kamowski frowned. "Oh?"

"I think he must have gone up to the hospital."

"I just came from there."

Rupert Canby looked up at him sharply. "Maybe you passed him on the way."

Kamowski nodded his head slowly enough to indicate he found that unlikely. He, of course, didn't know Arlen Canby from Adam. Yet something—the other man's extreme nervousness perhaps—made him withhold that information.

Rupert Canby sighed again and sat back in his chair. "The truth is, I don't know where he is. I came home from the funeral, directly here, and he was gone."

Arlen Canby's father didn't strike Dan as the kind of man who often—if ever—asked favors of anyone. It was a measure of his desperation that he looked up now and let his fear show.

"He hasn't really wanted to see Cassie. Not since that first night. She was all red and blotchy from the carbon monoxide. And he had to look at the children too, you know." The man shrugged one shoulder. "Besides, her parents are with her. You can understand."

Kamowski nodded. He didn't understand though. "Maybe he went out to get a paper or something," he said. "How long has it been since he's been out of the house?"

"Not since I got here, two days ago." Rupert Canby rubbed his forehead, squeezing his eyes shut. Then he looked at Dan again. "The other car's gone." He paused. "The station wagon's still there of course."

"Maybe he went for a drive—just to get away."

"I've been here over two hours."

"You're worried? About what your son might do?"

"Yes. He's terribly broken up. I know that sounds silly. Hardly adequate to the situation. His mother and I—we've scarcely been able to take it in ourselves, we've been so worried about him."

"Afraid of what he might do?"

"Yes. I mean, what would anybody do? But Lennie—" he gestured vaguely.

"Lennie's what you call him?"

"Yes." He laughed shortly. "He's always hated it. But that's how kids are, isn't it? No matter what you do, you're going to fail them, screw them up somehow."

Kamowski only nodded. He and Dell had no children, and the passion with which other people often spoke of their children, even grown ones, sometimes frightened him. "He's got a lot of conflicting emotions to deal with right now," Dan finally said. "He needs to get away for a while. If he's worried about work—the parish—I'm sure the bishop will arrange something."

The man bobbed his head up and down almost impatiently. "Yes, yes. But right now I just need to find my son. I'm afraid—"

"Of what?" Kamowski thought it would be better if Rupert Canby said it himself.

"All kinds of things could happen. I don't think he ought to go up to the hospital. Those people, Cassie's parents, they have enough to deal with right now. And I know how Lennie feels about that issue."

Kamowski frowned. "Issue?"

"The right to die. He's very philosophical. He's not a practical kind of person. Never has been. I've had to be practical myself."

"You mean . . ." Dan paused, waiting for him to fill in exactly what he did mean.

"I mean he might want to talk to the doctor about, you know, pulling the plug on the life support system. He doesn't think she could breathe on her own."

"It's a little early to be making that decision, don't you think? Has he said anything to you about this?"

"Last night. He talked about it a long time."

"Have you called the hospital?"

"Who would I talk to? The Armstrongs don't need to be disturbed any more. Lennie would be furious if I had him paged. Everyone would stare. And I don't know anyone there."

It was clear to Kamowski that they could do two things. They could sit here and wait for Arlen Canby to appear, or they could go out looking for him. But when he posed those two alternatives, Rupert Canby shook his head.

"What if he were to come back and no one was here? I don't think that would be good either. In fact, I'm beginning to think I shouldn't have left him alone even to go to the funeral. He shouldn't be alone. Not right now."

"All right then. I can go look. Or stay here. Whichever you think is best."

Canby stood up and began pacing back and forth in front of the window, stopping once to lift aside the drapes and look up and down the street. An automatic gesture, made without much hope or expectation. For the first time it occurred to Dan to wonder if the man was telling all he knew.

"I think I should stay here," he finally said. "If Lennie comes back, I need to be here. And I don't know the town at all."

"Neither do I," Kamowski said. "A parishioner brought me. But he's familiar with Somerville, naturally."

Rupert Canby looked alarmed at the mention of a parishioner.

"This man's a vestryman," Dan said. "And a bachelor. He'll keep his mouth shut."

Canby looked away. "Of course. Discretion—we'd appreciate that."

CHAPTER • TWELVE

TONY WINSTON WAITED TILL Father Kamowski and Jack Tatum left the hospital; then she took the elevator back upstairs to the Intermediate Care Unit where she had been waiting beside Cassie's bed when the Armstrongs returned from the cemetery. They had wilted in the Texas heat, and their exhaustion from their constant vigil at their daughter's bedside was plain. Maybe now that the priest had gone she could talk them into going to her place to rest a while.

Jane Armstrong had made it clear she intended to stick by her daughter's side for the duration. But did the woman understand that might turn out to be months? Even years? Cassie's condition appeared to have stabilized, but she was still on a respirator. Maybe the priest had talked to them about this, had guided them toward accepting the reality of their daughter's situation. While Tony and Jack had waited in the foyer, he had told her about Father Kamowski's prison history. Maybe the man was tough enough to make the Armstrongs face the facts.

It appeared, however, that the priest's visit, instead of consoling the Armstrongs, had drained whatever energy they had left. Jane Armstrong sat with her head resting on the bed in the crook of her elbow and holding Cassie's unencumbered hand. Her husband stood at the window, staring down at the sizzling parking lot below, his back rigid.

Tony was disappointed in the priest. His visit didn't seem to have helped at all. Maybe he was too tough for ordinary people. He was brusque, for a priest, and he didn't manage to conceal his own feelings very well. He'd certainly made no effort to disguise his sour mood in the lobby.

Well, someone has to do something for these people, Tony thought. Their own son-in-law appeared not to have had any contact at all with them, at least not after the night Cassie had been brought to the hospital. And considering the circumstances, that might be for the best. She would insist that they go to her apartment and get some rest.

"Jane." Though she said it quietly, the woman jerked her head up, startled. But her husband turned from the window with a look of relief in his eyes.

"I'm sorry to bother you again. You're awfully tired, I can see."

The woman smiled wanly, but said nothing.

"You need some rest," Tony went on. "You're both dead on your feet. Why don't you take the key to my apartment—it's not far from here—and go get some sleep. I'll stay right here the whole time. And I'll let you know if there's any change at all."

The woman studied Tony's face intently, looking dazed and uncertain. Then, for the first time, she looked inquiringly at her husband. She's about to give way, Tony thought.

"Come on, Janie," the man said. "The lady's right. We've both got to get some rest."

Jane Armstrong looked down at her daughter's hand and then back at Tony again.

"I'll be right here the whole time," Tony repeated encouragingly.

Jane Armstrong nodded and slowly let go of the limp hand. "All right," she finally said. "This is very good of you. We appreciate it." Her husband let out a relieved sigh. "You go on downstairs and wait for me," she said to him. "I need to—you know—" she pointed to the open door of the bathroom. "I'll be right there."

Tony gave him the key and directions to her apartment, and he left, clearly pleased that his wife had agreed. When he was gone, Jane spoke again. "First though . . ."

Tony looked up. "Yes?"

"I didn't want to say this in front of my husband, but I need to talk to someone, to tell someone. Just in case."

Oh no, Tony thought, sensing trouble. "In case?"

Jane looked down at the handbag she'd lifted into her lap and then snapped open the metal catch. "I'd like for you to look at something if you don't mind. I can't trust myself right now to think straight. You know how it is when you've gone a long time without sleep. You don't trust your own judgment."

"Sure," Tony murmured, trying to sound soothing.

Without saying anything, the woman opened the purse and pulled out a packet of folded paper. She unfolded it slowly—there were several sheets—and looked at it. Then she raised her eyes to Tony. "This is a letter from Cassie," she said. "The last one I ever got." Slowly she extended the folded pages.

Just as slowly Tony took them. She didn't want to. She had wanted to be helpful. But she didn't want to get drawn into any murky, emotional stuff. She hadn't been Cassie Canby's confidante—or even her friend really. How could she justify reading her letters now? But on the other hand, how could she say that to her mother?

Dear Mom, she read, *I hate to write this letter because I know it will only bring you pain. But I can't put it off any longer. I'm leaving Arlen.*

Tony looked up, but the woman only nodded for her to continue.

When I went on that retreat in Houston a while back, I thought it might help me somehow. And I did have a great time while I was there. I made some really good friends. A whole week with no one telling me how dumb I was! I know you and Dad don't think much of charismatics, but believe me, it was a wonderful experience. I felt like I'd been given a special gift from God—little nobody me! I was so excited. I thought my whole life would be different somehow.

But when I got home, things were just as bad as ever. I tried to tell Arlen about it, but he wouldn't listen.

There was a long smudge of white-out across the page at this point. Cassie had obviously thought better of telling her mother everything. Over the white-out she had written, *I just can't handle it anymore. I can't go into all the details, they're too bizarre and embarrassing—even to tell you. But I can't do all the things Arlen wants me to. I've tried to be a good wife. I try to please him as much as I can. He says I try to humiliate him and make him feel guilty, but that's not true. I know he's smarter than I am. I try to understand things the way he explains them, but I just can't. All I can say is he needs somebody different. I'm just too plain vanilla, I guess.*

Maybe I could have stuck it out a little longer, except for the kids. Things between Arlen and me are so tense that it's beginning to have an effect on them. Heather's gone back to sucking her thumb and Russell wets the bed every night. And Arlen gets real mad—he blames me for that too!

Maybe he's right. I just can't think straight anymore, I'm so confused. Anyway, I feel like I must get away for a while, just to sort things out. I met a woman at the retreat that I talked to a little about my problem. She has a beach house down at Galveston. She said if I ever needed a place to get away, I could use that. By the time you get this, that's where I'll be. I'll call you when I get there and give you the phone number.

Don't worry about me. The kids will love it, and I can just relax for a while. I know Arlen will be furious. I'm leaving him a note, but please don't tell him where I'll be if he calls. I don't know what will happen, but pray for me. For all of us.

Tony looked at the first page again. There was no date. She looked at Jane. "When did you get this?"

"Monday morning," she said. "We got the call from the hospital that evening." Her voice broke, and for the first time Tony saw her cry. Tony handed her the box of tissues from the nightstand and waited for her to speak again.

"If I'd known. If only I'd known sooner. Why didn't she call me instead of writing?" She blew her nose, ran her fingers through her disordered hair, and looked up at Tony.

"Maybe news like this is easier to tell in a letter. I had no idea things were this bad," Tony said. "I don't think anyone did."

Jane pulled another tissue out of the box. It made a ripping sound. "No." She paused and sighed heavily. "I don't think Cassie had many friends in Somerville. People she could talk to."

Certainly not at St. Barnabas, Tony thought. "I'm sorry," she said.

The woman raised her rough hands and then dropped them into her lap again. She shook her head, unable to speak for a moment. Finally she took a deep breath and looked directly at Tony. "But you can see, can't you?"

"See?"

"That she didn't do it. Cassie didn't try to kill herself."

Tony swallowed and rubbed her hands together. "She seems to have been very unhappy."

"But don't you see? She had a plan. She was doing something about it. She was leaving, getting away, taking the children to the beach. If she'd been contemplating suicide, she wouldn't have written this letter."

The fine lines between Tony's eyebrows contracted

as she considered that. "But you say you got that Monday morning. The same day—this all happened. That means she had to have written it—what?—three days earlier. Friday or Saturday at the latest. But she was still there on Monday."

"She would have stayed over for Sunday. I know she would. I know Cassie. She wouldn't have done this right before Arlen had to hold services on Sunday. She's always very thoughtful, very considerate, very—accommodating. She was like that even as a child. Believe me, I know her. She would have waited till Monday to leave. In fact, that's the very day she would have chosen. Arlen would have a whole week that way." Jane Armstrong had obviously thought this out.

"So—what are you saying?" Tony asked slowly. She thought she knew, but she wanted the other woman to actually put it into words.

Jane only crumpled a tissue up to her mouth and shook her head. She looked as though she might start crying again.

I don't want to do this, Tony thought. The congregation had at best ignored Cassie, at worst made a joke of her. Tony herself had felt a variety of things about the rector's wife—impatience, pity, even contempt. But never compassion. The image of Father Shields floated into her mind's eye, but she pushed it out again. She could imagine what he would say.

The silence continued. All right, she thought, and took a deep breath. "You think someone else did this to your daughter and the children." She said it as flatly as she could, not even raising the pitch at the end to make it a question.

Jane Armstrong sat back and rested her arms on the arms of the chair. "Yes."

Tony swallowed. "Arlen." There. It was the first time she'd said his name in months. It cost her something.

The other woman looked down at her hands in her

lap. "Arlen's always been ashamed of us. We're just ordinary farmers. Of Cassie too."

"But that's no reason—"

"No. I know. But something's not been right between them ever since New Orleans. That was his first big assignment out of seminary. I think it has to do with whatever she blanked out in the letter."

Tony looked through the pages until she found the white smudge again. *I can't go into all the details, they're too bizarre and embarrassing—even to tell you. But I can't do all the things Arlen wants me to. I've tried to be a good wife. I try to please him as much as I can.* What in the world was she talking about, Tony wondered. Something dishonest? Something kinky? Cassie's description of herself as "plain vanilla" seemed accurate enough. The rector's wife didn't strike Tony as the experimental type. She handed the letter back gingerly.

Jane took it and put it back inside the worn envelope. "What should I do?" When Tony didn't answer at once, she added, "Don't you think I should show this to someone? Am I out of my mind? What?"

Tony walked to the window and looked down at the tops of the pine trees edging the parking lot below. Cassie's letter certainly revealed more about the Canbys than anyone had known before—as far as she knew anyway. She was surprised that Cassie had planned to leave her husband, whatever their problems. But the letter could conceivably be either more evidence for Cassie's suicide or—something else. Tony shuddered.

"I know," she said, suddenly turning back to Jane. "Father Kamowski."

The woman frowned. "The man who was just here? The one who did the funeral?"

"Yes. I know he doesn't seem, well, very sensitive. But he's—he's had experience with this kind of thing. He'd know what to do. Why don't you show the letter to him?"

"Experience?"

Tony hesitated. "He's worked in prisons," she said. "He's gone out to see your son-in-law now. I could call him there."

Jane Armstrong's face had taken on its dazed look again, as though all this information was more than she could handle just now.

"And you," Tony added firmly, "need to get down to your husband right away. He's waiting for you. I'll call the priest from the phone right here. I'll never leave the room."

It wasn't until the woman had left and Tony was dialing the rectory number that she remembered Harriet. It was after three. A couple of hours had passed since she told Harriet she'd help unload the church paraphernalia from her car. Well, she'd go by there later. She couldn't be in two places at once.

It never crossed Mollie McCready's mind that Jack Tatum would call Wendy Sanderson to keep the nursery during the funeral. She assumed Jack had noticed the hole Wendy's absence had left in the dwindling corps of acolytes.

As a teacher at Somerville High School, Mollie had watched Wendy's transformation from a tidy, carefully groomed child into an intentionally grotesque punker. The girl's peers had been mildly shocked when she showed up with her bald face. But when she came to school a week or so later with one side of her head shaved and what was left of her long, honey-colored hair dyed bright red, they had openly gawked. And avoided her. All but a few who dressed in solid black and routinely defaced the "Just Say No" posters in the halls.

Mollie kept a careful eye on this metamorphosis. She had been expecting a change in Wendy at some point. Teenage girls didn't continue to play Alice-in-

Wonderland forever. "Her cork is in so tight, I'm worried about the explosion when it does come," she had told Denny. That's what Mollie thought had happened when she saw Wendy's new look.

Mollie team-taught the gifted and talented class Wendy was in. Kurt Felder, her teaching partner, handled the science and math and had taken particular notice of Wendy because of her interest in computers. Kurt hadn't seemed to notice the girl's missing eyebrows. But when she showed up with half her hair missing, he'd finally reacted. "What's going on with Wendy?" he asked Mollie. "Is that some new fad?"

She laughed. "In Europe or New York maybe. Not in Somerville. But the new fad is only a symptom of an old problem."

He looked bewildered, but Mollie didn't explain. She understood why the girls in the class called him "the Geek." She and Kurt worked well as a team, she'd decided, because they both stayed on their own turf. Very few details from his physical surroundings got entered in Kurt's database. And that fact had often turned out to Mollie's advantage. So as long as Wendy was doing well in class she decided not to press the matter.

Then one Friday toward the end of the semester, Mollie, who handled what was vaguely termed "communication skills," had assigned the class a story by Alice Munro—"The Wild Swans." The central character was a young Canadian girl going to the city for the first time who finds herself seated beside a man on the train who introduces himself as a clergyman. Taking advantage of her naiveté, he proceeds to slip his hand beneath her skirt under cover of his newspaper while pretending that nothing unusual is going on. Mollie had intended to use the story in a module she was teaching about rape and sexual assault. It was a touchy subject, she knew, and she'd already gotten a couple of calls from parents. She'd managed to reassure them, at least temporarily, by appealing to their fears for their daughters' safety.

She had found Wendy waiting outside her office the next Monday. "Hi, honey," Mollie said brightly. "What can I do for you?"

"That story you had us read," Wendy said.

"Yes? What about it? Come on in." Mollie unlocked the office door and deposited her books on the desk, indicating the chair across the desk for Wendy.

Wendy didn't sit down. "Whose fault do you think it was?"

"Fault?"

"You know. When the guy, you know. The one who pretends he's a preacher. Or maybe he is. I don't know."

Mollie sat down, placed her elbows carefully on the desk, and clasped her hands together. "You mean who's to blame for his putting his hand up her skirt?" Bluntness, she'd learned, was an invaluable tool in dealing with teenagers.

Wendy ducked her head once in an abrupt nod. She had recently adopted an attitude of sullen impatience to go along with her new hairdo.

"What do *you* think?" Mollie asked, sitting back and smiling. Now, she thought, it will come out, whatever's behind this transformation. "Remember our discussion in class about blaming the victim?"

"Nothing really happened though." Wendy was frowning in concentration.

"Didn't it?"

"Well, I mean, not really. He didn't rape her or anything."

"Maybe not technically. But if someone—stranger or not—stuck his hand up my skirt, I'd feel like I'd been personally invaded." Hearing the heavy tone of indignation in her voice, Mollie chuckled to lighten it and added, "Unless, of course, I'd invited him to." You didn't want to scare them away from sex either.

Wendy grimaced unconsciously, then sat frowning at the floor a moment.

Mollie waited, wondering if she should venture to ask if something similar had happened to the girl.

"But maybe she did want him to," Wendy said. "She didn't tell anyone." There was a note of supplication in her voice that made Mollie uneasy.

"That's a common reaction, don't you think? There's a certain—fascination—with one's body at that age—your age. You're just discovering your sexual feelings. And they're often confusing. This girl—I mean, who would she have told? Who did she have to talk to? Not that sister of hers. You have to understand the situation she was in."

"Yes."

"She's away from home, on her own. That's exciting. It feels good," Mollie went on. "To be out on your own in the world. But then this person, someone who's a trusted figure, supposedly a clergyman, makes a pass at her. What's she supposed to do? She's confused, isn't she? He's the source of both pleasure and shame—so what is she to do?"

"Yes?"

Mollie shrugged. "Well, that's where the story leaves us, isn't it? With the question. Is she the victim of a dirty old man, or did she cooperate in her own seduction?"

Wendy looked down at her feet.

"So what do you think?" Mollie asked cheerfully, leaning back and locking her fingers behind her head.

The girl's bald face contorted suddenly. "I don't know, Mrs. McCready! That's why I came to you."

Mollie sat there a moment, surprised by the intensity of the girl's response.

"I mean, why do people write stories like that if they don't know the answer themselves?" Wendy cried. "And if they know the answer, why don't they tell? It's not right not to tell!"

"But, Wendy—" Mollie began, softening her tone.

The girl cut her off, dashing the remaining long lock of hair out of her face. "Oh, just forget it. I've got to go. I told the Geek I'd be in the computer lab now. I've got to go." She reached for the doorknob.

Mollie stood up. Surely there wasn't any funny business going on with Kurt. "Wait, Wendy."

The girl stopped but didn't turn around.

"What's this project you're working on? Tell me about it."

"You wouldn't understand," Wendy said. "It's about reprogramming PROM systems."

Mollie laughed nervously. "I take it that doesn't mean a dance. You're right. I don't understand."

"No," Wendy said as she shut the door behind her. And Mollie felt certain she had meant more than computers.

Mollie called Kurt at home that evening. "Was there anything odd about Wendy this afternoon?" she asked.

"No. Not that I noticed."

Of course you wouldn't, she thought to herself. "What's she working on with you anyway? She was exceedingly scornful of my lack of expertise. I need to learn at least a few of the code words. She said something about PROM systems. I have no idea what that means. I made some stupid joke about a dance."

"Well, let's see." There was a pause while Kurt put together an explanation in ordinary language. "It's a system that could be in any of the electronic devices you might have around your house. A microwave oven. Garage door opener. Burglar alarm. That kind of thing."

"Okay."

"They do whatever they're programmed to do when you access them by means of a radio signal. PROM stands for Programmable Read Only Memory. When it gets a signal, a dual wave tone, its logic unit goes to work. Just like your touch-tone phone. Or your answering machine when you're away. You access that by pushing one of the keys on the phone you're calling from and it sends the radio waves—sound waves—that open up the logic unit. In some of these systems, information can be stored and then erased and new information put in. The older kind, you couldn't. They were dedicated—the programs burnt into the circuitry. But now you can store phone numbers on those easy-dial machines. And then erase them later and put somebody else's in if you want to. Wendy's been real keen on this."

"Could you put a bug in it somehow?"

"What do you mean? Like a recording device?"

"I don't know what I mean myself. It was just the first thing that came to mind."

"Hmm. We're talking about simple systems here. Why are you so interested in this anyway?"

"Just because I'm interested in Wendy. She's not a simple system."

Kurt made an indistinct murmur on the other end, which meant he felt inadequate to talk about Wendy, even as a system. Mollie decided not to say anything to him about Wendy's being upset over the story. School would be over in a couple of weeks. Summer always seemed to heal a lot of growing-up problems.

Grown-up problems, on the other hand, Mollie reflected after returning home alone from the cemetery, were not so easily taken care of. For instance, what did you do if your husband was in love with another woman?

She kicked her shoes into the closet and pulled her dress over her head, letting the air-conditioning evaporate the moisture from her body. In the mirror on the closet door she checked the demarcation lines between the tawny and pale portions of her skin. She'd only had a couple of weeks since school was out to work on her tan. When she was Wendy's age, girls used to compare their white and dark patches in the locker room. But now the contrast looked old-fashioned. She'd tried to talk Denny into vacationing someplace this summer where they had nude beaches. She could have tanned all over then. But he didn't even want to leave Somerville.

Mollie knew why. She had hoped it would be different now. But he had been to the hospital every day, even when they wouldn't let him in to see Cassie. How could he go on being infatuated with a woman in a coma? It didn't make sense, not for Denny.

She dropped onto the bed and ran her hands through her hair. She'd been understanding. More than understanding. She knew these infatuations happened. After all, that's how she and Denny had ended up together. But she couldn't afford to throw over another marriage at her age.

Why hadn't the woman died? It wasn't fair. Would he go on worshiping at her bedside as if it were some shrine? She knotted her hands and shook them toward the ceiling. "Why do you hate me?" she said in a fierce whisper.

CHAPTER THIRTEEN

KAMOWSKI HAD BEEN ON THE point of leaving the rectory when Tony Winston called. She said she needed to talk to him at the hospital before he left town. She didn't say what about. He asked her if Arlen Canby was there, but she said she hadn't seen him.

After he hung up the phone, Dan passed that information on to Rupert Canby, noting that the man seemed strangely relieved. Though Dan felt sure he had no idea where his son had gone, he couldn't shake the feeling that the father knew more than he was telling. And now Kamowski could feel Rupert Canby's pale eyes following him down the sidewalk toward Jack Tatum's waiting car.

The blue Ford sagged as he climbed in beside Jack. The professor looked at him expectantly.

"I gotta go back to the hospital," Kamowski said. "That woman you were talking to there—what's her name?—she called here. Besides, your rector's not at home."

"Tony Winston," Jack said. Then, "Not home?"

"Not according to his father." Kamowski wished Tatum would get the car rolling. He didn't like the feeling of being watched. "Someone's gotta go look for him."

"Mr. Canby's worried about Arlen?"

"You got it. He hasn't seen him since he came back from the funeral. His car's gone. And he doesn't want to leave the house himself in case his son should come back. Let's get going, okay?"

Jack put the car in gear and they rolled slowly away from the curb. Dan took a deep breath and held it. The professor's tentative way of driving irritated him. Tatum appeared to have gone into a deep state of meditation.

"I can't imagine where he might be," Jack finally said.

"He doesn't have any place he hangs out, anyone he likes to drop by and talk to?"

"Not that I know of. I usually only see him myself at the church or, you know, some kind of scheduled meeting." There was a pause. "I don't think he has any, well, what you might call friends. At least not here in Somerville, I mean."

"Maybe his father has something to worry about then."

Tatum looked over at Dan. He cleared his throat and pursed his lips, as though considering. Then he said, "Arlen got some letters a while back, anonymous letters, saying some pretty bad things about him."

Dan weighed this as they drove by the deserted guardhouse. Priests sometimes did get anonymous letters from disgruntled parishioners. But they usually didn't show them to other members of their congregation unless they intended to take some action. "Did he show these letters to anyone besides you?"

"I don't know. I . . . I wouldn't think so. Like I said, he didn't have any close friends here."

"Why you then?"

Jack shrugged and looked miserable.

"Maybe you should get some help looking for him," Dan said. "Someone in the congregation." He watched Tatum out of the corner of his eye, waiting to see if the man caught on to the fact that the job of hunting for the missing rector had landed in his lap.

Jack nodded slowly as the message sank in. Wearily he started going over the St. Barnabas membership in his mind, the currently active ones. Denny immediately came to mind. But involving Denny meant Mollie would find out—and then the whole congregation. The second person Jack thought of was Clyde Mapes. Clyde had the advantage of knowing the entire county better than anyone.

"I'll call Clyde Mapes from the hospital," he told the priest. "You remember. The fellow in the Stetson." He refrained from adding that Clyde wouldn't be happy about this request.

Back at the hospital, Kamowski found Tony Winston pacing the floor outside the Intermediate Care Unit. "How is she?"

"Fine. I mean, there's been no change. Can we talk in the waiting room?" He followed her to an alcove beyond the nurses' station. As they sat down amid the clutter of magazines and empty coffee cups, she unfolded several sheets of pink paper.

"Jane Armstrong showed me this letter she'd gotten from Cassie on Monday." She shook her head. "That seems so long ago now."

"Four days," Kamowski said.

"She thinks this letter proves Cassie didn't try to kill herself—or the children." She held the pages out to him.

He looked at them warily without taking them. "Why? What does it say?"

"That she was leaving her husband."

"So? Maybe she decided to leave the whole world and take the kids with her."

She shook the pages slightly. "Why don't you read it yourself and see what you think."

Kamowski frowned at the letter as though she were offering him a can of worms. "I don't know."

"Jane asked if I would give it to you. She doesn't trust her own judgment right now. She wants to know what you think."

"And then she wants me to do something about it," he muttered, half to himself. "The bishop's not going to like this," he added.

"The bishop," Tony said, and her tone made it clear what she thought of Kamowski's superior.

Dan took the letter and rattled the pages, holding them away from him as he read. "What's this retreat?" he said after a few minutes. "She says she was going to a beach house that belonged to someone she met at a retreat."

"A women's retreat. Run by Ursula Donleavy. Sort of a charismatic feminist, I guess you'd say. Have you heard of her? Leslie Rittenhouse—she used to be a member at St. Barnabas—told Cassie about it. It was several months ago. Down in Houston. Cassie's been different ever since." Tony stopped short, recognizing the irony of her words.

The priest sighed heavily. He had no use for either charismatics or women holding retreats, not unless they were nuns. He could see how it might cause some friction if a priest's wife suddenly started upstaging him with the Holy Spirit.

"Was she the hysterical type?" Kamowski asked when he'd finished reading.

Tony looked at him sharply. "Hysterical? No. That's not what I'd call Cassie. Just the opposite. Lethargic maybe. Even submissive. You like that better?"

Dan felt the edge in her voice. He shrugged one shoulder. "I'm just trying to figure whether to take this letter seriously. What do you think? That's not much to go on. Was there anything else? She says something about leaving her husband a note. Did they find anything?"

"If they did, I haven't heard about it."

"What did you think about how the Canbys got along? Did they fight a lot?"

"Not that I know of. Like I say, Cassie wasn't the aggressive or even the assertive type. He criticized her a lot, but she took it meekly. I don't know. It's hard for me to make any judgments. I've never been married myself."

Kamowski looked up at her and then down again at the letter. "What's this that's whited out?"

Tony said nothing, waiting while he read on.

"Oh," he said. He took a big breath and blew it out again noisily. "Why didn't Mrs. Armstrong show me this letter when I was here earlier?" he muttered, mostly to himself.

"Well." Tony let the word hang there.

He looked up at her, disgruntled by the implication of her tone and her raised left eyebrow. "So. When did she write the letter?"

"It isn't dated, but Jane says it ordinarily takes at least three days for Cassie's letters to reach them."

"So Friday maybe."

"Yes. And her mother said she would have waited until after Sunday to leave. She thinks Cassie was too—" she paused long enough to cause Kamowski to look up, "considerate to make her husband face his congregation on Sunday without her."

"Were you at church Sunday?"

"I haven't been there in months." She ignored his questioning look.

"I thought you might have noticed if she seemed upset."

"You could ask Jack. I'm sure he was there. Or Harriet Autrey. Or even the McCreadys."

Dan looked uncomfortable. "Me ask?"

"Jane Armstrong needs someone to listen to her. Hear her out," Tony said, and she looked at him imploringly. "Maybe she is grasping at straws. But I told her—"

"Told her what?"

"That you . . . would be able to help. She does need someone to talk to. Someone experienced. She thinks, well, she thinks Arlen . . . might have had something to do with it."

Jack called Clyde Mapes from a pay phone in the hospital foyer.

"Yeah, Jack. What can I do for you?" Clyde said when his mother called him to the phone.

Jack cautiously explained the situation. He could tell during the ensuing silence that Clyde was casting about in his mind for some way out.

"You know the whole county better than anyone, Clyde. That's why I thought of you."

"I don't see why we can't just leave the guy alone, Jack. Why do we have to go sticking our nose in his business?"

"His father's asked us to, Clyde. Mr. Canby's very upset."

"So why don't you call the sheriff. That's his job."

"The rector's only been gone a few hours, Clyde. I don't think the sheriff would want to get involved right now. Besides, if the newspaper knew the sheriff was out looking for the rector of St. Barnabas, well, after all that's happened . . . "

There was another long silence. "All right," Clyde finally said. "You want me to meet you or what?"

"I'm going over to the church to see if he's at his office. Why don't you drive by the cemetery on your way into town. Maybe he wanted to go there after everyone else was gone."

Clyde thought a minute. He didn't really like the idea. But he figured it wasn't likely he'd run into the rector there. "Okay," he agreed grudgingly. "I'll see you at the church after I check out the cemetery. It'll take me a while to get out there and then into town."

Clyde slammed the phone down and checked his pockets for his keys. His mother looked at him inquiringly, but he ignored her, grabbing his hat from its peg and slamming out the back door. The dust boiled up behind his pickup as he roared out the ranch gate.

Clyde got angry when he was scared, and he was scared now. He felt like he was being dragged into another person's nightmare. Someone else was doing the dreaming, and he was just a character in the dream, powerless to find a way out. He should never have gone to the funeral this morning, he told himself as the fields went by in a blur, whatever the bishop said. He should have stayed home, gone to the sale barn over in Leon County. Mixed with other people like himself—ranchers, men who got outside in the open air and worked for a living. Away from these priests and professors and dancing women.

He gunned the big pickup as he pulled onto the highway to the cemetery. Here he was out hunting down some priest like a runaway kid. This wasn't his line of work. That's what they paid the sheriff for. But at the thought of the sheriff and his own son's recent encounter with the law, Clyde cringed. Maybe Tatum was right. Maybe it was better not to call the sheriff right now.

Would Canby really go to the cemetery, he wondered. It would be the last place Clyde would go. He hated graveyards. Not that he was squeamish about death. He figured he saw more death on the ranch in a year than most people did in a lifetime. What he didn't like was all the fuss people made over it. Dragging it out. Goading themselves into grieving. He liked to get things over with. Not dwell on them. He didn't like having to imagine what Canby was feeling or where he'd be likely to go. Clyde had a hard enough time dealing with his own life without having to imagine somebody else's troubles. You started feeling sorry for people, pretty soon they took over your life. The way he figured it, everybody had to carry his own weight in this world.

He eased the pickup off the highway and in through the brick pillars at the entrance to the cemetery. The lane that wound among the graves was lined with alternating cedars and crepe myrtle trees. The wind stirred the leaves, and pink crepe myrtle petals drifted into the red dirt lane. It was peaceful here, he had to admit. He preferred this cemetery out in the country. He'd hate to be hemmed up in that old graveyard in town.

There was no sign that anyone was around, but Clyde let the truck roll to a stop under the trees and switched off the motor. It wouldn't hurt to take his time. Sort of relax and get himself together before he drove back to the church to meet Tatum. Clyde felt like he could use a little peace.

He climbed down out of the pickup, breathing in the dry, astringent aroma, a mixture of brown pine needles and oak leaves that carpeted the sandy loam where larger trees shaded the graves. It was a smell that always reminded him of fishing. When he was a kid, an uncle had taken him to a lake out in central Texas every summer. Around the lake the dirt was baked dry and shaded in spots with pin oak and mesquite. He always caught fish when he was with his uncle, and his uncle always told Clyde's father how lucky he was to have such a son.

Clyde took off his hat and let the slight breeze from the south lift the damp hair on his forehead. Wandering down the aisle of graves between the trees, he stopped to read the epitaphs on the tombstones of people whose families he knew. Sessions. Bodachek. Longineau. Maybe he ought to take Clyde, Jr. fishing sometime. He ran a finger over an old scar in a cedar tree. Standing there staring at the trees and listening to the sleepy whirr of crickets, he was gradually aware of the unexpected descent of peace. The taut muscles in his face had loosened, and he breathed in the scented air deeply and gratefully.

Then he caught sight of the two mounds of red dirt close to the wall of trees on the eastern boundary of the cemetery. That must be them, he thought. The two little kids—what were their names? He made his way slowly toward them over the uneven ground.

For several minutes Clyde stood shaking his head over the white and lavender carnations wilting on top of the red clay mounds. "Poor things," he said softly. "Poor little things."

Jack had just put the phone back in its cradle when he saw Father Kamowski lumbering off the elevator. He explained about his conversation with Clyde Mapes. Then he asked, "How's Cassie? Has there been any change?"

"No," the priest answered. "No change." Then, fixing his eyes on an array of stuffed animals attached by suction cups to the glass wall of the hospital gift shop, he asked, "You go to church last Sunday, Tatum?"

"Yes."

"See Mrs. Canby there?"

"I guess I must have. She's always there."

"Did she seem okay then? Was she upset or anything?"

"Upset? Mmm. Not that I noticed."

"Who else was there? Someone who might have noticed."

Jack's fleshy brow wrinkled in concentration. "Let's see. There was Mollie McCready. And Harriet Autrey. Both of them were there."

Kamowski shifted his gaze to the rack of get-well cards on the other side of the glass wall. "Any idea if the Canbys were having problems?"

Jack stiffened.

"Well, the rector showed you those letters, you said. I thought he might have confided in you if he was having other problems." Any priest who would do that is a fool, Dan added to himself.

Tatum shook his head. He obviously didn't feel comfortable talking about his rector's personal life.

"You a cradle Episcopalian, Tatum?"

Jack nodded. "Afraid so."

"I thought as much," Kamowski said. "Why don't you take me to pick up my car now."

CHAPTER • FOURTEEN

HARRIET AUTREY HAD NOT been the first, nor even the second person to arrive at St. Barnabas that morning. Denny McCready had come early to unlock for the mortician and turn on the air-conditioning. And after him had come Wendy Sanderson, slipping in unnoticed while the caskets were being carried in. She hadn't wanted anyone to see her. Though she was learning to enjoy the reaction her plucked face and shaved head got at school, to savor the shock and repulsion on people's faces, today she had wanted to be invisible.

She had intended to go directly to the nursery and stay there. But as she passed the foyer door at the rear of the nave, she peeked in through the small glass pane. The mortician and his staff were just leaving through the side door. Wendy stared for a long moment at the two small coffins, rocking slightly on her heels. Then, as though drawn into the nave with no exertion of her own will, she slowly pushed open the door and went in, closing it carefully and silently behind her.

She made her way up the aisle noiselessly, breathing heavily but taking care to make no sound, as though she feared to wake the children in the coffins. She went to the one on the gospel side first. Being careful not to let the white pall slide off, she lifted the lid and looked inside. She held it open so long that its weight made her arm begin to tremble. Then she lowered the lid silently and crossed to the other coffin. She looked inside, but lowered the lid almost immediately, her lips clamped between her teeth. Then she made her way back to the nursery.

Now Harriet Autrey was at the end of her rope. She had been sitting in the nursery with Wendy for what she thought must be an hour. Her head ached. Her feet hurt. She was getting impatient. She had been trying to get Wendy to leave, to come with her so that she could take her home to her grandparents, but the girl obstinately refused. "No," she said flatly. "I can't go back there."

Harriet had no idea what had happened to make the child behave like this. She decided she'd have to call Bert and Ilamae to come get their granddaughter. But the phone was in the office, and the office, Harriet knew, was locked. She'd have to leave the girl alone in the church while she went to call from the convenience store two blocks away.

She looked at Wendy, who kept rearranging the circle of dolls and animals around her. What if the girl bolted while she was gone? Then how would they find her? She was obviously in no shape to be out on her own.

For fifteen minutes Wendy had been explaining something about dances and garage door openers, though Harriet hadn't the vaguest notion what she was talking about. Dedicated systems? Logic units? Proms? She seemed to be going over and over the same ground as if trying to impress some point upon her. But all Harriet could make out was the girl's repeated insistence: "It's my fault. I know it. It's my fault."

"What's your fault, darling?" Harriet asked.

"The children. Heather and Russell. It's my fault they're dead."

"What?" Harriet thought she must have heard wrong. "What are you talking about?"

"He asked me to fix it. I didn't know. I didn't understand."

"Fix what, sweetheart? What are you talking about?"

"The phone. The new phone he bought. He said he knew I could do it. I was smart, he said."

Harriet frowned. All this was gibberish.

"I learned how at school, switching PROMs. It doesn't take long," Wendy said, starting her explanation over again. "In the Geek's class."

Harriet frowned. Greek? She thought the only foreign language taught in the Somerville schools was Spanish.

"He didn't care about my hair. We worked on it together. You don't think he'll get in trouble too, do you?" She looked beseechingly at Harriet, her eyes round under her bald brow.

"No, no, sweetheart. Nobody's going to get in trouble." After so many repetitions, Harriet said it mechanically now.

This was probably the girl's first experience with death. Maybe she'd grown fond of the Canby children. But why was she blaming herself? Of course, she was Jeanette Sanderson's daughter. Had she inherited her mother's instability?

"How could it be your fault, sweetheart?" Harriet asked gently.

"They'll find out. They always do. Even if he said they couldn't."

"Who, Wendy? Who said?"

"Him. You know." She gestured toward the door. "He knows."

Harriet turned and looked behind her. The doorway was empty. As the girl went on with her garbled monologue, it occurred to Harriet that she might mean the priest.

"Father Canby?" she interrupted.

Wendy held her index finger to her lips. "Shh."

"What does he know, Wendy? What does Father Canby know?" Harriet asked in a sharper tone.

The girl's eyes widened even farther. "Everything," she whispered. "More than anyone." She leaned closer to Harriet, her eyes strangely opaque. "He told me about her."

"Her?"

Wendy waited a moment, as though considering how to form an unfamiliar word. Then she said, bringing it out slowly, "Jeanette."

Harriet sat back in the rocker. No one ever mentioned Jeanette Sanderson around St. Barnabas anymore. How could the new priest know anything about her? The only ones who would have told him were the Sandersons themselves, and Harriet thought that highly unlikely. It was something they simply did not discuss, not even with close friends.

"Your mother?" she finally said.

The girl frowned. "Jeanette," she insisted.

Harriet sighed wearily. "Wendy, I must go now," she said. She had decided not to coax any longer, nor would she let the girl know she was planning to call her grandparents. Most likely she would stay put within her magic circle on the nursery floor till the Sandersons could get there. "You need to tell all this to someone else, someone who can understand what you're talking about. I can't," Harriet ended flatly.

Wendy said nothing. She didn't even appear to notice when Harriet slowly got up from the rocker and left the room.

Harriet left the church by the front door. She hadn't used it in years, but the convenience store was right down the street in that direction. After she called, she'd come back to the church and stay with Wendy till the Sandersons got there.

Leslie Rittenhouse had come home from the cemetery frustrated. Nothing had gone right that day. First, Tony had declined her invitation to ride with her to the graveside service, saying she'd promised to help Harriet in the sacristy after the funeral service. Leslie had never been on Altar Guild, indeed had never wanted to be. There were Marthas in the church, she told her friends, and there were Marys. Leslie considered herself one of the latter.

After the committal, she'd driven back by the church, thinking perhaps she and Tony could have a late lunch. She couldn't wait to tell her about Jane Armstrong's graveside speech. But Tony's car was already gone, although Harriet's was still there. Leslie struck the leather-wrapped steering wheel with her palm. Nothing was working out to her satisfaction.

She drove home and put a frozen dinner in the microwave. Then she noticed that the light was blinking on the answering machine. She pushed the button and heard Felix's voice. He sounded preoccupied.

"I forgot the notes I made on the Stubblefield carcinoma, Les. Could you bring them up to the hospital this afternoon by three-thirty? I have a meeting there with the oncologist from Houston at four and need to go over them first. Thanks."

She felt the dull beginning of a headache at the base of her skull. Why couldn't Felix come home for lunch and pick up his own notes?

The chicken divan was still cold in the middle. She ate around the edges and dumped the rest down the garbage disposal. Her headache was getting worse.

She went in the bathroom, took a couple of aspirin, undressed, and stretched out on the bed, trying to get her headache under control. The scene at the children's graves kept coming back to her. Jane Armstrong's passionate speech. The woman had looked the way Leslie always imagined the importunate widow in the parable would. Insisting something was wrong. Demanding justice.

Why didn't I do that when that jerk revoked my license, Leslie asked herself. At least Jane Armstrong had gotten everyone's attention.

And is that what you want, Leslie asked herself. For everyone to pay attention to you? Is that your real motivation here? Are you just concerned about your reputation? Is your ego hurt at having been driven from the field in humiliation?

It wasn't the first time she'd put these questions to herself. After her last encounter with Arlen Canby she had endured a week of sleepless nights, going over and over this same ground. She had even kept a journal to which she confided it all. That seemed to help. She talked to Tony. And to the priest at St. Cuthbert's. Gradually the questions had died away.

But the scene at the cemetery had brought them all to the surface again, as fresh as ever. She could still see Jane Armstrong's face, transfigured by her grief and passion. Afraid of no one and nothing.

Of course the woman was defending her child. Leslie understood that elemental urge. After her own divorce, when she felt like giving up on everything, she had struggled just to make a living for her two small children. Leslie sat up and stared across the room into the dresser mirror, distracted for the moment by the memories of her own hardships. The children, she thought. She still had the children. They were what had kept her going. Something elemental and, for once, beyond logic. The children needed her. That's why she had never entertained the thought of suicide. She'd felt that her whole life was a failure. But for their sake she'd gone on with life, hard as it was.

Had Cassie Canby's sense of failure been so desperate, so disoriented, that it had engulfed not only her life but her children's? An unhappy marriage might impel a woman like Cassie toward suicide, but what would make a woman, a mother, destroy her own babies?

Leslie grimaced at herself in the mirror. What about the reports of Cassie's behavior in church the last few months? Had that been a sign of instability? And what responsibility did she bear for that? She was the one who had gotten Cassie interested in Ursula Donleavy. Leslie frowned and turned away from the mirror. Staring at her reflection had left her mind open a moment too long, and the question had slipped in unbidden. She recognized it as the one she had been trying to ignore for three days now.

Leslie had been delighted to hear about the change in Cassie when she came back from the Donleavy retreat. And though she had taken Cassie's charismatic expressions no more seriously than Mollie McCready had, she'd relished their effects on Arlen Canby.

Leslie Rittenhouse, however, was not one to indulge herself in guilt. Her original intention in introducing Cassie to Ursula Donleavy had been well-meaning. And the possibility of her moderating the unsettling effects of the retreat she dismissed as too speculative a notion to treat seriously. Though she admitted to the sweet gratification she'd felt on hearing about the rector's public embarrassment, the question now was, what should she do about it? Anything?

She went in the bathroom and washed her face. Her headache was abating. She wished there was someone she could talk to. Tony had been her sounding board for months now, though for the most part their discussions only reinforced their individual discontent. As for Jack, it had been apparent for some time that she made him uncomfortable with her acerbic remarks about St. Barnabas. Who else was there?

She went back in the bedroom and started getting dressed again. What she really needed was a priest. The rector at St. Cuthbert's was on vacation. But that fellow today—what was his name? Something foreign. And he had an East Coast accent. Nevertheless, she'd been impressed with the way he'd celebrated Eucharist. His voice was strong and emphatic.

She found the diocesan directory in her desk drawer and thumbed through it, running her finger down the list of clergy names. "Something ending in 'ski'," she muttered to herself. It took her a couple of minutes to find him, since all she remembered was the ending to the name. The address was in a lakeside development halfway between Houston and Somerville.

There was only one ring before a woman's voice answered, sounding sharp with anxiety.

"Mrs. Kamowski? This is Leslie Rittenhouse from St. Barnabas in Somerville. Is your husband home yet?"

"No. No, he's not. I've been expecting him." She hesitated. "Were you at the funeral?"

"Yes, I was."

"I see. Well. Dan thought it would probably be over by noon."

"Yes. We were through with the committal by then."

The woman laughed nervously on the other end. "I guess I sound unfeeling. It's just that we'd made plans for this afternoon. I know your whole congregation must be suffering."

"Yes," Leslie said simply.

"Maybe there were people who needed to talk to him. I would have expected him to call though, to let me know he'd be late." There was a moment's pause. "Actually, I've been worried."

With some effort, Leslie switched her thinking from the original intent of her call to the other woman's problem. "Would you like me to see if I could locate him?" she asked. "I have no idea where he could be either. Possibly the hospital. With the Armstrongs. Mrs. Canby's parents. You understand the circumstances here." She turned the last part into a question.

"More or less. It sounds . . . very sad."

Leslie could sense the priest's wife was feeling sheepish about her own impatience. She repeated her offer. "I don't know where he might be, but I could check at the hospital. Even the church, though I doubt he'd be there now. Why don't I do that and give you a call back?"

"Would you?" Relief was evident in the woman's voice.

Leslie put down the receiver, feeling strangely relieved herself. At least she had something concrete to do now. She'd take Felix's notes to him and check upstairs in the Intermediate Care Unit for Father Kamowski. Maybe Cassie had taken a turn for the worse and he was there with the Armstrongs. And when she located the priest, maybe she could make an appointment to talk about her troubled conscience.

CHAPTER FIFTEEN

D AN STOOD, FISTS ON HIS HIPS, across the street in front of St. Barnabas. Tatum had dropped him off beside his van, parked in front of one of the university dormitories. A ticket the color of Chinese mustard was wedged under the wiper blade on the driver's side.

"This is the last straw," he muttered.

Dan had had a bellyful of this town. He longed to get out of Somerville and home to Dell. She must be having fits by now. She'd planned to go shopping for a new dryer this afternoon. For some reason she always wanted him to go along when she bought electrical appliances.

But the ticket complicated things. Anyone else might have ignored it, but it sent cold chills up his back. He couldn't just crumple it up and toss it away. Even campus police might be linked into the state computers now. All he needed was for his name to end up on a file and get flagged with his felony conviction. On the other hand, he balked at paying the ticket himself. Twenty-five dollars. He figured this one ought to be on St. Barnabas.

He climbed in the van and turned on the air-conditioner while he thought. What was the name of that woman Tatum said would remember Cassie Canby in church on Sunday? McCready. Something McCready. That was the junior warden's name too. The man had introduced himself that morning before the funeral. And he'd come to the committal—with his wife. Dan remembered her now. A thin woman with dark hair. The junior warden would definitely be the person to give the ticket to. Maybe he'd just go by the McCready house, drop off the ticket, and at the same time have a word with Mrs. McCready about Cassie Canby. He could call Dell from there too. Surely the missing rector would have turned up by then.

Canby's disappearance was a sticky situation for Dan. The bishop wouldn't want him getting involved in the congregational politics of St. Barnabas. But he would expect him to offer comfort and solace to the family, at least for today. Did that include hunting for the missing priest? Well, tomorrow the bishop would be on the scene himself. Then he could handle the problem.

Dan pulled in to the Circle K at the bottom of the hill to check the phone book for the McCready address. If he could find it, he decided, that would be a sign. If there were a whole string of McCreadys, or if they weren't listed, he'd just call the Canby home, check with Rupert about his son—he'd probably turned up by now anyway—and take off for home.

He had to wait for an old lady to get off the pay phone outside the convenience store. She looked vaguely familiar. Had she been at the service that morning? She seemed distracted. He waited till she'd rounded the corner of the building before he got out of the van. If she was a member of St. Barnabas, he definitely wanted to avoid her.

He ran his finger down the second page of M's in the Somerville directory. Only one McCready in Somerville. Dennis McCready. Milam Street. That must be it. He asked the kid at the counter where Milam Street was.

The boy, staring at his clergy collar, pointed toward a tourist map of the town tacked up beside the cash register. The directions sketched in his mind, Dan climbed back in the van, remembering how Father Berkowitz had told him that wearing clergy black would be better than prison white. There were days when he wasn't so sure.

He found the McCready house with no trouble. About a mile from the church, north of the courthouse square in an area thick with pines and magnolias, the low brown brick rectangle showed years of dark tannin stains on its roof from the overhanging trees. He rang the doorbell, and a woman eventually appeared, one hand clasping a beach towel at the top half of a bikini.

"Mrs. McCready? Dan Kamowski," he said, holding out his beefy hand awkwardly when she opened the door.

"The priest today," she said with a half-mocking, half-eager smile, stepping back to invite him in. "Come on back." She led him through the house and onto the back deck where she'd obviously been sunbathing.

He sat down on a picnic bench, not sure that the white plastic chair she offered him would hold up under his weight. She stretched out on a chaise longue and put on her sunglasses.

"Mrs. McCready—"

"Mollie, please."

"I have a favor to ask of your husband."

Her mouth smiled below the sunglasses and she raised a limp hand. "Hey. Join the crowd. What can he do for you?"

"I parked across the street from the church this morning. I didn't know it was a restricted area. My van had a ticket on it when I got back just now."

"Just now?" She arched an eyebrow above the rim of her glasses. "It must be after three."

He shifted uneasily and the bench squeaked beneath

him. "I went by the hospital to see Mrs. Canby and her parents. And out to see the rector's father too." Actually it was none of her business how he'd spent the afternoon, he thought. And what was she doing inviting strange men in when she had practically no clothes on?

She rolled onto her side and propped an elbow on the arm of the chaise longue. "Really? How were they doing? I was thinking about taking a casserole over for them."

He shrugged and let that do for an answer. "Do you remember Mrs. Canby being at church last Sunday?"

The sunglasses tilted to the side and the woman leaned back again. "Let's see. Yes. I'm sure she was."

"How did she seem then? Upset or anything?"

"Mmm. Let me think." She pressed her lips together. "Cassie's not a real expressive person, you understand. At least not till lately when she's gone charismatic on us." She put a tanned hand quickly to her mouth in a gesture of embarrassment, her sincerity patently feigned. "Oh, goodness. I didn't mean to say that. I hope you're not—"

Kamowski raised a wide palm. "I've heard about that," he said, cutting her short. "Just go on. How did she act during the service?"

Now she seemed genuinely embarrassed. She sat up and crossed her legs to one side. "The kids were acting up. In fact—oh, yes, now I remember—she left with them right after church school. We don't have anyone to keep the nursery anymore. Of course they're too big for—" She stopped suddenly and bit her lower lip.

He waited for a long moment without saying anything. She reached over and pulled the beach towel across her lap. Her hands fidgeted with the thick cloth for a minute.

"You may as well know," she finally said, her voice abruptly flat, "I wasn't a fan of Cassie Canby's. Of course, the children . . . it's terrible."

Dan sensed the woman's brittle defenses slipping. "And why was that, Mrs. McCready?"

The dark glasses tilted upward toward him. "My husband is in love with her." She said the words abruptly. There was a long pause. Finally she took a deep breath and went on. "He still is. Even after she gassed herself and the kids. He's probably up at the hospital right now, keeping vigil at her bedside."

Dan sat there with his hands dangling between his knees. What was wrong with women these days? Didn't they have any shame? What was this more-than-half-naked woman doing, bluntly confessing to a strange man that her husband was in love with the rector's wife? *Not to a man*, he heard Berkowitz say in the background of his mind, *to a priest*.

"So if I seem unfeeling," she gave a short, bitter laugh and leaned back again, "you have to forgive me. Of course, the children—that's a terrible tragedy," she said again. "But Cassie. Why didn't she just go ahead and die?" She had wrapped one fist tightly in the towel, and now she put it to her mouth.

Land mines everywhere you go in this town, Kamowski thought. He stared morosely at the woman's long lean body. What about her? Could she have tried to do away with her rival? She certainly seemed brazen enough for just about anything. And what about Cassie Canby herself? Had there been more going on at St. Barnabas than she had let her mother know in the letter?

Letters. What about the hate mail Arlen Canby had showed Jack Tatum? Dan looked at the woman across from him. No. Why would she send anonymous letters to the rector? To his wife, maybe, but not to him.

"So you think your husband and Mrs. Canby—"

"I don't know what to think, Father." She sat up again, wearily this time, as though finally surrendering her jaded pose. "Cassie? I don't know if she was capable of carrying on an affair. It would take a lot of calculation and stamina, neither of which Cassie seemed to have. But Denny? Definitely. She's just the soft, helpless type he'd go for."

Which no one could accuse you of being, Kamowski thought to himself. "But you have no evidence?"

She turned her head away from him. "The evidence wives get is usually of a negative kind. The sins of omission, if you get my drift."

He swallowed and said nothing. He never had liked marital counseling.

"He was up at the church all the time," she went on, "supposedly fixing leaky faucets or replacing light bulbs."

"But he's the junior warden. That's his responsibility."

She gave him a disdainful smirk from behind the glasses. "I think some of those leaky faucets must have been at the rectory."

Kamowski considered this. Maybe Cassie Canby had indeed intended to leave her husband. But maybe there was going to be someone else at the beach house in Galveston. Denny McCready. That wasn't the kind of thing she'd be likely to tell her mother in a letter. But it also wasn't likely she would try to kill herself if she was running away to meet a lover. Maybe her husband had found out about it.

Dan looked over at the woman in the sunglasses. Maybe Mollie McCready had found out about it. "Then why do you think Mrs. Canby tried to kill herself?" he asked.

The woman shrugged her bare shoulders. The bikini top slipped a quarter of an inch. "Guilt. Frustration. Despair? How do I know? She and Arlen didn't—don't— have the ideal marriage. Under other circumstances I could feel sorry for the woman. She'd gotten into this charismatic thing, you know. Sort of an emotional outlet probably."

"Which she wouldn't need if she had your husband."
The words were out of Dan's mouth before he knew it.

She looked at him and her forehead furrowed above
the glasses. "No. Maybe not. I hadn't thought of that."
She turned her head away again and appeared to be staring off into the trees behind the house.

"You really think your husband's up at the hospital
now?"

"I'd stake my life on it," she said flatly. "I may be
wrong about Cassie, but not about him. He obviously
prefers a comatose Cassie to a conscious wife."

He stood up. "Maybe I'll take this ticket to him
there," Dan said. "I should talk to the Armstrongs again
before I leave."

She didn't offer to get up. "Suit yourself," she said.

"Likewise," he said as he stepped off the deck and
headed around the house to the van. He had meant it literally. And Berkowitz, he thought, might have said the
same.

The Sandersons' phone had rung a long time, but no
one had answered. Now that she thought about it,
Harriet couldn't remember their being at the funeral
today. Where were they anyway? She brushed a damp
string of hair off her forehead as she made her way back
up the hill from the convenience store. Would Wendy
still be at the church waiting? Where were her grandparents? What should she do? Why had this problem
landed in her lap anyway? She was old. Old and alone.
Younger people ought to be taking care of things now.

She stopped a moment to lean on a railing in front of
a dormitory and catch her breath. The sun made the
asphalt in the street black and oozy around the edges.
She could see the heat shimmering on the horizon of the
hill.

A pack of young girls about Wendy's age brushed

past her, dressed all alike in chartreuse shorts and orange tops. A camp, Harriet reminded herself. A cheerleading camp. The university rented out its dormitories during the summer for such things. Band camps. Math camps. But these must be cheerleaders, she decided, looking after their bobbing ponytails held up by some kind of green and orange wrapping. Why wasn't Wendy a cheerleader? Such a strange child. Why had she disfigured herself so? What was wrong with her? Bert and Ilamae were too old to be raising a teenager today.

She certainly wouldn't have undertaken such a task. Things were so different now. Drugs. Sex. Crazy music. How did anyone know what to do with them? She put her hand to her chest. How did she know what to do now? Maybe she should have called someone else from the store. Mollie McCready, for instance. She was a teacher. She'd know how to handle the situation.

Harriet looked up the hill at St. Barnabas shimmering in the afternoon heat. Then she looked back toward the Circle K, cars crowded in front of it.

What could she do if she went back to the church anyway? She hadn't been able to convince Wendy to leave. And she couldn't get to the phone in the office. It would be best to go back and use the phone at the store again. This time she'd call Mollie McCready. Mollie was such a capable person. She was the one to handle this.

Wendy had known it would be like this once she stepped outside the magic ring; her protection would be gone. She hadn't wanted to leave the toys on the nursery floor, but there was nothing else she could do. He knew best. He had always known everything—everything about her. She moved down the hall like an automaton, silent and stiff. Nothing could protect her now. Not even him. This was the way it had to be, the way it was supposed to be.

Across the stone floor of the foyer, up the aisle. The door to the sacristy was standing wide. She stepped inside and it closed behind her. Then she felt the oil running over her face, down her neck. The anointing. A sacrifice always has to be anointed, he'd explained to her.

It was dark here. Dark and warm. The way she had expected. The way it was supposed to be. She dropped to the floor and pulled her knees tight against her. Soon now things would start crawling over her. Up her arms, under her clothes. Probing all the hidden places she had wanted to keep to herself. But he had known about the hidden places too.

She had read a fairy tale once about a bad girl who sank down into a marsh, sucked under the slime and mud to a place where toads and snakes and things without eyes lived. Things that twined and curled themselves in her hair. Made her their nest. Wendy could hear them hissing at her now. She knew she was bad too, like the girl in the story. That's why she was here now, in the warm, suffocating dark. A sacrifice. That's where she deserved to be. He had explained all that. It was the only way, he said, to make things even. Everything had to come out even. Like the conservation principle in physics, he said. Matter and energy. Pleasure and pain. Everything has to come out even. No more, no less.

For a brief moment, a light leapt up behind her. A fire. A fire for the sacrifice. Behind her the door opened and closed again swiftly, and the key turned in the lock. Then the light sputtered, gradually faded, leaving her in darkness again.

She wanted to stay here in the warm, suffocating dark. This was the way it was supposed to be, the way to make things even. Russell and Heather were under the ground in a dark place too, suffocating. This would make it even for them too. It would make things better for everyone. Even Jeanette. It would all be even now.

CHAPTER SIXTEEN

L ESLIE WAS SURPRISED TO FIND
Tony sitting by Cassie's bed, reading a
book. She glanced at the body on the bed
amid the tangle of tubes. "No change?"

"No," Tony said, closing the book.
"The Armstrongs went to my place to sleep a few
hours."

"What about the priest? Father Kamowski?"

Tony stood up and stretched. "He left here over an
hour ago. He's probably home by now." She didn't want
to tell Leslie about Cassie's letter. The Armstrongs were
private people. They might want justice, but not expo-
sure.

"No. He's not," Leslie said with an irritating note of
finality. "That's why I came up here. I talked to his wife
and he hasn't come home. She's worried about him. I
thought I might find him here."

"Maybe he went by to see the Armstrongs before he
left," Tony said offhandedly. She had given the priest
her address before he left the hospital. "Leslie," she
went on, trying to maintain her casual tone, "did Felix
say anything to you about finding a suicide note from
Cassie?"

Leslie looked at her closely. "No. Why?"

"I just wondered. They usually do, I understand. Leave notes."

"Felix only saw her here in the emergency room. The police would have kept anything like that for evidence."

"And he didn't hear them say anything about a note?"

"Not that I know of. What is it? What's up?" Leslie planted herself in the chair by the bed. "Is there some doubt about . . ." She gestured toward the inert body on the bed beside her.

It was sweltering in the stairwell, and by the time Denny made it to the third floor he was breathing hard. He'd promised himself he would use the stairs instead of the elevator. This was the time, right after he left the office, when he usually went by Nautilus and worked out. Climbing the hospital stairs had become a substitute for that routine.

He hadn't said anything to Mollie about coming to the hospital, but if she found out he was visiting Cassie every day, he had decided not to deny it. She'd have to understand this was something he had to do. And how could she possibly be jealous of the poor little scarecrow tied down with tubes upstairs? The raw redness caused by the carbon monoxide had receded from Cassie's skin after three days, leaving her a mottled yellow and purple. Already she had lost the roundness he had loved.

He loosened his tie and took the last few steps slowly to retard his heart rate. He didn't want to look like a wild man. Cassie's parents might be there, though he hoped that they were getting some rest. He wanted to have a little time alone with Cassie. He could sit there and hold her poor punctured hand and murmur what he had never been able to tell her in health.

It would be all right for him to tell her now, he reasoned. There was no chance he could presume on that love. He wouldn't be able to take advantage of her weakness or exploit her unhappiness. Somehow they had both been protected from their own irresolute natures. He recognized now that it would have taken no more than an upward glance, a pressure of the hand on her part, for his own full heart to burst its bounds and engulf her.

It had not occurred to Denny to wonder how such a woman, admittedly weak and vulnerable, had found the courage to attempt to take her own life and the lives of her children. Because his own will was so malleable, Denny rarely considered intent or choice as the cause of a person's actions. He was a man to whom things happened, not one who caused and shaped events. He had no more willed to love Cassie than he could have willed himself to stop loving her. Though his heart had broken when he'd seen her lying in the hospital bed, helpless and inert, it did not occur to him to seek for reasons or assess blame. The tragedy had simply happened, and, with the humility that sometimes accompanies acknowledged weakness, he judged no one, least of all Cassie.

After all, he could see that it was Cassie who was paying an immeasurably high price for their souls' protection. This insight, however, did not come to him in an analytical way. He merely felt, amid his grief, a certain humble gratitude to her. And he knew of a certainty that at this point his place, as ordained a position as he had ever occupied in life, was by her side, caring for her, whatever that meant, the rest of her days. He made no separation between love, price, and duty.

Passing the nurses' station, he nodded to the women he'd learned to recognize over the past few days. The one who monitored Cassie's unit raised her coffee cup in greeting.

Before he entered her room, he set his face into a smile, confident that, even though she couldn't see him, it helped Cassie somehow when he smiled. Then he pushed open the wide door, and the smile drained away.

"Denny," Tony said, half in greeting, half in relief.

Leslie looked up at him from the bedside and frowned. "Hello, Denny," she said.

He stood in the doorway, not really wanting to go in while the two women were there but unable to back out now. "I just came by to see about . . ." He motioned wordlessly toward the figure on the bed.

"No change," said Leslie.

What did they mean, "no change," he thought. There's always some change. Cassie's hair, for instance, showed signs of having been washed. It wasn't pasted down to her skull like it had been the day before. And they'd put her in a different hospital gown, one with little yellow checks instead of the plain pale green. She was a little thinner, too, and her hands were beginning to curl inward.

Leslie stood up. "Denny, you wouldn't mind staying with Cassie a little while, would you? Her parents have gone to get some rest, and Tony promised them she'd stay right by her. You know how devoted they are. Mrs. Armstrong is afraid she might wake up and be alone." She glanced at the woman on the bed. "Not much chance of that. Anyway, Tony and I need to run an errand. It shouldn't take long. Would you mind staying for just a little while? Mollie wouldn't mind, would she? It's only a little after four."

Tony looked at her friend sharply. She knew exactly what Leslie had on her mind.

Before she could protest, however, Denny came over to the bed and pushed a stray wisp of hair back off Cassie's forehead. Then he sat down in the chair. "Sure," he said evenly. "I'll stay."

"Come on, Tony." Leslie took her friend's elbow firmly. "We'll be back soon," she said over her shoulder to Denny as she propelled Tony out of the room.

"What are you doing?" Tony demanded as soon as they were far enough down the hall to be out of earshot.

"First of all, I want to know what all this is about a suicide note."

"Nothing. There's not a suicide note—you said."

"I said Felix didn't know about one. But why were you asking? What have you heard that made you ask about one?"

Tony didn't lie very well. "Nothing," she repeated, even less convincingly than the first time.

Leslie crossed her arms and looked at her friend steadily.

"It's just that . . . Father Kamowski . . ."

"Yes?"

"He asked about one when he came back by the hospital." That was, after all, the truth, Tony told herself.

"Well," Leslie said, seemingly satisfied, "I need to find him. His wife—I told you—is looking for him. How long have the Armstrongs been gone?"

"We can't bother them," Tony protested. "They're supposed to be resting."

"I'll call," Leslie said, starting toward the nurses' station. "Just to find out if he's been there."

"No." Tony caught her arm. "You'll wake them up."

Leslie frowned. "Was he going anyplace else?"

Tony thought a moment. "Out to the Canbys'," she said. "He hadn't seen Arlen yet."

"Oh." Leslie considered. The rector's home was the last place in the world she wanted to call. What would she say if Arlen Canby answered? Ask to speak to Father Kamowski? She could do that. And if the rector's father answered, he wouldn't even know who she was. "All right. I'll call there."

"Let's go downstairs," Tony said, nodding toward the three women in white behind the counter who had been watching them curiously.

The phone only rang once before a voice on the other end answered. "Lennie? Is that you?"

"No," Leslie said, startled. "This is Leslie Ritten-house. I'm looking for Father Kamowski."

"Have they found him? Lennie?"

Puzzled, she took a moment to respond, during which the voice added, "Arlen, have they found Arlen?"

"I, uh, I'm not sure," Leslie stuttered. "I was looking for the priest. Father Kamowski, I mean. Mr. Canby?"

"Yes, yes. This is Rupert Canby. The priest isn't here. I'm waiting to hear from him. I haven't heard anything. Tell him to call me. I don't know what to do. Just tell him that."

"All right, sir. I certainly will. I'll find him as soon as I can." She said this while widening her eyes at Tony and slowly nodding her head. Then the line went dead at the other end.

Jack had been surprised to see Harriet's car still in the back parking lot after he dropped the priest at his van in front of the church. He supposed she was per-forming some kind of Altar Guild duty after the service. The Altar Guild was a mysterious force in the church to Jack, one he didn't fully comprehend. But he knew enough to stay out of their way; they guarded their duties jealously and neither expected nor appreciated help.

The rector's white Toyota was not in the back lot, however, so Jack circled the block slowly, thinking per-haps the priest had parked on a side street, trying to avoid parishioners. There was no sign of his car any-where though, and Father Kamowski's van was gone by the time he made it back to the front of the church.

Jack kept driving, through the campus area first and then farther afield, around the courthouse and the post office, going slowly enough to scan the sidewalks and infuriate the motorists behind him. After the third angry driver had blasted his horn at the pale blue Ford wavering across the center line, Jack decided to give up his aimless search. He briefly considered driving out to the cemetery to meet Clyde, but had the feeling his company wouldn't be welcome. And there seemed no point in going back to the hospital. Tony Winston was already there.

In the end Jack decided to go by his office and pick up some papers he needed to grade for his summer school class tomorrow. He checked his pigeonhole in the mailroom first, and while he was sorting through it his department head, Wayne Gribble, sauntered in. Gribble, a short, thin man with two kids in college and two more in high school, had taken Jack's class for him that morning.

"There's a reporter hanging around outside your office wanting to interview you," he told Jack, his voice half eager, half envious.

"Me?"

"Yes. Knew you were on the board of elders, I guess." The department head was Church of Christ.

"Vestry," Jack said.

"Whatever. Be careful though, Tatum. Don't bring the school into this," Gribble added. "You'll be back in class tomorrow, won't you?"

Jack nodded and escaped into the hall, thinking perhaps he could slip down the stairs and avoid the reporter. But before he could reach them, he saw a young woman coming eagerly toward him. At first he didn't recognize her. But by the time she was extending her hand to him, Jack could see it was Beth Marie Cartwright, who'd been coming to St. Barnabas as long as he could remember. She'd done something with her hair, and her face looked brighter than he remembered it. And now that he thought about it, he hadn't seen her at church in some time. Harriet Autrey had told him the girl had finally gotten herself a boyfriend—a deputy sheriff, if he recalled correctly. Then, just as he started to smile in greeting, he remembered that she wrote a column for the local paper. Was she the reporter Gribble had warned him about?

"Dr. Tatum," she said, putting a lean brown hand in his and looking up at him shyly. "You remember me? Beth Marie?"

"Of course," he said, more heartily than he felt. "What a surprise to see you here. It's been a while—"

"I know. I haven't been around much." She paused for a moment as if she might explain her absence, but then made a gesture as if to brush the matter aside. "I haven't kept up very well with everyone, I'm afraid. I was wondering if you could tell me what's been going on. This accident with the rector's wife. And the children. It's awful. The paper—I hate to say this, but when they found out I was a member at St. Barnabas, they thought maybe I could find out some more information."

Jack had already put a hand over his mouth, and his forehead contracted into troubled creases.

She touched him lightly on the sleeve, her own face mirroring his alarm. "Oh, you don't have to worry, Dr. Tatum. I know how upset everyone must be. The whole town, in fact. I mostly just want to know for myself. I won't tell the paper anything you don't think I should."

He glanced up and down the hall nervously. "There's not really much to tell, except what you already know. Everyone's devastated. Father Canby especially. The funeral was today, you know."

"Yes," she said, stepping back, looking down at her own folded hands. "I should have come. It's just that, well, I didn't want anyone to think I was there for the wrong reason. Just because of the paper."

Jack took a deep breath and let it out slowly. "No. Well. I mean, I'm sure we'd all have been glad to see you."

She raised her eyes to his shirtfront, a slightly sardonic smile pulling at her mouth. "Thanks. Okay. Well. That's all. I just wanted to stop by and find out—" she jerked a narrow shoulder in a shrug, "if there was anything I could do."

"Really appreciate that," Jack said, deliberately leaving the comment vague. "I'll let you know. It's great to see you, Beth Marie. Really glad you stopped by."

"Sure," she said. She flicked her fingers at him in a little wave as she turned away and headed for the stairs.

His heart sank as he saw her head bob out of sight. He hadn't known what to say. He only had this vast sense of failure.

On his desk were two telephone messages, one from Lanelle Chambers and the other just a phone number. He stuffed them both into his shirt pocket, sat down at his desk, and slid the stack of papers over in front of him, staring at them blankly. Maybe he'd work on these for a while. It was something he knew how to do.

Driving back into town, Clyde Mapes felt suddenly very weary. That was the way he put it to himself—not tired, but weary. Weary was the word his mother would use. It meant more than just tired. He felt washed-out, empty. Not irritable the way he usually did when he was tired.

The sudden sadness that had overtaken him at the cemetery by the children's graves was like a wave, its power having the force of an entire ocean behind it. There had been nothing to do but submit to it. Now, the wave having receded, he felt something had been washed out of him. And he wasn't sorry to see it go. In its place was something else he couldn't name. So he called it weariness. A desire, deep in his bones, a longing for rest.

Clyde didn't ordinarily spend time worrying his feelings or trying to find names for them. All he knew as he swung the pickup into the rear parking lot at St. Barnabas was that he wanted to get home to his family.

He was surprised to see Harriet Autrey's old grey Oldsmobile still sitting by the back door of the church. Just can't tear herself away, he thought. Poor old lady. St. Barnabas was all she had left and now it's gone. She must still be mooning around the place.

He was also surprised to find the back door locked. Maybe she was worried about being in the building alone, he thought. He went back to the truck and got out his big ranch key ring where he kept the one for the church.

After unlocking the door and stepping into the windowless parish hall, Clyde had to wait a moment for his eyes to adjust to the darkness. Then he tiptoed across the empty expanse of the room. He always felt like tiptoeing when he was in the church alone.

"Harriet?" he called out.

The stillness swallowed up his voice. He checked the kitchen and the front parlor across from the office but found them empty.

"Harriet?" he called out a second time.

He checked all the Sunday school rooms, the nursery, even the bathrooms, all without success. He frowned. Maybe Harriet's car wouldn't start and she'd gotten a ride home with someone else. He tried the office door on the off-chance it might be open. As he started to turn the knob, he thought he heard a noise inside—maybe a drawer sliding closed or someone moving in a chair—but the door was locked, as he'd expected.

He waited a moment to see if he could hear anything else, but it was quiet. Maybe it was the rector. He knocked once. "Father Canby?" he called out. There was no response.

What should he do? The sound was probably just one of those noises an old building makes on a hot day. He called out once more, louder. "Your father's looking for you!" He felt foolish, shouting at what was probably an empty room. Or the man might just be waiting for him to go away and leave him alone.

Clyde considered. The only thing he could do, he decided, was wait awhile, at least till Tatum or that big out-of-town priest showed up. He felt sorry for Canby. He'd just as soon leave the guy alone. On the other hand, his father would have the whole county out looking if he and Tatum couldn't find him.

Clyde crossed the stone floor of the foyer and paused at the door of the sanctuary, looking in through the little window. Maybe Harriet was still in the sacristy, clearing it out. He opened the sanctuary door quietly and went up the aisle, tiptoeing again.

The sacristy door was shut. "Harriet?" he called softly. He thought he heard something stir inside. "Harriet?"

Clyde reached for the doorknob, pausing only a split second as he caught a whiff of a strange, sharp odor. He opened the door and switched on the light. His heart lurched. Dropping to his knees beside her, he realized he didn't even know the girl's name.

CHAPTER SEVENTEEN

MOLLIE DROPPED HER TOWEL on the back of the sofa and picked up the phone.

"Mollie? This is Harriet."

"Yes, Harriet. What can I do for you?"

"I've got a problem. You know Wendy Sanderson, Bert and Ilamae's granddaughter?"

"Yes? She's a student of mine. What about her?"

"I found her in the nursery here at church. I stayed on to clear out the sacristy. After Tony Winston left—she was helping me, you see—"

"Yes." Mollie sat down on the sofa.

"After she left I found Wendy back in the nursery—I don't know why she was there to begin with—but she was in a terrible state. I don't really know how to describe it. She's sort of babbling and not making sense and she won't leave. I tried to get her to come with me so I could take her home, but she said if she stepped outside the circle something terrible would happen. You see, she has this circle of toys all around her and—"

"Did you call the Sandersons?" Mollie broke in.

"I can't get them. They're not at home. Wendy mentioned something about you. I thought you might be able to help. Since you're her teacher. You know her a lot better than I do. Maybe you could persuade her to go home."

Mollie held the phone away from her ear for a long moment.

"Mollie?"

"Yes. All right," Mollie finally answered. "I'll get dressed and be right there. Don't leave her till I get there."

The three women in white smocks looked at one another as Dan passed the nurses' station for the third time that day. He walked with a measured, deliberate pace. It was a way of walking he'd learned on the Bronx streets and that had served him well in prison—not exactly challenging but definitely announcing his determination. With each step, he looked as if he were claiming territory.

At present, it was a way of masking his indecision. What should he advise the Armstrongs to do? Go to the sheriff with their daughter's letter? Backing the plaintiff was an uncommon role for Kamowski, one that he didn't feel particularly comfortable in. Besides, what business was all this of his? The bishop would probably exile him to the darkest part of the East Texas Piney Woods for getting involved in this.

On the other hand, Cassie Canby's letter worried him—especially after his conversation with The Bikini. Now *there* was a woman to reckon with. He figured she had enough bitterness and bile in her to take out the woman she saw as her rival. But the kids? Would she go that far? Besides, considering the circumstances, it was hard to see how this could be anything but suicide. Why else would anyone sit in a closed garage with the car windows up and the motor running? Dell would know better than that. Wouldn't she? But then he considered Dell smarter than most women.

The person he really needed to talk to was Arlen Canby. That was another thing that kept him hanging around. Surely the bishop would expect him to stay in Somerville until the rector of St. Barnabas was accounted for. He couldn't afford more clergy suicides in his diocese. Had Canby told the bishop about the anonymous letters he'd gotten? Maybe they'd come from Denny McCready. Well, when they finally found Canby, Dan figured he could get some answers to these questions. Meanwhile, he'd see what he could get out of McCready himself.

He found the junior warden, just as his wife had predicted, beside Cassie Canby's bed. The man sat hunched over, staring at the floor, his elbows on his knees, but holding the woman's limp hand.

Kamowski stepped inside the door. The Bikini obviously knew her man.

Denny heard the step and looked around. "Father Kamowski?" He placed Cassie's hand back on top of the smooth sheet and stood up.

Kamowski raised a hand in silent greeting and then took the one Denny had extended to him.

"Do you do healing?" the man blurted out.

"What?"

"Some priests are into that. Father Shields used to do the prayer for healing—you know, in the prayer book—down at the altar if anybody wanted it. But what about here? In the hospital. I mean, maybe it would help. It's worth a try, don't you think?"

Dan stared into the man's urgent face. An Israelite without guile, he thought. Not with faith, maybe, but no guile either. "Sit down, McCready," he said.

The man sat down again slowly, still facing Dan who continued to stand.

"You in love with this woman?" Kamowski asked.

Denny dropped his eyes a moment, then looked over at the figure on the bed. "Yes." His voice was so low Dan could only catch the final sibilant sound.

"What about your wife?"

The man looked up at him. "You mean—do I love my wife?"

Kamowski shrugged. "I mean what about your wife?"

The other man sighed heavily. "Cassie needed me. She was all alone. There was no one for her here. She was all alone."

"You didn't answer my question." Dan folded his large arms across his chest.

"Mollie." Denny drew a deep breath as though tackling the subject of his wife required more effort than he was equal to. "Mollie doesn't need me. She never has. She's intelligent, brilliant, I guess. She figures things out so quick. She has all this energy. She's strong. She doesn't need me," he repeated. "I don't know what she ever saw in me."

"She married you, didn't she? Musta been something." Kamowski dragged another chair from against the wall and sat down facing him. "I just came from talking to your wife."

Denny looked up quickly. "She doesn't know about . . . this."

"You wanna bet? She's the one who told me you'd be up here." He paused while shock registered on the junior warden's face. Then Dan fished the parking ticket out of his pocket. "By the way, I'd like you to take care of this for me."

Denny took the mustard colored slip without looking at it. "You think she knows?"

"She figured this thing out long ago, McCready. You said yourself she was brilliant."

The other man sat back. "It wasn't Cassie's fault. She never . . . we never . . . ."

"Never, huh?"

"Never. Cassie's, well, pure and sweet. I don't know if she was even aware of how I felt."

"You never laid a hand on her?"

"No. I swear."

The priest rubbed his face with his massive hand, churning the furrows up and down. "Well," he finally said, looking up at Denny, "I think the healing you need to be praying for right now is your wife's. I'm not sure but what she don't need it more." He stood up. "That is, if you expect God to do anything for this woman here. This isn't a magic trick we're talking about, you know. God ain't a fairy godmother, McCready, with nothing better to do than go around granting wishes. In fact, just the opposite. You're the one supposed to be granting his wishes."

Denny frowned up at him. "What do you mean?"

"Doing God's will—you church people throw it around awful easy, I notice. Well, that's what it means—granting God's wishes."

"God's wishes? How can God have any wishes? He can—"

"Do anything he wants?" Kamowski sighed. "Maybe. Maybe not."

Denny continued to stare at him. Dan felt completely out of his depth, like a bad swimmer who can barely make out the shoreline. "You know the ten commandments, McCready?"

Denny's glance wavered. "Sort of."

"All right. Think of those as God's wishes. And you're supposed to grant 'em."

"And if I do—" Denny looked over at Cassie.

"Will he make this lady well? I don't know. How's your record been so far? Got any extra brownie points stored up?"

Denny puffed out his cheeks and let out the air slowly.

"So. Looks like the deal's already blown."

"Are you saying God did this to her just to get even with me?" For the first time there was an angry spark in the junior warden's eyes.

It was on the tip of Kamowski's tongue to say, No, but your wife might have. Instead, he said, "No. I'm just saying don't plan on making a deal with God when you can't deliver."

The spark flickered dully. "There's got to be something I can do for Cassie. Anything. I'd do anything."

Dan looked over at the figure on the bed. "You think you know what's best for this woman? You really want her to wake up so she can find out she's killed her kids? Is that your idea of mercy?"

"No," Denny said, and Kamowski was surprised by his grimness. He leaned forward over his knees again and dropped his head. "As a matter of fact, I was thinking maybe the best thing I could do for her was to pull the plug on that whatchamacallit." He pointed to the tube feeding from the wall into Cassie's nostrils. "Maybe that's all I can do for her now."

Kamowski laughed suddenly—a hard, barking sound that he tried to stifle too late. "That's good. That's really good. It may be because of you that she's in this shape to begin with. Now you think you can fix things up by a simple little twist of the wrist. It ain't that easy, McCready."

The spark was smoldering in Denny's eyes again. "What do you mean? How am I responsible?"

Just then a nurse put her head into the cubicle. "Father Kamowski?" she said. "There's a call for you out here at the nurses' station."

Kamowski looked at the nurse, then back at McCready.

"I'm all right," the man said, raising his hand. "Don't worry."

Dan followed the nurse out of the room and picked up the phone at the desk. "Yeah?"

"Father Kamowski?"

"Yes?"

"He's there, isn't he?" It was The Bikini.

Dan paused for only a moment. "Yes."

There was a longer pause on the other end. "Well. Anyway. We need him."

"We?"

"At St. Barnabas. We need to get into the office. I'm calling from home. Something's wrong there. I'm not sure what, but we may need to get into the office, and the office is locked. Denny's got the only key besides the rector's."

"He's not there then, the rector?"

"I guess not. I'm leaving right now myself. Maybe you better come too. I don't really know what's going on. Wendy Sanderson—" She stopped. "It's too complicated to explain over the phone."

"All right," he said. "We'll be there."

Tony and Leslie had seen Father Kamowski step onto the elevator at the end of the corridor just as Leslie hung up the phone after talking to Rupert Canby.

"There he is," Leslie said. "At last." She had started toward him when Tony caught her arm.

"Wait."

"What do you mean, wait? I've been trying to get hold of this man for hours. His wife wants him. Rupert Canby wants him. I want him."

"Just be still, will you? We know where he is now. And I think it might be good if Denny got a chance to talk to him upstairs. Alone."

"What are you talking about?" Leslie turned and looked up at the taller woman.

"Come on, Les. Surely you've noticed."

"Noticed what?"

"The way Denny is. About Cassie." And in answer to Leslie's blank stare, Tony added, "Boy, you may be logical, but you're not very—what's the word?" She described convolutions in the air with her hands.

"Intuitive?"

"Intuitive. You don't catch the undercurrents sometimes."

"So you think—"

"I don't think anything. I've just noticed. How attentive Denny always is to Cassie. Sympathetic. Protective."

"But nothing—"

Tony shrugged. "Who knows? Let's go sit in the lounge. He's got to come out this way again. We'll see him."

Reluctantly, Leslie followed her to a sofa in the lounge, checking her watch every five minutes. Finally the elevator doors opened and the priest emerged, followed by Denny McCready.

Leslie jumped to her feet and hurried toward the two men, intercepting them in the lobby. "Father Kamowski. I've been looking for you. Your wife needs you to call her. And Rupert Canby too."

He looked at her as though trying to recall who she was. "Fine," he said, and continued toward the door. Denny was already through the glass panels.

"You can call them from here," she added quickly.

He stopped and looked at her vaguely. "Say, would you mind doing something for me? Call my wife and tell her I got held up. Say not to expect me for another couple of hours. And Mr. Canby. I'll get back to him as soon as we get to the church. Thanks." And the door slid closed behind him.

Leslie put her hands on her hips and stared after him. Then she turned to Tony. "How do you like that? What does he think I am, his secretary?"

"Did you see the look on Denny's face?" Tony asked. "He was in no mood to stop and chat. I wonder what they're going to the church for?"

The expression on Leslie's face underwent a slow transformation from affront to curiosity. "Maybe they've found him."

Jack put the cap back on his pen and pushed the stack of papers to the edge of the desk. He checked his watch. After five now. Gribble was sure to be gone. And Clyde would be waiting for him at the church. He started to put the pen back in his shirt pocket and discovered the telephone memos he'd put there earlier. He pulled them out and looked at them again, dropping Lanelle's back onto the desk. The number written on the other pink slip looked familiar. Of course. Why hadn't he noticed the first time?

He pulled the phone toward him and dialed the number. It rang three times, and he was on the point of replacing the receiver when he heard the phone picked up on the other end. At first he thought it was the answering machine they'd bought when they couldn't afford a secretary any more. But there was only silence. Then he heard someone draw a long, shuddering breath.

"Hello? Hello?"

"Jack? Is that you? Thank God. I need to talk to someone. A priest. Father Kamowski. Is he still around? Can you get him for me? Please, Jack. Please."

"Sure, Arlen. Are you all right? I'll be right there."

CHAPTER • EIGHTEEN

HARRIET PUSHED OPEN THE back door of the church, grateful for the cool darkness. After her walk back from the Circle K her clothes were sticking to her. She stood there in the dark parish hall, letting the heat drain from her body before she started back to the nursery. It would take Mollie a few more minutes to get there, and she dreaded facing Wendy again alone.

In the distance she heard the office phone ring once and then stop. The answering machine must have switched on. Wearily, she started down the corridor of Sunday school rooms.

The door to the nursery was closed. Harriet frowned. She was certain she had left it open.

"Wendy?" she called, and pushed on it cautiously. The circle of toys was scattered. The stuffed elephant and a red plastic truck had been pushed out from Wendy's magic ring. The girl wasn't inside it any more.

Harriet crossed the room quickly to the small rest room at the back of the nursery and flipped on the light switch. Empty. She checked under the crib in the corner. A small stool and some blocks, that was all. She stood up and took a deep breath. She should never have left the girl, not in her condition. Maybe she was still in the building somewhere.

She checked the outside door at the end of the hallway. The thumb latch was still on. Of course, Wendy could have locked it if she'd left that way. Harriet hurried back up the hall, stopping to look briefly in each of the Sunday school rooms. She was checking the last one when she heard someone come in the back door—or was it someone leaving?

Harriet hurried into the foyer. But just as she rounded the corner, a figure emerged from the shadows of the parish hall.

"Mollie! Thank God, you're here!"

Clyde stooped down and picked up Wendy's limp arm, feeling for a pulse. His heart was pounding so hard he couldn't tell if what he was feeling was the tremor of his own pulse or a flutter along the girl's vein. He sat back on one heel and tried to decide very quickly what to do. Should he pull her out of the tiny room, elevate her head, not move her at all? What had happened to her? How did she get in here?

I've got to call the hospital, he thought, get an ambulance, the police. But the phone was locked up in the office. Fortunately, he had his truck with the CB in it. He could call from that.

He stood up and backed away from the girl, still trying to catch some sign of life. Then he thought he heard voices out in the foyer. He turned and ran down the aisle. Thank God. Someone to help.

Mollie and Harriet stared at him as he came bursting into the foyer from the nave.

"Help," he said hoarsely. "We've got to get help."

"What?"

"That girl. Ilamae and Bert's girl. The one with the shaved head. She's in there."

"In *there*?" They started toward the door.

"She's—something's wrong. Don't move her. I'm going to call."

"Denny's coming," Mollie said, pausing in the doorway. "He has the key to the office."

"Can't wait," Clyde yelled over his shoulder as he headed toward the rear entrance. "I'll use my CB."

He had parked his truck under a tree at the far end of the parking lot. He opened the door on the passenger side and pulled out the speaker. The CB was just crackling to life when he saw Jack Tatum's blue Ford heaving up the driveway into the parking lot.

Jack got out of his car. He saw the truck, but not Clyde on the far side.

"Tatum!"

Jack turned toward the pickup and saw Clyde's hand motioning to him from the other side of the truck. He was halfway across the expanse of asphalt, cooling now as the evening came on, when he heard another vehicle— Father Kamowski's van—laboring into the driveway.

Denny jumped out of the passenger side. Kamowski emerged more slowly from the driver's seat.

"What's going on?" Denny shouted.

"I'm trying to raise the ambulance and the police on the CB," Clyde yelled over the roof of the truck.

"I just got here myself," Jack said, looking from one man to the other. "I got a call. Earlier this afternoon at the office. I didn't return it right away—"

Denny shook his head impatiently. "Is Mollie here?" Jack looked baffled.

"What about Wendy?"

"I don't know. I just got here myself," he repeated.

"Here." Denny dropped a key in Kamowski's hand. "You open the office," he said. Then he loped across the lot and disappeared through the back door.

"What's going on?" Jack asked the priest, whose eyes had narrowed as he took in the scene of confusion.

"Tell me about this phone call," Kamowski said to Jack.

"I only returned the call a few minutes ago. I recognized the church number when I looked at it again. Arlen answered. Father Canby. He wanted to talk to you. He sounded very upset."

Kamowski nodded curtly and started toward the church door while Jack was still speaking. Jack followed him into the dark parish hall. The priest flipped on the light switch and an uneven pattern of recessed bulbs glowed overhead. He stood still a moment, scanning the big empty room, then proceeded deliberately toward the foyer at the far end.

They could hear muffled voices in the sanctuary.

"What's going on?" Jack asked.

"Why don't you go see," Kamowski said, motioning toward the nave door.

Left alone, Dan contemplated the door of the rector's office. How long had the man been in there? All afternoon? Obviously Canby hadn't felt like making his presence known to his parishioners. Was he trying to find some solitude, a place to escape people's sympathy? Or had he enjoyed the sensation of sitting silently in the center of a storm? And had he been alone?

On the way over from the hospital, McCready had told Dan that Wendy Sanderson used to baby-sit for the Canbys. A troubled teen, he'd called her, whatever he meant by that. What had she been doing here at the church? Dan hadn't noticed any teenagers at the funeral. And from McCready's description of her, she'd be hard to miss.

Kamowski raised his hand to knock, then dropped it and inserted the key McCready had handed him in the parking lot. The knob turned easily.

"What's going on here?" Leslie said as she and Tony

pulled into the St. Barnabas lot. "Harriet's still here. And there's Jack's car and Father Kamowski's van. And Mollie's Mustang."

Tony pointed to the far end of the lot. "Clyde's truck, too."

"In fact, there's Clyde himself."

The rancher was just slamming the door to the pickup.

Leslie pulled her Mercedes alongside the truck. "What's going on?" she repeated to Clyde as she got out.

He looked at her warily. "I don't know. The Sanderson girl—"

"Wendy?"

"Something's happened to her. I was just calling an ambulance."

"An ambulance? Is she hurt?" Tony asked.

"I don't know. Something's wrong. I found her in the sacristy."

"The sacristy? What in the world was she doing there?"

"Nothing. She was—unconscious."

"But I locked the sacristy before I left," Tony put in.

"How long will the ambulance take?" Clyde asked, looking at Leslie.

"Who knows? Is she bad?" But before Clyde could respond, she had already opened the church door.

At the front of the nave, they found the McCreadys and Harriet kneeling around Wendy Sanderson's prone figure, the light from the sacristy falling on the girl's pale face. Jack stood back, looking down at the group, his face slack with shock.

"This is my fault," Mollie was saying. "I should have known."

"Is she all right?" Leslie asked sharply. "What's wrong?"

Denny sat back on his heels. "I don't know. I can't get a pulse." He looked up at Clyde. "Is the ambulance coming?"

Clyde nodded.

"Here. Let me see her," Leslie said, putting her handbag down on the organ and kneeling beside the girl.

"What happened?" Tony asked.

"I don't know," Clyde said. "I came back to meet Jack here and saw Harriet's car. I figured she was cleaning out the sacristy, so I came in here to see if she needed any help while I waited. That's when I found her." He pointed to the girl on the floor. "Harriet wasn't here," he added, looking at the older woman as if for an explanation.

"I went down to the Circle K on the corner to try to call the Sandersons," Harriet said. "I found Wendy still in the nursery after I'd finished cleaning out the sacristy. Something was wrong. She was talking all crazy. I tried to get her to let me take her home but she wouldn't leave this circle of toys she'd made around herself. She said nothing would happen as long as she was in the circle. I didn't know what to do. The Sandersons weren't home. So I called you." She looked at Mollie. "She said something about you. That she'd promised you something. That's why I thought of calling you."

The man behind the desk was tall but thin, just as Dan had remembered. Even with the age difference, he figured he'd be able to contain whatever happened in this room. And the police would be here soon.

CHAPTER • NINETEEN

SHUT THE DOOR."

Leaning back in the chair behind the desk with his legs crossed, one knee jutting angularly toward the ceiling, Canby gave every appearance of feeling in command of the situation. Dan shut the door.

"Lock it."

His hand was still on the knob. Dan snapped the thumb latch in without taking his eyes off the man behind the desk.

"They've found her."

Though the words weren't spoken as a question, Kamowski chose to take them that way. "I guess so," he said. "I haven't seen her."

"Sit down." Canby gestured impatiently toward the folding chair on the other side of his desk.

Kamowski studied the chair a long moment, nodded once, and sat down. Condolences didn't seem to be what Arlen Canby was looking for. "Your father—" he began.

Canby stood up suddenly and waved a long arm, brushing the word aside. "You've met him. Yes. Well, you can see what he is." He didn't look at Dan for confirmation of this vague accusation, but moved across to the one, chin-high window in the office, peered out, then turned and began idly pulling books forward and pushing them back in his bookcase. Then he crossed to the desk again and, with the same distracted air, riffled through papers while he spoke. "He's always been concerned with keeping up appearances. He never wanted me to be a priest. But he wanted me to go to the funeral this morning."

Canby sat down again, looking suddenly weary, and ran his thin fingers through his hair. "But never mind that," he went on. "I'm a priest. I am a priest." He stared across at Kamowski, as though daring him to contradict this claim.

Dan said nothing.

"And you're a priest." The way he said it seemed to carry some further implication. He stood up again suddenly. "I want to confess."

Other than shifting his eyes upward to meet the man's gaze, Dan kept his own face perfectly motionless. It was an old prison skill. He watched silently as the man paced back and forth in the narrow space between the window and the desk.

All at once Canby turned and stared at him. Then he jerked a prayer book from between the bookends on his desk and held it in front of Dan's face, shaking it slightly. "Here," he said. "Page four forty-seven."

Dan did not take the book immediately, but continued staring up at him. Canby flapped the slackbound prayer book in front of him again. Slowly Dan reached out and took it. Canby pulled another prayer book from a shelf and quickly found the page he wanted.

Dan turned the pages slowly. This was not a part of the prayer book he used often. At the top of page four forty-seven in bold letters it said, "The Reconciliation of a Penitent."

As soon as he saw that Dan had found the proper page, Canby came around the desk and dropped to his knees in front of him. Involuntarily, Dan stiffened in his chair. Canby seemed not to notice. He glanced around the office as though searching for something, then, still on his knees, shuffled back around the desk and pulled a loose cushion from his chair. Shuffling back again, he arranged the pad under his knees. Then he opened his prayer book again.

"Bless me, for I have sinned."

Dan looked down at the book. He cleared his throat and read, "The Lord be in your heart and upon your lips that you may truly and humbly confess your sins." Then, from long habit, he raised his right hand to sign the cross over the kneeling figure.

Felix Rittenhouse was downstairs in X-ray with the consulting oncologist when the ambulance call came in. Just as he was starting back upstairs, he saw the EMTs rushing out the side door of the emergency room.

"Dr. Rittenhouse," the young clerk at the ER desk called to him. "Did you hear about the call that just came in?"

He turned and raised his eyebrows, affecting weary inquiry.

"St. Barnabas. They found a girl there. She may be a DOA. Isn't that your church?"

He dropped his charts on the ER counter, not answering her question. "Send these upstairs," he said, and hurried through the side door. The EMTs were already backing the ambulance out, but he beat them to the church.

He wasn't surprised to find Leslie there, nor to see that she had taken charge of the situation. She had the girl covered with an old tablecloth Tony had found in the kitchen.

"Go tell the EMTs where we are," Felix called to Jack as he came up the aisle. "They should be out there by now." He scanned the girl's face and body quickly, then knelt down and put two fingers to her throat. He waited a moment, pulled them away, and rubbed them with his thumb. "What's this stuff on her?"

Leslie felt the rigid throat herself. "Suntan oil?"

"What's that smell?" Felix asked, looking at his wife. Everyone sniffed and murmured vaguely.

"I smelled something funny when I first opened the door," Clyde said.

"Smells like—" Tony sniffed again, "I don't know . . . high-pitched."

Denny stepped inside the sacristy. He bent down, as though to pick up something, and came out again, his hand covered with soot. "There's something in there with the same smell. Looks like an old oily rag," he said. "But it's burned. Completely burned to ash."

Leslie stood up and closed the door to the sacristy. "We better not touch anything else."

Just then the EMTs came banging through the side door with a gurney. Jack trailed after them. Felix stood back while they lifted Wendy's limp body and strapped it down.

"Is she going to be all right?" Harriet asked, looking at him imploringly.

He stared back at her blankly, then scanned the circle of faces surrounding him. "You people!" he said angrily. "What do you expect?" Then he turned and followed the emergency team out the door.

Inevitably, everyone's eyes slewed toward Leslie. She got to her feet, brushing her hands on her skirt and keeping her eyes down to avoid their questions.

Mollie, who had been kneeling beside Wendy, now slumped sideways, sitting on the floor in an awkward heap. "It's my fault," she said again.

"For crying out loud, Mollie," Tony broke out irritably, "stop saying that. We don't even know what happened to her."

"She's dead. Or dying. That's what happened to her."

Denny bent down, took his wife's elbows, and lifted her to her feet. "Hush," he said. "It's not your fault."

"Yes. It is. I saw Wendy was having problems. I should have done something about it. I was her teacher. But I told her not to talk to her grandparents about it. I was afraid they wouldn't understand. I made her promise. I didn't know—"

"Hush," Denny said. He led her over to the lay reader's bench and sat down beside her, leaning forward to screen her from the others.

Leslie looked at Harriet. "Is this where you found her? Here in the sacristy?"

"No. She was in the nursery. She was talking strange, all garbled. I couldn't make much sense out of it. The only reason I left her was to get help. She wouldn't leave with me."

"She was here all alone. I guess she could have done this to herself," Leslie said.

Jack looked up nervously.

"Where's that priest?" Clyde asked him. "Father What's-his-name. Didn't he come in with you?"

"Not exactly. Denny was with him. They came in his van." Everyone glanced over at the McCreadys and then quickly away again.

"But you came in with him," Clyde persisted. "I saw you. Where'd he go?"

Tony broke in. "Please, Jack. Just this once, answer straight, okay?"

They were all staring at him, waiting. "I think he's in the office," he said. "Denny gave him the key."

"To call?"

"Well. Yes." That wasn't exactly a lie, Jack told himself. And if the two priests were talking, it was better that they not be interrupted.

"Good," Leslie said. "I never did call his wife. And we need to contact the Sandersons."

Harriet got to her feet. Clyde wiped his forehead

with his upper arm and put his hat back on. Only Tony kept her eyes on Jack. A worried frown puckered his forehead.

"What else, Jack?" Tony said. "About the office." They all stopped and looked at him again.

This is what Arlen must feel like all the time, Jack thought. That everyone's staring at him, waiting for him to make a wrong move. How he must hate us all.

"Father Kamowski's in there talking to someone, I believe," Jack said stiffly.

Arlen Canby reminded Kamowski of a couple of guys he'd met in prison. One was a little wiry fellow who never stopped moving. He constantly feinted and dodged in spasmodic jerks so that you could never tell what he might do next. He had put a shiv into another prisoner in the exercise area once. The motion was so swift and casual, no more than an extension of the little guy's constant fidgeting, that the guard was unaware of the stabbing until a trickle of blood began to puddle on the asphalt. In fact, the bosses never discovered who the culprit was, and the blame had been distributed among them indiscriminately.

The other prisoner Canby reminded him of was completely different—a soft, chubby fellow they called Dough Boy. He had reddish blond hair, fine as a baby's, and sun-reddened smudges on his cheeks like a cartoon character or a doll. He collected crimes, soliciting stories from new inmates intent on establishing a tough reputation among the prison population. Dough Boy retold and polished the stories, mumbling them over to himself in his cell at night, gradually making them his own. Sometimes he even went to the warden with them, confessing to crimes he'd only heard about.

The warden had learned to ignore him after he discovered some of the crimes Dough Boy confessed to were committed after his own incarceration. But when his official audience dried up, Dough Boy began grabbing other inmates, his eyes bulging and the pink inner lining of his protruding lips glistening while he urged his guilt upon them, inventing new details to gain their attention.

Arlen Canby moved like the thin, wiry prisoner; he seemed to find it impossible to be still for very long. And he had the confessional obsession of Dough Boy. Kamowski didn't want to believe the things the man was telling him. But, like Dough Boy, he described the details with relish and plausibility.

"She started coming by the office several months ago," Canby said. "She had this adolescent crush on me, I guess. I was trying to deal with it the best I knew how. I didn't want to just cut her off completely. She has a very sad history, you understand. Her mother abandoned her when she was born. Her grandparents have reared her. Naturally, she's a very insecure young person. You can imagine. I've been trying to work with her, build up her self-image, her self-esteem. She was worried about not having any boyfriends, not being attractive."

"So just what were you doing?"

"Oh," he jerked his shoulders in a shrug, "I tried to encourage her in a more positive direction. She's a bright girl. I was trying to stimulate her to concentrate on her strong points, her intellectual abilities. I told her the other would come in good time, not to worry."

"The other?"

"You know. Her body developing. Sex. The flesh." He said the last word sardonically, emphasizing the sibilants, but the look he gave Dan was like a challenge.

"Go on."

"She was a real science nut. Kids know so much these days, technology and computers. I never was good at any kind of science. So I'd let her explain her projects to me. It seemed to bolster her self-confidence. I guess it gave her a feeling of power too, control. We spent some time together after school a couple of times a week. I thought of these sessions as regular counseling appointments, built them into my schedule." He gestured toward a weekly calendar lying open on the desk.

"Unfortunately, I think she got the wrong idea. It didn't occur to me at first that she was, well, responding to me sexually. I was a fool." He broke off and rubbed his forehead with his fist.

Dan waited.

"She was taking chemistry last semester, in the spring. Doing experiments with gases. Figuring out toxicity levels on her computer. That was her special project."

He paused and Dan nodded cautiously.

Canby dropped his eyes to his hands again. "I was trying to build up her trust level. She needed an adult she could trust." He paused. "At least that's what I thought."

"Go on."

Arlen Canby sighed heavily and sat back on his heels. "Can I sit down now?" he asked abruptly.

Kamowski motioned to the chair behind the desk, and Canby got to his feet. He went back to the other side of the desk, where he sat down and began opening and shutting his desk drawers compulsively.

"Cassie and I were having problems. You probably know that if you've talked to her mother. I shouldn't have said anything to Wendy about it though. I can see that now. It gave her ideas. Though maybe she could tell anyway. Maybe the whole church was talking about it, I don't know. But she must have gotten the idea that— well, she could make me happy where Cassie had failed. If you see what I mean." He suddenly dropped his head into his hands and covered his face.

Dan took the opportunity to relax his own expressionless gaze and silently draw in a deep breath.

After a moment, the other man raised his head and went on. "She came in here one day when I was really down and started telling me how sorry she felt for me. How no one else appreciated me here. That kind of thing. She said she wanted to do something really nice for me, something to cheer me up. I didn't understand what she meant right away."

"And you—"

"Of course I turned her down." Canby gave Dan a wounded look, then stood up slowly and went to the window. He put his hands in his pockets, staring out at a squirrel climbing a pecan tree. "I don't know how Cassie found out. Wendy used to baby-sit for us until she started this punk thing. Then Cassie didn't want her around the kids anymore." He turned from the window suddenly. "So don't you see? I'm afraid that's why Cassie killed herself. Wendy must have told her we were lovers. That's why I blame myself for all this."

Dan's eyes followed Canby as he moved back to his desk. Otherwise his face was absolutely still.

Canby sat down. "Aren't you going to say anything?" he demanded, as though the silence irritated him.

"Is that all?"

The man opened and shut the pencil drawer again. Then he sighed. "You mean—" He gestured toward the door, indicating the general area of the sanctuary.

"The girl. What's happened to her?"

"Okay. So I guess I'm to blame for that too. But you can see she's not in touch with reality. She wanted us to go away together. Can you believe it—after all that's happened? 'Live happily ever after.' Those were her words. I came up here this afternoon thinking I'd pick up my mail and get out of the house for a while. Away from Dad for a few minutes anyway. I hadn't wanted to see anyone. You can understand. Anyway, when I saw Harriet Autrey's car here, I slipped in the back door by the nursery. I figured I could come up the hall to my office and no one would know I was here. I had no idea Wendy was in the nursery. She spotted me and called me in there. That's when she started talking about my being free now. Us going away together. How happy she would make me. I couldn't stand it. As if I hadn't been through enough already—" He stopped with a strangled cry.

Dan swallowed soundlessly and waited.

"I had to literally pull her off and push her away. Then I came in here and locked the door. I had to get away from her. From everybody. I couldn't deal with Wendy just then. Later I heard Harriet talking to her. I thought that was good—she'd take her home to her grandparents. Maybe she would tell them some cock-and-bull story, but so what? At this point, who cares? What else do I have to lose?"

He drew a deep breath and went on shakily. "But then Harriet left—alone. As soon as she was gone, Wendy came to the door and started banging on it, pleading for me to let her in. She said her life was ruined unless I let her in."

His voice was growing shrill. "I admit. I was a cow-ard. I just kept very quiet, pretending I wasn't here. Finally she went away. I'd been through so much already. I just couldn't deal with any more. I didn't care what she told anyone. I kept waiting for someone to come for her. Surely Harriet wouldn't just go off and leave her like that. I waited a long time. Then I decided I'd better check on her. I looked all over. Finally I heard her there in the sacristy, crying. I begged her to come out, but she wouldn't. So I came back in here and locked the door again. I was afraid someone might come any minute." He put his head down on the desk and his shoulders began to heave as though he were sobbing.

Kamowski remained immobile, listening intently for footsteps out in the hall.

Gradually Canby's sobs grew quieter. He cleared his throat. "So what should I do?"

Kamowski looked down at the prayer book. *Here the Priest may offer counsel, direction, and comfort,* it said in italics. Dough Boy and the little wiry guy—he couldn't get them out of his mind. The other prisoners wouldn't have anything to do with Dough Boy after a while, and the source of his stories dried up. Dan had heard later from Berkowitz that he'd been transferred to the unit at Gainesville for the criminally insane.

"He stopped eating," Berkowitz told him, "went on a hunger strike. Shriveled up to nothing. You wouldn't know it was him. All that skin just hanging off of him, empty. The warden here didn't want the press getting hold of something like that, so he shipped him up to Gainesville. It's all right if they starve themselves there. Then they can call 'em crazy and stick an IV in them."

The wiry guy, the one who never stopped moving, had gotten out on parole. Berkowitz hadn't heard any more about him after that. "It's easy to get lost in the free world, you know," he'd said.

Canby broke the silence first. "It's obvious I've got to leave. I know that. The bishop—he'll crucify me."

Kamowski looked at him levelly. "No. He'll sign you up for some kind of recovery program in Houston. He can't afford even a whiff of publicity about this. And he can't risk shipping you off to another diocese now. That won't work this time."

Canby looked at him narrowly, started to speak, and then stopped himself.

"That is how you got here, isn't it?" Kamowski asked. "Something happened back in New Orleans. It was this little hick town or nothing, wasn't it?"

Canby didn't answer directly. "Maybe I'll just leave," he said. "Disappear. That might be best for everyone."

Kamowski pulled at his lower lip thoughtfully. Was the wiry guy still out there, he wondered. He watched Canby pull at the knuckles of his long hands.

"Is this the only way you could think of to get out of

it?" Dan said, hearing his voice asking the question as soon as it had framed itself in his mind.

"What do you mean?" The long fingers twitched spasmodically. "Out of what?"

"Out of this little backwater town, out of being a priest, out of a marriage, out of being who you are."

Arlen Canby sat back in his chair. Then he flattened his hands on his desktop deliberately. "I see. You think you've got me figured out. A little amateur psycho-analysis."

Kamowski shrugged. "You're the one who wanted me to hear your confession. But I've got to hear all of it." He leaned forward now. "I've been where you are. I screwed up my life too, Canby. Then I got lucky. I got caught. I couldn't run away. That's the only counsel I have to offer you. Get caught. Whatever you've done."

For a moment Dan thought the man was actually considering the idea. His face drained, turned a putty color. He stared across the desk at Kamowski, and his lips jerked once as though he were about to speak. Then he looked down and pulled the prayer book over in front of him on the desk.

"That's it," he said. "Page four forty-eight."

Out of the corner of his eye Kamowski saw Canby check his watch.

"No," Dan said. "That's not it. I think you better finish your story."

CHAPTER • TWENTY

THE POLICE ARRIVED JUST AS the gurney was being lifted into the ambulance drawn up at the side entrance of St. Barnabas. After a hurried consultation with the EMTs, the officer in the patrol car radioed back to the station for an investigative team. The ambulance pulled away with its yellow lights revolving.

Inside the church, the two patrolmen found the little knot of parishioners still clustered down at the front of the nave. Denny moved over to the sacristy door when he saw the policemen coming down the aisle.

"We found her in here," he volunteered.

One of the uniformed men nodded. The other pulled a small notebook from his pocket. "The door was closed?"

Clyde spoke up. "Yes, sir."

"You the one who discovered her?"

Clyde nodded.

"All right. You folks just have a seat. Let's get your names first." The patrolman with the notebook began writing down the information while the other asked the questions.

Mollie had wiped the mascara smudges from under

her eyes. Her chin was tilted slightly up, but her face
was tight as a drum. Denny resumed his place beside
her, one arm over the back of the pew. They weren't
quite touching.

Tony sat on the other side of Mollie. She would have
liked to reach out and pat Mollie's hand or make some
other comforting gesture, but she was afraid the woman's
composure might break completely. Besides, Tony
sensed that any gesture of consolation from her might
intrude on whatever subtle readjustments were going on
between the McCreadys. She had never seen Denny
assume quite such a protective attitude toward his
wife—nor Mollie so grateful for such attention, for that
matter.

Tony wouldn't have minded a little solicitude herself
right then. Mollie and Leslie were lucky, even if they
didn't know it. She and Harriet were the ones who'd be
alone tonight, with no one to listen to them go over the
terrible events of the day until they could sleep, and no
one to breathe beside them if they couldn't. She looked
across the aisle where Harriet had taken her usual spot in
the old lady's pew. The policeman sitting beside her asking questions was probably the first man to occupy that
pew in years.

Harriet felt near collapse, hunched over and dabbing
at her eyes. Her weariness had become a kind of vortex,
sucking all rational thought down into confusion and
oblivion. All she could remember clearly was the sight of
Wendy sprawled on the floor of the sacristy, enfolded in
that sinister, acrid smell. How had the girl gotten in
there? Why had she left the ring of toys, her circle of
safety? If I had stayed, Harriet moaned inwardly, if I
hadn't left her alone. How am I ever going to tell Ilamae?
I'm no good to anyone here. Not anymore.

Across the aisle, Leslie turned around in her pew,
staring at the rear door of the nave. Why didn't Father
Kamowski join them? No one had yet told the police

that the visiting priest was in the church too. Leslie had been on the point of going to find him in the office when the police arrived. Who was he talking to there? Arlen Canby? What was going on? There were too many unanswered questions, and she suddenly felt unnerved.

Leslie's only acquaintance with Wendy was from seeing her perform her duties as an acolyte months back. Thus, when she saw the young girl sprawled on the floor outside the sacristy, she had been almost as shocked by her bizarre looks as by her condition. And what had she been doing in the church this afternoon anyway? Tony had told her that even the usually compliant teenager had finally abandoned her duties at St. Barnabas, but she hadn't mentioned anything about a shaved head.

Disjunction. Incongruities. Ambiguities. Leslie liked none of these. Reason seemed to collapse under their weight, like a roof overstressed by a deluge. Her mind, desperate to make sense of the situation, could only register data, facts. But there was no way to put the facts together so that they added up to an answer. In the place of reason, what filled her orderly mind now was a welter of unexplained sensory images. The two little coffins. The newspaper headlines. The rutted lane at the cemetery. Jane Armstrong's anguished voice. The smell of coconut that hovered around Wendy's inert form.

Her husband's anger was the only thing Leslie understood. Whatever had happened to Wendy Sanderson, it was clear Felix blamed them for it. The members of St. Barnabas. Herself included. She had heard the note of injured outrage in his voice, as though they'd let him down. He had expected more from them. What that was he might not have been able to say. But in his eyes they were responsible. For this. For everything.

Though he kept his gaze trained on his hands, Jack was watching Leslie out of the corner of his eye, hoping for once she'd keep her mouth shut. He could tell she was anxious to disclose Father Kamowski's presence in the church as soon as the detective got to her. Jack intended to tell the officer himself about the two priests in the office, but he had a feeling Arlen needed all the time alone he could get with Father Kamowski. Jack remembered the sound of desperation in the rector's voice, even though he couldn't recall now exactly what the man had said. Lately Arlen's voice had been like a dark cloud in Jack's mind, smothering and obscuring thought, blocking clarity. At times he could scarcely make out the man's words, much less their meaning.

To be honest, Jack didn't know what to believe any more. At one time it had all seemed so clear. Love. That was the key. He worked hard at it. He tried to treat his students with courtesy and understanding. He drove to San Antonio every month to see his mother whose demands increased with age. There were also two prisoners he visited regularly. And he could see that, though not every effort was an unqualified success, the condition of the cosmos was better off, even if only by some minuscule amount, because of these efforts.

But it hadn't worked at St. Barnabas. He'd tried to mend the bridges between the members and the rector. He had tried to do what he thought was love. But his efforts only shriveled or turned to something else. Alienation. Resentment. His love hadn't done either the church or Arlen Canby any good, and he didn't know why. Love was supposed to be like a talisman. If you stuck with it long enough, it would heal any situation. Now he wasn't sure. And he was afraid. He could only hope, in a kind of desperation, that Father Kamowski could succeed with Arlen Canby where the rest of them had failed.

As for the Sanderson girl, Jack was completely at a loss. He'd had no idea when he'd called her about keeping the nursery that she had changed so much. He'd hardly recognized the body slumped on the floor in the sacristy. Now Mollie McCready was blaming herself for this. But he was the one who'd asked the girl to come to St. Barnabas today. What else was he responsible for?

Clyde sat behind the others in a pew by himself, certain that the policemen had been looking at him suspiciously ever since he told them he was the one who'd discovered the girl. The peace that had descended on him at the cemetery had evaporated. Now he was back to feeling vaguely guilty again. Guilty and cornered. His chest ached with the need to get outside and smoke a cigarette. What might he have done wrong? What could he have done differently?

And the peace—where had it gone? Had it just dissolved? Had he been the romantic type, Clyde might have been tempted to think he had only imagined that interlude of clean sweetness as he wandered among the graves. But Clyde knew he wasn't the romantic type. He never imagined anything. What had happened had happened. What he didn't understand was why the feeling hadn't lasted. All he knew now was that he wanted to go home.

Just then the forensic team came through the back door of the nave and started matter-of-factly setting up equipment on top of the organ, their faces expressionless. The two patrolmen herded everyone farther back to the middle pews, while one of the men attached a yellow plastic ribbon to the organ and the altar rail to cordon off the area. Another man in a short-sleeved shirt and a tie drew the two patrolman off into one corner to talk.

After a few minutes, one of the officers came over to the group, his arms folded across his chest. "Won't be much longer, folks. Soon as the detective here gets through asking you a few questions, you can go."

He had just turned back toward the detective when there was a distant, heavy thunk from somewhere in the church. The policemen and the detective stopped talking and looked at one another. A man holding a small brush and a clear plastic bag in his gloved hands stepped out of the sacristy and looked around. "What's going on?"

"That wasn't thunder," said one of the patrolmen, and started toward the door at the rear of the nave. He was halfway down the aisle when a blast splintered the door inward.

When Kamowski asked for the rest of the confession, Canby had looked at him warily for a long moment. Dan could see him waver in that instant, consider protesting, assess how much he had to barter. Finally, Canby sat back, checked his watch again, and smiled with one side of his mouth.

"So you don't believe me. I should have known." He opened and shut the middle desk drawer with an air of exaggerated weariness. "It's never been any different. There's no one I can trust. Not my family. Not my wife. Not the church. They all turn against me eventually. Try to trap me. Make it my fault." He jerked the drawer angrily. "Do you think I don't know what's been going on here? I try to do my job. But they're all against me. I find someone I think I can trust, and sooner or later I find out he's against me too."

"Who do—"

"Shut up!" Canby drew his hand suddenly from the drawer. He was holding a small revolver. "Just because you're big, don't think you can intimidate me." He was yelling now.

Kamowski kept his eyes on the man's face, but he was mentally estimating distances. Across the desk. To the door.

"The bishop sent you here because he thought you could intimidate me, didn't he?" Canby lowered his voice menacingly. "He's looking for somebody to blame when he shuts down St. Barnabas. Well, I'm not intimidated, you hear?"

Kamowski stared fixedly as the man leaned toward him across the desk and leveled the gun at his forehead. A long moment passed. Then the barrel sagged and Canby sat back.

"No. You're not getting off that easy. You're going to listen to me first. Someone's going to hear this." He took a shallow breath and looked at his watch again, obviously calculating. "We've still got time."

He got up and came around the side of the desk, positioning himself between Dan and the office door.

"Cassie was making sure I failed here in Somerville. Just like before."

"In New Orleans," Kamowski said in an even tone.

The rector's thin nostrils flared and his jaw clenched before he went on. "She should have wanted to make me happy. It was her duty. Even her beloved Bible she was always quoting says that, doesn't it? If she believed it, she should have submitted. That's all I wanted—submission." He looked at Kamowski and blinked several times. "I wasn't going to hurt her."

Dan exhaled silently. "And when she didn't—submit?" he asked, keeping his voice flat.

The muscles around Canby's mouth jerked convulsively, the desperation to explain struggling with the cunning he habitually relied on for survival. The need to assert the reality of his own experience alternated with an unbending force that considered neither the man's body nor mind, both of which appeared perilously close to breaking.

No wonder Tatum pitied him, Dan thought. And pity had prevented the professor from seeing that the anonymous letters, full of hate and accusation, were self-inflicted.

Canby lowered himself slowly onto the side of the desk, holding the gun loosely. "There's lots of opportunities in New Orleans," he answered, grinding the words between his teeth. "Places where you can pay people to submit. But it's all a pretense then, isn't it?" He looked balefully at Kamowski a moment, then closed his eyes.

"But it was real enough when the bishop found out," Dan said, with more of an edge to his voice than he'd intended. "That's when they got rid of you, wasn't it? This diocese must have owed him a pretty big favor to take you on."

Canby's long hands knotted into fists. "I've had to submit—all my life. To my father, to my teachers, to the bishop. I'll be damned if I submit to a woman!" He struck the desk with the fist. "She was going to leave me! That would have been the last straw, wouldn't it? How can you control a parish if you can't even control your own wife." He took a deep breath and laughed shortly. "But no. She wouldn't stay. Not even when I begged her."

He broke off and looked around the room wildly. "Can you believe that? I begged her! Me, a priest! After she got involved with those lunatics, that— woman!—I could see it was all over. It wasn't enough to humiliate me in church. Oh, I know what they do at those retreats, those women. It's disgusting. And then she wanted to go away to that beach house. I knew what she was going for. Who she would meet there. She couldn't fool me."

He sat back, panting. "No. I even got it out of her— what she was up to. She thought she'd be able to sneak off with the kids, leave me to face everyone alone. But I found out. Cassie was no good with secrets."

A smile of satisfaction glinted briefly on his stark features. "I couldn't get her to stay, but you should have seen her face when I told her I'd go with her and the kids to the beach house. That we'd work it out together. What could she say then?"

He was still holding the gun loosely, bracing himself with one arm on the desk. I could take him now, Kamowski thought. But Canby wasn't through with his confession. And this might be his last chance to make one. At least they were getting closer to the truth.

"Wendy had fixed the garage door zapper for me so that I could use it to make the new phone ring," he went on. "It wasn't easy, of course, leaving them there in the car while I went back inside to get the phone call. But what else could I do? I could see what was happening. The rope was tightening around my neck. Soon I'd be jerked along to the slaughter. The scapegoat of St. Barnabas, the one everyone blamed. A failed priest. A failed husband. How else could I escape?"

He looked up quizzically at Kamowski. The anger and pain seemed to have drained away. In their place was something worse, something beyond reason.

"How else could I start over?" he smiled. "I had to cut myself off from everything that went before. It was the only way. I had to make a new beginning. A new life." He laughed and the sound was nearly normal, like a prelude to a joke. "Think of it, padre. To be born again. In California!"

It was a moment before Kamowski spoke. "The girl," he finally said, keeping his voice level. "Wendy. Tell me what really happened, Canby."

The side of Canby's face that smiled dropped as Kamowski said the girl's name. "She had this hang-up about her mother—the town slut for all I know—who'd gotten herself pregnant in high school, then left town after Wendy was born. Wendy was obsessed with finding her. But at the same time she was scared the same thing would happen to her, that this was some kind of genetic flaw or something."

"So how'd you handle it?"

Another barking laugh erupted from Canby's throat. "Reality therapy. She wanted to know what it was like. I showed her."

"You—"

Canby waved the gun, the barrel pointing at the

ceiling, to cancel Kamowski's question. "Books. I showed her books. None of that 'Pretty Woman' stuff, but real, working hookers." He stopped momentarily, considering. "That's when she started dressing funny. Shaved her head. I don't know. I guess she was going through some kind of weird identification with her mother."

"And this was your idea of counseling? Looking at dirty pictures with a kid?"

Canby straightened himself and improved his grip on the gun, though he seemed to have scarcely heard Kamowski's question. "I must have been crazy. I thought for a while she was the answer. I could lead her along. She was young. I thought I could shape her. She would do what Cassie refused to do. Be what my own wife refused to be. What she should have been. A vessel. An earthen vessel for me." His smile returned momentarily, then gradually disappeared altogether. "But even that well was poisoned."

He glanced at Kamowski, an earnest look on his face. "I think I've finally come to believe in original sin, you know. Everyone eventually betrays me. That's what it is, original sin. Inevitable betrayal. Even Wendy. Fresh, innocent Wendy." His face grew rigid. "She wouldn't go with me, you know."

"And you were afraid she might give you away if you left her behind—say something that wouldn't fit with the story you were concocting."

Another change seemed to come over Canby. He suddenly became more animated. Sitting forward, he gestured mock-helplessness with his arms. "Hey. The girl's obviously been hanging around with some bad types. Shaving her head. I don't know. Maybe she even got involved with a cult. Somerville will eat that up. They like to think of themselves as important enough to attract the undivided attention of the devil."

"Had she figured it out? How you'd used her?"

"She couldn't put it all together. Not at first. I made

sure of that. She'd given me a copy of her project on poison gases. I'd suggested it, of course. It had all the information I needed. I told her I was interested in her work. That we needed to share everything. All our secrets." He barked out a laugh. "We even share the guilt. I think she was beginning to see that herself." He raised an eyebrow to underscore the irony. "I guess you could say she was my research assistant."

"And you were afraid she might give you away."

Canby's lopsided smile was back in place. "Not on purpose, of course. She was in love with me, I told you. It's an occupational hazard. You know that, padre. But how could I go on with that after this tragedy to my family? I'd come to my senses, seen the error of my ways. I had to break it off. So—" He threw up his hands and cocked his head to the side, mimicking regret. "Despairing of keeping me, and remorseful over what she'd done, Wendy took herself off to the sacristy—note the symbolic setting—and choked herself on phosgene, another toxic gas covered in her report. Burn a rag soaked in heavy-duty degreaser and you get phosgene. It makes carbon monoxide look like fresh mountain air on the toxicity scale. You don't even have to inhale deeply. It penetrates the skin. Especially after you've rubbed on a little suntan oil. It really soaks in fast then."

"But your wife and kids—that was just carbon monoxide."

Canby's face switched to mock gravity. "Please. My wife. My children. A terrible tragedy. Cassie was crazed by jealousy when she found out about Wendy, you see. But she's no rocket scientist. Carbon monoxide is about the most you could reasonably expect Cassie to come up with for a suicide attempt. And even then she failed."

"You used Wendy's research for that too."

"I told you. The girl was in love with me. I taught her some things—and she taught me other things. It was a symbiotic relationship, you might say. By the way, did you know that 10,000 parts per million of carbon monoxide can kill you in a couple of minutes? Well, make that five for you, padre, considering your size. Why, people have died on the open sea from breathing engine exhaust on a cruiser. A closed garage on a hot day with the air-conditioner running, sucking in the fumes, it's even more effective. And a little paint thinner on a rag stuffed in the intake vents speeds up the process considerably. Wendy used the correct terms, of course, in her chemistry report. Ethylene chloride, not paint thinner. It's all there in the report, safe at school. I even encouraged her to make a backup copy off her computer. You never know, I said, what might happen. You wouldn't want all that work to be lost. Now it's sitting there waiting to be discovered by the police."

"I don't believe the girl knew anything about it," Kamowski said. "How you intended to use the information."

Canby shrugged. "I'd also gotten her to switch the innards somehow on the new portable phone I'd bought and the garage door gizmo. Not only could I make the phone ring with the garage zapper, I could operate the garage door with the phone. I got the phone to ring just before we took off for our family outing at the beach. And I made sure Cassie couldn't get the garage door open while I was inside on the phone. Of course I had to use the wall phone to call 91—supposedly when I came home and discovered them in the garage. My only mistake was I didn't wait long enough before I called for help."

"But the girl didn't know—" Kamowski broke in.

"I told Wendy I'd use the rigged zapper just for a joke, just a little party trick. Of course, afterwards, well, she was beginning to see how she was implicated. And to quote Calvin, 'who knows what evil lurks in the heart of man'—or words to that effect. Or in the heart of a troubled teenager, for that matter. Her fingerprints are all over both gizmos. So far as anyone knows, I wasn't even there. A young girl's insane jealousy. Oh, it's not a pretty story." He looked over at Kamowski. "And one you'll never tell, padre."

"And now you've faked her suicide. That's how you got her into the sacristy, isn't it? Convinced her she was the guilty one."

"She was a gibbering idiot. Something snapped. Who knows what she might have said or done. I couldn't risk it. You can see that." He frowned in irritation and checked his watch again. "I had hoped you could pass along my original confession to the police after I was on my way. That's why I wanted us to have this little chat. As you said, my plan gets me out of everything I hate— this town, this church, these people who want to eat me alive."

He stood up, the gun gripped firmly again. "If you'd only believed in my penitence—and my first confession. Why didn't you have a little faith in me, padre? It could have saved your life—and a lot of other busybodies. I wasn't sure of you though, so I provided myself with a backup too. When my father shows them the confession he found in his prayer book this morning, complete with all the grisly particulars of my involvement with a troubled girl determined to win my love, an anguished statement full of self-recrimination, the conclusion will be inescapable. Overcome by guilt, I've taken off for parts unknown. I'll be fairly safe. True, my father will be humiliated. A shame. He's probably been frantic to find me all day, before anyone else found out. Now it's too late. It'll have to come out. I have to admit to a certain satisfaction in that—Dad having to tell the police the whole sordid story. I think they'll go for it, don't you? No one would believe I'd sacrifice my career, my reputation, if it weren't true."

"Hey!" He flung his arms out again suddenly. "Haven't I been in here confessing to you all this time, repenting in dust and ashes? Jack Tatum can corroborate that. Too bad you'll be in no shape to confirm the story, padre." He put his left hand in his pocket and pulled out something that looked like a TV remote.

"What a clever girl Wendy was," he said, punching several buttons on the face of the plastic rectangle. "The darling of her science teacher. They spent hours fooling around with electronic stuff. At least that's what she said they were doing. She certainly taught me everything I know about these gizmos, though we kept that our little secret. Anyone who knows me will attest to the fact that I'm no good at all with machinery of any kind. On the other hand, she's got a reputation as a computer whiz. The conclusion will be inescapable, I believe."

It was then Dan heard the first explosion from the direction of the parish hall.

"What's that?" he said, starting up from his chair.

Canby held up the box for Kamowski to see. "Another garage door zapper. Simple really. Uses radio signals. Wendy reprogrammed it for me only last week, putting in the code I needed for the blasting devices. Can you believe they keep that stuff just sitting around on trucks at construction sites? That's Somerville for you."

He leveled the gun at Kamowski. "You wanted to hear the rest of the story." He pushed another series of buttons and there was a second deep thunk. The office window rattled and a framed diploma fell off the wall.

Dan started toward the door.

"Sit down."

"What are you doing this for, Canby? Is this just spite?"

"Please," Canby said with his wry smile. "Give me a little more credit than that. After all, I'm saving them the cost of demolition. Actually, padre, you're responsible. I wouldn't have had to do this if only you'd believed me. I was hoping to slip quietly off to California. And you could have vouched for the fact that I had ample reason. But you've left me no choice. I've been receiving hate mail, you see. Anonymous letters. Ask Jack Tatum. And eventually they'll discover Wendy wrote them too. I added them to the same disk where they'll find her chemistry report. Poor girl! She was obviously trying to punish me for not leaving my wife—setting up the church to blow after her suicide in the sacristy. Taking us all down with her. Like I said, it's amazing the things kids know these days. Unfortunately, after the blast under your chair goes off, you won't be around to set them straight."

CHAPTER TWENTY-ONE

AS HE STUMBLED THROUGH THE debris blown into the foyer by the explosion, Jack could see a dull red glow coming from the parish hall. Already he could hear beams splintering and cracking in the fire. Just as he reached the rector's office he heard a noise he thought was a third explosion, smaller but sharper. Then the office door burst open and Arlen Canby rushed out.

The rector stared wildly at Jack, then grabbed his arm. "What's happening?" he cried.

"The building's on fire. Just get out!"

As if in response to the command, Arlen started across the foyer toward the Sunday school hallway, half-dragging Jack with him. "This way," he shouted.

"Canby!"

Jack looked back and saw Father Kamowski in the office doorway. He was bent forward, clutching his side.

Canby dropped Jack's arm, turned, and pulled a black plastic rectangle from his pocket. His thumb jerked over its surface several times as he stared at Kamowski for a long moment, then down at the black box in his hand.

"It's over," the priest in the doorway grunted. "Give it up."

Then Jack saw the man beside him hurl the black box at the figure in the doorway. Kamowski, his head lowered but his eyes fastened on Canby, lurched toward them.

"No!" Canby screamed.

Kamowski fell just as he reached them, groping to wrap his arms around Canby's legs. The rector jumped back, and, as Kamowski's body hit the stone floor, he kicked the side of his head.

Just then the front door to the church jerked open. "Get out!" Clyde yelled at them. "It's spreading fast." The open door sucked flames into the foyer from the parish hall.

Jack turned toward the door, then back to the body on the stone floor. Flames were already licking around the foyer entrance, making a bright ring like a circus hoop of fire. He felt the rector release his arm and begin backing away. Then Jack heard him running down the hallway toward the nursery exit. He didn't turn to look.

"Help me," he shouted to Clyde. "Father Kamowski's hurt. I can't move him."

It was only as they tugged and shoved the unwieldy body across the foyer to the front entrance that Jack noticed the trail of blood smeared across the stone floor. They were struggling to lift him over the metal threshold when the two policemen suddenly appeared. Stumbling and swearing, the four of them were able to carry the priest across the street to the safety of the dormitory lawn.

As they rolled him over onto his back, Kamowski's eyes opened a moment. "Canby. Where is he?"

Clyde looked at Jack.

Jack shook his head. "I'm not sure."

"You mean he still might be in there?" Clyde shouted at him. He was on his feet again, running back toward the church before Jack could answer.

One of the policemen was stripping away Kamowski's black shirt. Jack looked down at the priest's flaccid belly, the ragged tear almost concealed in a fold of flesh. Kamowski groaned.

"Keep still," the officer ordered. "The ambulance will be here soon."

Jack glanced up to see Leslie running toward them. In a moment the others who'd been herded out of the church by the side door crowded around the priest.

"Is he hurt? What's happened?" Tony cried, dropping to her knees beside him. Behind them, Harriet sank to the grass unsteadily. Mollie clutched her husband's arm.

Jack got to his feet and slowly backed away as the others crowded around the figure on the ground. He took a few more steps backward, then turned and trotted across the street. He could hear the fire sirens, still a few blocks away. He spotted Clyde just as he was opening the side door of the church, apparently intent on rescuing the rector.

"No, Clyde! He's gone!" Jack shouted, but the door had closed behind him. Jack ran up the steps and pushed open the heavy doors into the little vestibule. The fire had already crept into the sanctuary. The high rafters were ablaze. He had not imagined a fire could burn so swiftly.

Through the smoke, he saw Clyde moving slowly up the aisle toward the chancel. Jack dropped to his knees and crawled along behind the back pews. Clyde had wrapped his bandanna around the lower part of his face, but he was inching backwards now, almost overcome by the billowing smoke. Jack scrambled toward him, keeping as low to the floor as he could.

"Get out!" Jack cried. "He's not here." He groped toward Clyde, looped an arm around him, and hauled him down the aisle. Pushing the door to the vestibule open with his foot, he half-dragged, half-rolled Clyde through the door.

"We've got to get him out," Clyde said between gasps, flat on his back.

"He's already out, I'm telling you. I saw him leave by the back hallway," Jack shouted down at the face darkened by the smoke.

"No. He came back in. Just ahead of me," Clyde insisted. "He was running. The fool must be trying to save something."

A long, crumbling crash inside the sanctuary jarred them both. "It sounds like the ceiling's giving way," Clyde said. He looked up at Jack. The hesitation in the other man's face suddenly clarified everything for Clyde. Jack can't do it, he thought. And the others need him.

Clyde rolled over onto his stomach and pulled his knees up under him. His breath was steadier now in the protected vestibule. Shifting his weight from his knees to his toes and hands, like a runner on the mark, and not bothering to wrap his face this time, he hit the door of the vestibule with his shoulder and vanished into the fire.

The police had told them all to wait on the dormitory lawn across the street from what was left of St. Barnabas while the ambulances were being loaded. A sheriff's deputy stood nearby to keep away the crowd that had collected. Jack had rejoined the group, and now they all stood or sat on the grass in the summer twilight, mesmerized by the glowing skeleton of the burning church.

One more explosion had shaken the building, but by then the roar of the fire muffled the blast so that it was felt more than heard. Then the fire had eaten away the roof and rafters, and after they collapsed, the roar had diminished. Now there was only the crackling of the flames and the hiss of steam as the firemen played their water hoses over the charred remains.

The police questioned Jack first. "How come you didn't tell anyone the priest was in the building?"

"I told Father Kamowski. We'd been looking for the rector all afternoon. His father hadn't been able to find him since the funeral this morning."

"We? You and who else?"

"Father Kamowski. And Clyde Mapes. Then when I went by my office, I got a call from Father Canby. He was here at the church. He said he needed to talk Father Kamowski. He sounded upset—desperate. So I came right over. I got here about the same time Father Kamowski and Denny McCready drove up."

"And you told them you'd found the missing priest?"

"I told Father Kamowski about the rector wanting to see him."

"But not the others? You didn't tell anyone else that he was in the building?"

Jack hesitated. "No. As I said, he sounded desperate. He said he needed a priest, and I believed him. I wanted to give the two of them as much privacy as possible. I was afraid Arlen—Father Canby—was about to go over the edge."

They were sitting in a patrol car in the gathering darkness, the door open and the dome light illuminating the pad on which another detective was making notes.

"So tell me why you tried to stop this other guy—" the man asking the questions looked over at the other detective's notebook, "Clyde Mapes—from going back inside."

"I thought the rector had left. I'd seen him running down the back hallway. It has an outside door. I didn't expect him to come back."

"Why? Did you see him shoot the other priest?"

Jack rubbed his damp palms together, remembering the smear of blood across the stone floor. "I wasn't sure what had happened."

The detectives exchanged glances.

"Any idea why he did go back into the church?"

Jack shook his head.

"Is it your opinion that, once you got inside the building the second time, Mapes was trying to save him, this other priest?"

"Yes. Clyde told me so when I dragged him out into the vestibule."

"What happened after that? Just tell me in your own words."

"I couldn't make out much. There was so much smoke, it was hard to see."

"Just tell us what you did see."

Jack hunched his shoulders together. "I edged the vestibule door open. I couldn't see Clyde at all at first, the smoke was so thick. Then, down in front of the altar, I saw them both." He stopped.

The detective handed him the paper cup of water he'd been sipping from. "Take your time."

Jack drank from the cup, his eyes closed. How could he tell this man what he had seen? The two of them before the altar, Clyde's arms locked around the priest in a powerful embrace. The flames had not yet reached the chancel, but the back of Clyde's shirt had caught fire on his way down the aisle, and his hair. Arlen was trying to struggle from his grasp, but Clyde, the stronger of the two, wouldn't let go.

"It—" Jack stopped and made a gesture in the air, flinging his hands upward— "erupted," he said. "Exploded. The altar. I saw it fly apart. The two of them were thrown backward. Up into the air. Then I couldn't see anything else. And the flames." He stopped. His voice was hoarse.

"You're on the board here, aren't you?" the detective asked unexpectedly.

"The vestry. Yes. Yes, I am."

"Did you know anything about the demolition plans for the building?"

Jack frowned. "Only that it would be next week sometime."

"You didn't know that the truck parked across in that north lot had the explosives on it?"

Jack looked vaguely around, as though trying to locate north. "Truck? No. I didn't know." That seemed to be his answer to everything, he thought.

"I know this is hard," the detective said, "but we need your impressions while they're still fresh. This isn't just a case of arson, you know."

"I'm all right," Jack said. But the rest of the questions he answered in a stubbornly desultory way. Leave it to the others, he thought, to fill in the details about Arlen Canby's marriage and his troubles with the congregation. He'd done all he could for now. He'd seen the bodies the firemen had pulled from the blazes. What was left of them.

But as he was climbing out of the patrol car at the end of the interview, he paused. "If it's all right with you, I'd like to go out to the Mapes' ranch and tell the family myself." He felt responsible for Clyde. He should have stopped him, somehow. Now all he could do was carry the news. Like the messenger in Job. *I only am escaped alone to tell thee.* It was the least he could do now. Clyde's wife and mother shouldn't have to hear the news from strangers. It should come from someone they knew. One of them, one of the congregation.

He walked wearily back across the grass to the group, all sitting on the curb now, and told them he was going out to the ranch.

Leslie looked up at him, a hundred accusing questions in her eyes. But what she said was, "Take my car. Yours is in the back lot. They won't let you in there." She stood up and fished the keys from her purse which she had somehow managed to keep with her throughout the confusion.

"And Jack," she said as she handed them to him, "tell them Clyde tried to save him. That you saw it—Clyde risking his life. They need to know that. Tell them that."

He took the keys and started to turn away.

"Jack," she said, handing him a handkerchief she'd pulled from the purse, "here. Your face."

The handkerchief was sheer and scented. He wiped his face, surprised to see how it blackened the thin cloth, and handed it back to her.

"It wouldn't have done any good if you'd gone back in there again, Jack. You'd only have been killed too. Then no one would have been around to tell them."

He looked away, across the street where kids were crowding the dormitory windows. "Maybe," he said. "I don't know."

There was a lot of bad news to be delivered, Leslie thought as she watched Jack drive away. She wished she could go with him out to the Mapes' ranch, but she knew he wouldn't want her along. Besides, it would be best for them to hear about Clyde from Jack alone. They trusted him. If she were there, a woman they only knew as someone who had made difficulties for their husband and son, their grief would be complicated with anger. And they would be angry enough later.

Leslie looked over at the patrol car where the officers were taking Harriet's statement now. She still couldn't sort it all out. What had been going on in this building that was now evaporating into the night air? If she'd looked for Father Kamowski at St. Barnabas after she'd talked to his wife instead of going to the hospital, she would have been there to help Harriet with Wendy. None of this might have happened then.

And what *had* happened anyway? What had Wendy done to herself in the sacristy? Was she trying to kill herself? Why? And Arlen Canby—had he actually shot Father Kamowski? Had the man finally lost it completely, gone berserk? And the building blowing up. Who was responsible for that? All she knew for sure was that St. Barnabas Episcopal Church had put two people in the Watson County Hospital tonight, and two in the morgue. And that didn't even count Cassie and the children.

Leslie shuddered, suddenly feeling cold despite the heat still radiating from the remains of the church. Dead bodies, burning buildings. It was all so physical. She'd felt prepared for spiritual battles, moral conflict, a war of ideas. But dead bodies, charred flesh. She hadn't been prepared for that. For the first time in a long time she felt like she was in over her head. And the worst part was she wasn't sure she would ever find out the answers to her questions. She needed to know. She wanted explanations. She didn't like being in the dark. It made her feel weak, blundering. Yet she had this terrible feeling she was never going to find out.

Tony came toward her from the direction of the clustered patrol cars. She turned and faced the smoldering fire as she spoke. "I called the bishop," she told Leslie. "They let me use the radio telephone before they started on Harriet. He said he was on his way up here. He wants to talk to all of us."

"Ha!" Leslie's laugh was brittle. "It's a little late now."

"I think he realizes he's going to have to take some heat for this," Tony said.

Leslie turned away from the church, staring into the thickening darkness, her arms folded. She didn't care about the bishop. She wanted Felix here. Surely he'd heard about the fire by now. Why wasn't he here?

She looked over at Mollie and Denny sitting on a blanket one of the firemen had given them. Mollie was leaning forward over her knees. Her dark hair had fallen across her cheek so that Leslie couldn't see her face. From time to time Denny idly stroked her bare arm as he stared at the illuminated skeleton of the church building.

"He'll be here," Tony said to Leslie.

As though on cue, a dark sedan pulled across the

intersection and in among the maze of fire trucks and patrol cars. Felix was out almost before he turned off the ignition.

Tony watched Leslie turn as he called her name, then run the few yards to meet him. Tony turned away, hugging herself and trying not to look at the McCreadys either. Here she was, alone again. No better off than when she'd first come to Somerville and left Mance behind.

She took a deep breath, as though to fill up the space inside. The cavity within her was so empty that she felt like any minute her ribs might collapse, just like the rafters of the burning church. She didn't want what had filled the emptiness before—not Mance, not even performing. She wanted what she had found at St. Barnabas—and lost. Tony didn't try to put it into words. All she knew was that the hot, burning ball that had once lit up and filled that inner cavity was somehow enclosed within the conflagration gradually dying across the street. What would be left when St. Barnabas was no more than ashes? She almost envied Clyde. She would rather have been consumed by that fire than to see it die.

She could see one of the patrolmen helping Harriet out of the lighted automobile now. The older woman clung to his arm, trying to stand upright and blinking at the shadowy figures around her.

"Tony?" she called in a thin voice.

"I'm here," Tony said.

The detectives had let Tony take Harriet home with her after asking only a few questions.

"You shouldn't be by yourself tonight," Tony told her. Nor me either, she added to herself.

The day's events had shaken Harriet badly. She needed support to walk and her head nodded spasmodically on her thin neck. She kept asking about Wendy, making Tony repeat the same meager information several times. As she unlocked the door to her apartment, Tony was relieved to see that the Armstrongs had left for the hospital again. She didn't want to have to go over it all again with them. Tomorrow maybe. But not now.

She settled Harriet in the guest bedroom and stretched out on the sofa until she was sure the older woman was asleep. Then she got up quietly, wrote a note in case Harriet woke up, and left for the hospital.

At the front desk she learned that Wendy was still in critical condition. Dan Kamowski, however, was already out of surgery and awake. She went upstairs and found a tall woman sitting by his bed. Her hair was still as bright as Tony's had been ten years ago.

"He's all right?" Tony asked, without introducing herself.

"He's going to be. The bullet didn't hit anything vital," the woman said.

"The bishop should be here soon," Tony said. "I talked to him over an hour ago."

The priest, looking like a sallow walrus beached on the high hospital bed, groaned and opened his eyes. "Then sit down," he said to Tony. It sounded more like an order than an invitation. "I got something to say to you before the bishop gets here. Dell, you go outside and hold him off if he comes poking his nose around."

The woman stood up and looked at Tony appraisingly. "I'll be right outside."

Tony took the chair she had just vacated. The priest's eyes had closed again, and she thought perhaps he had drifted off to sleep.

"They're going to need you," he suddenly said, his eyes still closed.

She frowned.

"Look," he went on, his speech a little slurred, "think how this is going to shake everybody up. The whole community, not just the people at St. Barnabas.

What'll be going on in their heads? What'll they make of it? A crazy priest blowing up the church?"

Before they'd put him in the ambulance, Dan had only told the cops in a general way that the rector of St. Barnabas had been talking crazy, unbalanced by his family's death. But sooner or later, he knew, the story of what the man had done to his own family would come out. They couldn't do much in the way of damage control there. The bishop was going to have a coronary, but the Armstrongs deserved to have their daughter's name cleared, even if the truth would be little consolation to them.

Canby had set him up with that confession business, hoping that Dan would eventually tell the police the version of the truth he'd heard in the rector's office. But it would never have worked that way either. If Dan had believed there was a moment when the guy felt so much as a grain of repentance, he would have protected the inviolable nature of confession. He was no stranger to tangled motives himself.

What Dan couldn't figure out was what had made Canby go back inside the church. He had obviously rigged the altar to blow too. Did he think it would fail to go off because the charge in the office had? Was his rage so great that he'd die just to make sure he took the whole thing down with him?

And then there was the Sanderson girl. What was her life going to be like now, supposing that she survived? Dan had already decided, while he'd waited on the gurney in the emergency room before they put him under, not to say anything about Wendy to the police for the time being. The Sandersons needed to hear the story first, and from someone besides the police. Someone they knew.

He opened his eyes and looked at the tall woman sitting by the bed. "It's going to be in all the newspapers. Somebody'll swear there was devil worship going on there. Satanists. You name it."

"The truth is worse," Tony said woodenly.

"What do you mean? The girl? Wendy. Has she died?"

"No. Not yet anyway. They said she'll be in danger for at least another week though."

"If she lives," he said, blinking at the light, "she's going to need your help. Her grandparents too."

Tony shook her head. "Don't say that. I can't do any more. None of us can. It's all too much for us. Cassie and the children were already too much. And there's the Armstrongs. Arlen's father. The Sandersons. Where does it stop? I don't understand it. It's too much for us. Too much—" she shuddered, "malice. Too much misery."

You don't even know how much yet, he thought, closing his eyes against the fluorescent glare from the tube over his head. "You'll be all right if you stick together."

She shook her head again. It was asking too much. "We'll be like some terrible secret society or something. Accomplices in this—this ordeal, this horror."

"It's what you've always been," he said. "You just didn't know it. Now you do."

She sat there silently for several minutes. Then she said, "I hated him. He's the only person I believe I've ever really hated. Now there's not even that. How can you hate someone who's dead? I feel like he's crushed me, crushed us all. Like we're all trapped in that building, burning with him."

"Maybe you are," he said. "Maybe we all are. Maybe it needed to happen." He felt foolish talking in this picturesque way. "All I'm saying is," he went on doggedly, "you're at the bottom now. But it's good to get to the bottom. The bottom is a place to stand. The truth is at the bottom. Any illusions you might have had are gone. Maybe you won't—we won't—ever know all the facts. But you won't have any illusions. And you don't have to worry about the truth. It can take care of itself. It's the others, the ones who'll read what they think is the truth in the paper—they're the ones who'll feel like they're falling through space. Like there's nobody they can trust, not even a priest." He turned his head towards her. "Somebody needs to already be there at the bottom waiting for them."

She closed her eyes. She could still see flames licking the charred skeleton of St. Barnabas. "You have a lot of confidence in us."

"Not particularly," he said. "I just know about the bottom. And what can happen after you've been there."

Kamowski's wife came to the door. "The bishop's here," she said.

"I'll go," Tony said, standing up.

A gentle, bubbling snore came from the bed.